Praise for Ally Kennen's novels

BEAST

"Rings with talent and compelling detail . . . a tense, funny and touching tale. I really love this book"
Amanda Craig, *The Times*

"*Beast* has a tension that never lets up. Ally Kennen is already a remarkably assured writer"
Nicholas Tucker, *Independent*

"An extraordinary imaginative achievement . . . this is a compassionate story from an exciting new voice"
Bookseller

"Sharply and wittily observed . . . An exceptional first novel"
Books for Keeps

WINNER of the Manchester Book Award
SHORTLISTED for the CILIP Carnegie Medal, the Booktrust Teenage Prize, the Branford Boase Award, the Berkshire Book Award, the Leicester Book Award and the Bolton Book Award

BERSERK

"This absolute nail-biter, written in clever and convincing teenage vernacular, has an ending of stunning ingenuity"
Sunday Times

"Written with a verve and confidence that never lets up. Very funny . . . this excellent novel well deserves the large audience it should get"
Independent

"The sure-footed blend of deadpan humour with gritty, urban realism in this sharply observed novel will readily engage young adult readers"
Guardian

"Chas and his troubled mates flirt with danger, girls and law-breaking in this humorous, gritty story . . . an irresistible farce-come-thriller"
Booktrusted.com

WINNER of the North East Teenage Book Award and the Leicester Book Award
SHORTLISTED for the Manchester Book Award, the West Oxfordshire Book Award and the Coventry Inspiration Book Award

BEDLAM

"A hot paced, nail-chewing thriller with enormous brio, great style and a frosting of wicked wit"
Guardian

"*Bedlam* grips right from its opening pages. Kennen builds tension almost unbearably, leaving the reader guessing the possible outcome almost to the end"
Books for Keeps

"Kennen's usual mix of villainous and vulnerable characters come together to create a chilling, atmospheric thriller"
Bookseller Children's Buyer's Guide – Highlight of the Season

"I absolutely loved reading this book . . . tense and intelligent . . . Dark humour bubbles below the surface and just as you're getting slightly breathless, a sucker punch catches you straight from leftfield and you find yourself in fits of laughter"
Thebookbag.co.uk

"Readers will be gripped from start to finish by this dramatic and compelling book"
Booktrusted.com

LONGLISTED for the CILIP Carnegie Medal 2010

QUARRY

"I cannot fault Kennen when it comes to originality. From her story setting and characters to her dares, all are completely original. She managed to take a simple game of dares and turn it into a thrilling story that gave me chills. Excellent!"
YA Book Reads

"The author has a creative skill that draws the reader into the world of the characters. So if, like me, you haven't read any of Ally's other books, then I would recommend reading them just on the strength of this book"
Mr Ripley's Enchanted Books

"This is all excellent, page-turning stuff. . . *Quarry* will reassure [Ally Kennen's] older fans that her grip on noir is as muscular as ever"
Guardian

"Gripping to the last, and teeming with wonderfully drawn characters. . . Kennen has created a wonderful, likeable character struggling to keep his sanity in this entertaining thriller"
Bookseller: Children's Bookseller's Choice

"This is both involving and scary, and presents an ultra-modern story with a twist"
Telegraph

ALLY KENNEN comes from a proud lineage of bare-knuckle boxers, country vicars and French aristocracy. Prior to becoming a writer, she has worked as an archaeologist, a giant teddy bear and a professional singer and songwriter.

Her first novel, BEAST, published in 2006, was shortlisted for the Booktrust Teenage Prize and the Carnegie Medal, and won the 2007 Manchester Book Award. Her second novel, BERSERK, won the North-East Teenage Book Award and the Leicester Book of the Year Award 2008. In total, her dark and thrilling teen novels have been nominated for over eleven literary awards.

Ally lives in Somerset with her husband, three children, four chickens, and a curmudgeonly cat.

No woman has ever beaten Ally in an arm wrestle.

Also by Ally Kennen

SPARKS

BEAST
BERSERK
BEDLAM
QUARRY

BULLET BOYS

ALLY KENNEN

First published in the UK in 2012 by Marion Lloyd Books
An imprint of Scholastic Children's Books
Euston House, 24 Eversholt Street
London, NW1 1DB, UK
A division of Scholastic Ltd.
Registered office: Westfield Road, Southam
Warwickshire, CV47 0RA

ISBN 978 1407 12990 7

A CIP catalogue record for this book
is available from the British Library

Printed and bound by CPI Group (UK) Ltd, Croydon CR0 4YY
Papers used by Scholastic Children's Books are made
from wood grown in sustainable forests.

1 3 5 7 9 10 8 6 4 2

www.scholastic.co.uk/zone

For Arthur

CONTENTS

"One for all and all for one. . ."

Alexandre Dumas,

The Three Musketeers

Alex

Alex never killed hares. He'd despatched hundreds of rabbits, dozens of foxes, a couple of injured deer, one blind ewe and a nest of bloody-minded wasps. He'd also shot pigeons, crows, rooks, rats, grouse, moles, mink, a road-damaged cat, a sheep-worrying lurcher and a frothing, coughing badger. He'd set snares and traps, laid poison and strung small furry bodies on gibbets. He'd plucked and gutted, skinned and beheaded. But he couldn't bring himself to shoot a *Lepus* because his mother had said it was unlucky.

The sun burned the back of his neck as he sprawled in the heather. He adjusted the rear-sight and curled his finger round the trigger of his air rifle. Below him, in the shimmering heat-soaked valley, a grey-brown blur moved stealthily through the gorse towards the river gorge. It was unusual to see a hare in the open in high summer. Maybe it was diseased. The animal was within his range, caught in the cross hairs. Alex's finger tensed. Dad said, There's nothing crueller than nature. He said if it wasn't for gamekeepers like him, the whole country would be overrun with vermin.

Alex loosened his grip, put on the safety catch and pushed the gun away. Hares didn't do any harm. Deep in the valley, the creature sniffed the air, smelling the danger maybe. Then it vanished in the grass. Alex sat up and wiped his face with the back of his hand. Helena, his mother, also said hares were magic and could make time stand still.

Alex turned to the sun. He loved to feel the heat creep through his skin. Tim, his dad, got dizzy and stupid with too much sun. Not Alex. He could lie still for ages on a baking rock, soaking up the heat like a reptile. A movement on the far hill caught his eye. Alex shouldered the gun and looked through the sight. A line of army boys dotted the rocks and heather, following Irishman's Wall down Belstone Tor. A small squad had been out training since the early hours and were now on a gruelling run. There was a ten-mile circuit from the army barracks over the open moorland of Rowtor, past Strangeways Farm, then up and over the rock-strewn slopes of Belstone and down the other side. Next they would follow the river for a mile or so, through bog, bracken and beef cows, and battle back over the sheep paths round the hill to the camp. The military had a licence to train over huge swathes of the desolate north moors. Their presence was a part of the landscape of Dartmoor as much as the rocks, the tors and the straggly sheep.

Alex counted the soldiers, one, two, three, four. Where was number five?

Earlier this morning Alex had hidden behind the vast stones of the prehistoric settlement that squatted on the side of Cosdon slopes, and had trained his sights on the old mining leat as one by one, five soldiers disappeared into Cosdon Drain. This huge drainpipe ran underground through the valley and the men had to crawl up and down in the darkness and wet.

"It's a dangerous job." That's what Quartermaster Sergeant Furzey said. He sometimes drank in the same pub as Alex's dad. Furzey said the recruits arrived at the camp as big boys in uniforms and left as human weapons. He said the harder he trained them, the more likely they were to survive. The 8th Battalion, Dart Rifles, or The Bloodhounds, as they were known locally, were a small outfit of three hundred soldiers. They had recently come back, eleven men short, from a twelve-month tour in Afghanistan where, amongst other things, they'd been involved in controlling insurgents in a remote mountainous settlement. The Bloodhounds' barracks was situated on the next tor and was also used as a training base for soldiers from all over the country. Dartmoor was a harsh, testing place to train. There were three hundred and sixty-eight square miles of moorland scrub, steep tors, rivers, gorges, lakes, bogs, boulders and forests. Alex had seen soldiers struggle through blizzards, weighed down with their packs, even as he helped dig snow-bound sheep out of snowdrifts. A few winters ago there had been a couple of fatalities; the first was a young soldier on a seventy-two-hour exercise. He'd got lost in freezing fog and died of hypothermia in the sub-zero temperatures. Just a few weeks later a Lance Corporal had fallen out of a tree, where he'd been keeping watch for twenty-four hours, and had broken his neck.

Quartermaster Sergeant Furzey obviously wasn't feeling merciful today and it was a full hour before the first wet soldier emerged from the drain into the boiling moorland heat. He fell into the heather, rubbing slime from his eyes. Alex waited another minute before the second and third soldiers appeared, gasping and coughing. They helped pull the fourth man out of the mouth of the drain. He blinked at the light and was sick all over his boots.

Alex waited. Minutes passed. He watched one of the men shout into the pipe. He could hear him from up here.

"BAZ."

And then there was Furzey in his jeep. A door slammed, there was a radio conversation, but still no fifth soldier. Alex looked at the yellow-brown grass and black reeds of the valley floor. Somewhere, under there, not far from the surface, a human was struggling to get out. Alex felt a prickle of alarm. The drain was four feet high and the water was often two feet deep.

Then at last, fifteen minutes after his mates, the fifth soldier emerged, red as a demon, minus his hat and coughing and spewing as he lay, face down, in the bog, his white-blond hair plastered to his head. Alex watched as one of the soldiers steadied him, gave him a drink from his canteen and walloped him on the back when he began coughing again.

Minutes later, Furzey had the lot of them up and pounding the sheep paths back on the training circuit.

Sometimes Alex wondered what it would be like to be a soldier. He was only a year or two younger than some of them. He wore similar clothes, greens and browns. He carried a gun when he was working. He kept his hair cut very short. He was interested in the techniques of stalking and shooting. But that's where the resemblance ended. The bottom line wasthat these men were being trained to kill other men. Sure, some of them were engineers and logistics specialists, some of them were communication experts and skilled mechanics. But there was no escaping the brutal reality, the blood, of their job.

Now the soldiers had vanished into the bracken in a heat haze.

Alex skirted the hill, stepping carefully to avoid the marshes, weaving through the long grass and stones. He picked bilberries as he walked, spreading them on his tongue and tasting the sweetness. As the moor gave way to a set of wild fields, bordered by ancient walls made of large grey stone, he heard a guttural cawing and saw three black crows harassing a buzzard. They'd kill it if they could. Crows were vicious. They attacked the lambs and killed the young pheasants. They ate huge amounts of the pheasants' food. They were also breeding like mad. Tim said he had never seen so many crows this year; they had overpopulated the area to such an extent that there was less birdsong in the evening round the house. Alex had watched a couple of crows raid a nest of fledgling birds and carry off the young to feed their own. He'd watched them take chicks from the pens, before they'd put the netting up, the little fluffy bodies squeaking in the sky. Alex checked the ammunition in his gun, put it up, aimed at the nearest bird and pulled the trigger. The gun kicked into his shoulder and Alex felt a charge as he watched the crow plummet. A direct hit. He wished Tim had been here to see. The other birds scattered in the sky and Alex jogged down the hillside to retrieve the corpse.

The bird had fallen in amongst the mature trees that lined the river. This was Golden Combe, the boundary between the five-hundred-acre Stonebridge Estate, where Alex and his dad worked, and the moor. Gold was allegedly buried in this valley, hidden centuries before from the Viking marauders. When Alex was a little boy, he'd come out here with a spade and Gaffer, his dog, and dig for it, turning over bright stones and mud in the riverbed.

The sun beat on Alex's neck as he searched the reeds for the fallen bird. The river was slack because of the crazy heat. And here was the dead crow. It looked so perfect, like it could spring into life. It was a huge bird, with a long, sharp beak, still-bright black eyes and curving claws, sharper than knives. Its blue-black feathers gleamed.

Alex remembered a passage in one of his mother's letters.

Crows are like creatures from another world, a world of dark fairy stories. They fly easily from the world of humans to other worlds of magic and darkness. Hades or spring; it is all one to them.

"She had quite an imagination, your mother," Tim had said. "She saw things differently to everyone else."

Alex wouldn't know. She had died when he was five years old. The birthday letters and an album of photographs were all he had. He dropped the limp, feathery body into a small hessian sack and tied it up with a length of string. Then he dumped his satchel and his gun on a wide, flat rock at the water's edge and removed his boots and socks. He dipped his feet in the cold water and watched as the tiny brown sprats darted around his toes. Mature trees, beech, oak and ash, had grown down here, sheltered from the moorland winds. The grass, sheep-nibbled to a perfect turf, was soft and comfortable. A thick curtain of ivy hung between the pair of elderly beech trees that stood either side of the river. Their fat roots coiled down the banks and entwined in the sparkling water. Alex shut his eyes and listened to the sounds of the moor: the wind in the leaves, the bees, sheep, the rushing, gurgling river, and now something else. There was another noise, like some kind of animal, snuffling and moaning, coming from downriver. Alex peered through the greenery, unable to work it out. He withdrew his feet from the water and pulled on his socks and boots as grunting and splashing noises drew nearer. Whatever it was, it was in the river. A big animal – a deer? Something injured? It sounded like a bloody bear! Alex was about to dart behind the tree when a gasping, muddy, sunburned face emerged beneath a low branch. It was a soldier and his face was twisted with crying. Shocked, Alex backed away, dipping to pick up his gun. If he slipped through the fall of ivy, maybe he wouldn't be seen at all. Alex edged back, taking great care not to crackle the leaves. The soldier was carrying an assault rifle with a powerful optical sight. He was grunting and moaning, making hoarse, animal sounds that reminded Alex of the crow in his bag. He sounded desperate; he was breathing heavily, coughing and snorting and clawing at his burning red face. He wore a helmet covered in webbing and grass and reeds. His combat trousers were wet and coated in mud, and his loose khaki T-shirt was damp and grimy. He was carrying a large heavy-looking backpack and a hydration kit. The soldier stopped dead in the river, saying OH OH OH, then collapsed so that he was sitting right in the water.

Hardly breathing, Alex realized he recognized him. This was the fifth soldier in the pipe, the one who hadn't come out for ages. His name may have been

"Baz". He wasn't very old; maybe eighteen or nineteen, a year or so older than Alex. Had he got his rifle wet? Surely he knew better than that? Drips of water shone from the barrel. The lad was a long way downstream from the usual training runs.

Alex manoeuvred himself round the trunk of the beech, deliberating whether he should offer assistance. But no soldier would want to be seen in this state. Now he was rising from the river, water and steam coming off him. What a mess! He was obviously exhausted and overheated. The river was the right place for him. He must have got separated from his mates. It was very easy to lose your bearings on the moors, especially if you were dehydrated, and this lad must be shattered after his ordeal in the pipe this morning. Soldier boy took off his helmet and ran his fingers through his blond hair. As he raised his arms, Alex caught the stink of him and saw a blue tattoo in the shape of a dagger on his wrist. He leaned into the water and splashed his face over and over, the water soaking his neck and shoulders and running down his chest. Paint and mud dripped from his fingers into the water. He shook himself and rubbed his face. He sniffed. Alex waited. He took a compass out of his pocket but as he opened it, it slipped through his fingers and fell into the river. The soldier swore and threw down his pack. He plucked the compass from the water and sat on the flat stone, sniffing. Then he dipped his hat in the current and washed off all the camouflage. Alex watched the mess of leaves and vine and bracken float downstream.

The soldier looked around him, seeming to take in his surroundings for the first time. Then he stiffened. Unnerved, Alex followed his gaze.

The crow bag lay in a pool of sunlight.

The soldier stood carefully and looked round, long and slow, like he had obviously been taught, and Alex suppressed a shudder. He did not want to be on the end of that stare. He could see the boy's face through a weave of ivy. He had a long chin and bulgy blue eyes. His hands were red with sunburn and smeared with mud and he had a cut on his elbow.

The soldier prodded the bag with the damp barrel of his rifle. He hooked it up and drew it close. When he saw what was inside, he dropped it.

The gift of a dead crow to Her Majesty's army was unlikely to go down well, and the bird was still warm. The expression on the soldier's face switched; he was no longer desperate and weeping but looked as malevolent as that dark old crow.

"Where are you hiding?" he growled in a voice smeared with menace.

Alex bit the inside of his cheek and waited. He had no intention of offering help now.

"Show yourself," roared the soldier.

8th Battalion: The Bloodhounds

Two shots ricocheted out over the valley and the soldier swore. More shots followed. Cursing and coughing, the soldier picked up his hat and his rucksack and blundered over the river, scrambled up on to the bank and pushed through the scrub. Alex watched until he was just a stick man, winding unsteadily through the heather and stones to the curve of the hill. Alex came out from the ivy. He supposed those shots were some kind of army code. He didn't want to hang about so he collected his crow bag and was about to make for home when he spied something lying in the weeds by the side of the river.

The soldier had left his gun behind! He must have lost his mind. Everyone knew this was the one thing a soldier must never, ever do.

What kind of a soldier was he? Alex stared at the weapon. It was a Heckler and Koch assault rifle. His punishment would be unthinkable.

Alex pulled at his lip. There was a footpath on the

other side of the river. This was a place people visited. Someone would find the gun pretty soon if army boy didn't come back for it. But you couldn't just have anyone finding the gun. Guns had to be licensed, and stored under lock and key. What if a kid found it?

But if Alex picked it up and handed it in, then the soldier would know it was he, Alex Jebb, who had seen him cracking up. Alex had witnessed his humiliation and had seen him lose his gun. He could be thrown out of the army for less. At the very least, his reputation would be destroyed forever.

Tim would know what to do. Alex could hand over the gun to his dad and let him take it back to the barracks. He could give it to Quartermaster Sergeant Furzey with a nod and Alex could stay anonymous. He didn't want this desperate guy to know he even existed. Alex picked up the gun and opened the magazine. The chamber was empty. The barrel was scratched to pieces and the wood of the handle was smooth with use. The serial number was stamped on one side, though another number on the other side had been seared off. He shut the gun and held it on his shoulder. He looked through the sights up the hill. The scope on this weapon was more powerful than his, although the lens was scratched. There was that hare again! What was it doing out in broad daylight? Alex watched the hare until it vanished into a copse of gorse. Then he turned, lost his footing and stumbled into the stream behind him. As he rose from the water, he grabbed at the bank. A helmet had passed by the stone wall, not one hundred yards away. Now another shadow chased down the wall, heading this way. Alex tried to think. If he ran in the direction of home they'd see him exposed on the hillside. But if he fled upstream they'd probably track him down.

His only choice was to hide.

Three men tipped into the glade. One was the blond soldier-boy with red-rimmed eyes. The others were just as bedraggled and dirty as he, with hot, tired faces, wearing helmets, backpacks and carrying identical rifles.

"This is the place," gasped the blond soldier, sweat pouring off him, trickling into his eyes and down his cheeks like tears. "Oh hell!"

"Calm down, Baz. We've still got time." A tall, dark-haired soldier who seemed in better shape than the others searched the riverbank. He was the only one of them who had a mouthpiece attached to a radio around his belt. His voice wavered. "So where did you leave it?"

"I can't remember." Baz looked terrified. "I'm done for. I'll be thrown out of the army, won't I?"

The dark-haired soldier touched his shoulder. "Calm down and start looking."

"You'll have the whole barracks in confinement," muttered the third soldier, stepping through the water. He was short and muscular and had a gruff voice. "You'll get us all done for gross negligence. I'm ashamed to be your brother."

The younger man went rigid. "I nearly passed out, Riley," he moaned. "People die on these moors in this heat."

"Getting lost on the moors for four hours is nothing to lose your gun over, Baz. Nothing is bad enough to lose your gun over. They say even if you get shot, you make sure you're holding on to it when you go down." Riley moodily parted the reeds with his sodden boot. "It's bad enough you cracking up in the bloody pipe earlier. And now this."

"Belt up and look for the bloody thing," said the dark-haired soldier.

But after a few minutes' searching, Baz collapsed on the bank.

"I'm dead," he said. "I'm well and truly dead. We'll never find it. I remember now where I left it – on that rock." He pointed to the flat stone. "And it's gone!"

His brother swore. "Stop being such a bloody fairy and help us."

The dark-haired soldier with the radio suggested that everyone form a line and sweep the area systematically. Baz heaved himself to his feet and began looking again.

"What's this?" Riley, the muscular soldier, toed the dead crow over the grass.

"That's what I haven't told you," said Baz. "I think someone was here just now. The bird had only just been killed when I got here. I thought I heard the shot. I thought it was Riley." He looked at the third soldier. "That's why I came here."

His companions exchanged glances.

"You've let an army weapon fall into civilian hands?" asked Riley. "That's it then. No leave, no chow, no socials. Just hours of drills and more drills and turn-outs and an almighty lock-down." He took off his hat to reveal a shining bald head. "There may even be a court martial."

"He can't have got far," said the older soldier. "It's a twenty-minute walk to the road, and there's nothing else in any direction. You were here, what, ten minutes ago? He's still close."

"But who would come out here, Saul?" asked Riley.

"Walkers, farmers, kids," Saul answered. He toed the dead bird. "If we can find him before he reports the gun, we're in the clear. Look for tracks, freshly disturbed soil, broken twigs." He pointed to the stone. "We'll start there. We've got thirty minutes before we'll be missed."

"But what about the others? The exercise?" asked Riley, rubbing his bald skull.

"We've already messed up," said Saul. "Now it's damage limitation."

He put a pair of binoculars to his eyes and scrutinized the surrounding hills.

The other two radiated out, treading softly, eyes to the ground. Baz was still having trouble with his breathing, but this new fear seemed to be reviving him.

Riley paused at the base of the big dead beech. He parted the ivy with the tip of his rifle.

"Here's something," he said. He held up a grid of dried mud, like the corner of a waffle. It was a square of mud from the tread of Alex's boot.

The others waded over.

"He's close," said Saul.

Barely inches away and hidden inside the tree, Alex stood with his arms pressed to his sides, his breathing so shallow and quiet he thought he might faint. He was pressed in on all sides by soft, crumbling, rotting wood and had just one tiny peephole to the left of his face. How quickly his day had changed direction. He could see the river and now the tip of Saul's gun. He hadn't had any time to think when the soldiers came sneaking down the hill; instinct had made him hide. Alex had known about this tree forever. He'd come across it when he was a lad, chasing squirrels with Gaffer. He'd crawled inside and stood up. When he tilted his head back he could see the sky. It was like being in a chimney.

Now he was beginning to question his decision. If anything happened to him, in this tree, no one would ever, ever find him. Thank goodness Tim had taken Gaffer with him today. There's no hiding with a dog.

"Hello?" Saul called out, so close Alex felt the vibration of his voice through the dead wood. "We just want the gun back. Nothing else."

Alex didn't believe him.

Then Saul swore. "Look at that." Alex saw a glimpse

of shoulder and arm as Saul reached up and unhooked the gun from the branch. Alex hadn't wanted to leave the gun lying in the puddle. Now he wished he had.

He felt the vibration of feet and relieved grunts.

"How did it get there?" Baz exclaimed.

Saul stepped back from the tree and Alex had a clear view of Riley.

"You drive me mental," he said.

"I can't reach that high," said Baz, ignoring his brother. He took the gun and examined it. "Thank God."

Alex had a cough building in his throat. It was an itching, burning sort of cough, made worse by the dusty soil around him and the lack of air. His throat tightened. He was going to explode.

"Sod it, let's just go," said Saul. "Q might let this go if we get back now."

"You mean you're not going to radio the checkpoint and tell all?" asked Baz, a break in his voice.

"Move it," said Saul.

The cough was just there, boiling away in Alex's throat. His eyes were watering. Gingerly he manoeuvred his hand to his mouth. He stuffed his fist inside, unable to stop a tiny grunt escaping.

Baz heard him. "What was that?"

The others looked at him.

"Come on," snapped Riley.

"It came from over here," said Baz, coming back to the tree. He put his hands on the trunk and looked up at the leaves.

"Who the hell cares, now we've got the weapon," said Riley, following Saul out of the river hollow to the grass beyond.

Baz spied the hole and, to Alex's horror, put his eye to it. Alex felt a deep, paralysing fear as Baz's pupils dilated in surprise. This was very bad.

Time seemed to stand still as they gazed at each other.

"Move it, soldier," came a voice from a million miles away.

"*You're dead*," mouthed Baz soundlessly.

He drew back and disappeared. Minutes passed and nothing happened.

Alex looked up to the circle of light above him, assessing whether he could climb up and punch his way out of the rotten wood. He couldn't just wait here for whatever they were going to do to him. But now there were splashing noises, hoarse breathing and the sound of running feet. Then, there was quiet.

Alex closed his eyes. The silence was intense, oppressive. Alex counted to one hundred before he allowed himself to take a deep, deep breath. The cough had vanished. He waited a full five minutes before he began to lower himself to the ground. What if Baz was waiting for him outside? This could be an ambush. But pins and needles were creeping up his legs. He had to get out. He knelt and slowly, slowly moved towards the hole. The air hung with the sweat of the three men. He waited by the hole, not daring to stick his head out.

This must be how bloody rabbits feel. Then he saw a buzzard fly low down the hill and spotted three figures travelling at speed below it. Alex crawled out of his hiding place and rolled on to the riverbank.

Max

I, Max Cosgrove, will be very lucky if I get out of this place alive. My ears are still ringing with the sound of trumpets and I am hemmed in on all sides by pompous stooges, all resplendent in their passing out uniforms. My brother is standing like the Colossus beneath the walloping crystal chandelier in the centre of the room, and is dressed in a black serge jacket with gold buttons, red-striped trousers, peaked hat and boots polished to a liquid shine. He looks like someone has just unpacked him out of a box. The carpet is thick with others like him, chucking back the wine and trying to impress their mothers and girlfriends with their newly officered ways.

I am reasonably costumed in a brand new navy suit, my white school shirt and my brother's yellow tie, but I'm the one who feels ridiculous. I'm pretty certain that every soldier in this place knows what I have done and hates me for it.

Beneath each shorn skull and polished brow they are thinking up ways to humiliate me further, and I'm trapped, friendless, here by the banisters. Even the waiters hate me. One passed by just now with a loaded tray of wine and I offered to make his burden lighter but he just ignored me, even when I told him he looked like the offspring of a penguin and a sausage. Anyway, I swear I look at least twenty.

Later, there will be a massive party with a band, fireworks and more boozing, but for now it is all polite conversation.

I hate polite conversation.

I slump against the stairs, fingering the woodwork and leaving smears on the highly polished wood, and watch my mother yakking on the other side of the room. Her jaw is moving so vigorously the feathers on her hat are trembling like a peacock in a tornado. Next to her taupe festooned figure, my fearsome father stands, his ramrod back betraying his military background. Stupid old fool. He's wearing his meagre collection of medals, like anyone here would be awed.

My parents gaze fondly upon Simon, my brother, glowing in his uniform, his officer's buttons ceremoniously taped up until midnight. I hate to admit it, but I'm impressed with him. It's hard to reconcile my big, soft brother, who could eat an entire tub of ice cream and who insisted, up to the age of fourteen, that babies came out of women's poo holes, is now an officer of the British army, holding court with all his admirers ranged around. Here we are at Sandhurst, the stuff of legend and culmination of our parents' dreams. Simon's girlfriend, Andrea, is here of course. Like my mother, she's wearing enough feathers to denude an entire ostrich colony. She has a high-pitched irritating voice and a too-big nose, but I have to admit even she looks good, in a tight-fitting red suit that shows off her legs and long shining blonde hair that covers her ugly-beautiful face. She's standing there looking adoringly up at Simon. I think I might be sick fairly soon. I have drunk twelve glasses of orange juice in the last hour because there has been nothing else to do and no one will give me any wine. I would head into the kitchens and swipe a bottle at source but I absolutely do not want to draw attention to myself. I'm trying very hard to stay under the radar. I do not wish to cross this new crop of military might. I don't want to make any more enemies.

The string quartet stationed in the far corner start playing the same jaunty neo-classical number they've played three times already, but everyone except me is too tipsy and happy to notice.

I feel a tap on my shoulder and headbutt the banister in alarm.

"You next, hey Max?"

I looked up into the grisly old face of Colonel Proctor: an old crony of my father's.

"I don't know if the army is going to be my thing, Colonel," I say, in my best Risings voice.

"Nonsense," says the old man. "It's in your blood. Your father was a fine soldier before his injury and it looks like your brother will do very well."

We look over at Simon, who salutes smartly as a superior glides up for a chat.

Colonel Proctor obviously hasn't heard about me yet. "How old are you now, anyway? Just finishing school?"

"I've finished school," I say. "Or rather it finished with me. I've been expelled."

"What?" Proctor leans closer, blasting me with whisky breath. "I can't hear you."

Suddenly my father looms out of the crowd, his grey egg-head creased in irritation. He gives me a "shut up" look and greets old Proctor jovially, taking the old man's elbow and moving him aside.

I am swept back by the current and wash up against the wall. Watching my old adversary – the waiter – approach, my foot lashes out of its own accord, sending his tray of drinks crashing to the floor. Red wine soaks into the pale blue carpet amongst shards of sparkling glass. The waiter shoots me a look of pure hatred as noise in the room quietens for a moment or two (I guess the military are skittish about loud crashes). The lull is brief but all eyes are on me and I feel like I am turning inside out. I hadn't planned this. I bend to help but the waiter tells me to wee off.

In minutes, legions of fresh lackeys are mopping and clearing up as I stand helplessly by. I don't know what to do with my hands because I haven't got a drink or anything to fiddle with. I must look like a boy ape, with my knuckles hanging by my sides.

"Max," snarls my mother through her polished teeth. Her feathers quiver with disapproval.

"It was an accident." I can hear the whine in my voice. I wish that sometimes things would go right.

"Why do you have to spoil everything?" she spits. I resist the urge to pull out a feather and tickle her on the chin. I know I am being childish. I'm jealous of Simon, I admit it. It's extremely simple. I have never been able to live up to the guy. He's Scooby-Doo, I'm Scrappy. He's Jesus, I'm John. I've never had the same billing. It doesn't help that my brother is a pretty decent sort of bloke, a good all-rounder who deserved a better brother than a fink like myself.

I begged to be allowed to stay at home but there had been no question of that. Mother had been so caught up in it all, she'd insisted on having the oven steam-cleaned and the windows washed in honour of the occasion, though it made no sense at all as our house on the edge of Dartmoor is over a hundred and eighty miles from Sandhurst.

Mother is completely mad.

"You should be proud of your brother," she says.

I am proud of Simon in my own mean little way. I know how tough my brother found the army at first, and how homesick he had been. Despite our family's military background (Dad had been with the Rifles for twelve years before retiring to work for the army estates), the first few weeks of Simon's training had been a real shock.

"They even tell you how to shower," he told me on his first trip home.

"At last," said witty me. "You haven't seemed to be able to do it properly so far, judging how you stink."

But Simon has changed; he's got tougher. His body has changed shape. His skin looks tougher. Even the bristles on his chin look sharper. Most striking of all is his new, easy confidence. Even our father now talks to him with some semblance of respect (imagine that!).

But now I really have been left behind, and, after what I did at school, I'll never catch up. I'll always be the freaky little brother in the funny clothes. The child people don't like to ask after. I'll be remembered for the rest of my life as the child who terrified an entire school.

Simon appears at my elbow. He looks taller than ever. Maybe they give newly commissioned officers boots with wedges.

"All right?" he grins. His curly hair has been cropped so short, you can barely tell he used to have ringlets. "Mother is having the time of her life."

I smile at him. "Congratulations," I say, and I mean it. "Second Lieutenant Cosgrove, you're going to be fantastic."

When it's just me and Simon, things are simple.

"Are you OK?" asks Simon. "Have you started at the new college yet?"

That is just like Simon. This is his day of glory and he's asking after my squalid little life.

"I start on Monday," I grimace. "I'm not looking forward to it."

"Girls!" says Simon nodding, upbeat. "At least you've got girls at Hammerton College."

I smile politely. Females are the least of my worries. I shoot a look at Andrea's legs. Except maybe that one.

"Are you really all right?" asks Simon. There is not a fleck of dust on his black-and-red-striped uniform.

"Well." I am about to list my woes when our dear father breaks the surface like a shark, bows in and draws Simon towards him.

"Proctor, you remember my son Simon. . ."

Another tsunami of congratulations begin and I am left alone as my hallowed brother is borne away on a tide of admirers.

Gloomily, I reach for my thirteenth orange juice. If I vomit, it will be a cheerful orange colour.

The passing out parade had been stunning. Hundreds of young officers were drilled in the yard with their ceremonial swords and bayonets. They were flawless. I wondered how they did not fall over, or trip over the fellow in front.

The friends and relations sat in a grandstand at the side as the cadets received their stripes. Ladies sat fanning themselves and everyone was dressed like they were attending some uber wedding. When I'd spotted my brother's face in the line-up I'd felt an annoying prickle behind my eyes. Simon! My brother; my fighting partner, parent deflector and fart-buddy. We'd shared a room for twelve years. Now he was a soldier and belonged to the army. I'd glanced at my father, who had a proud yet stern look fixed on his face. That would be right; Frank Cosgrove wasn't one to let his hair down. My mother was drunk with happiness, taking photographs willy-nilly and watching her beloved elder son so hard, I wondered if her eyes would pop out. I was desperate to *do* something, shout out "DOWN WITH THE MONARCHY" or run flashing out on to the parade ground, and skip in and out of the columns of men, willy waggling. But fear held me back. These men were powerful.

My father had caught my eye as Simon received his stripes, before docking his gaze safely back on his oldest son.

Can't get it right / I lost the good fight / I'm a different flavour / to what my pa favours. . .

There will be no second passing out parade, no matter how hard my parents wish for it. I could no more march in that perfect coil of human machinery than I could fly to Mars. I am made all wrong.

Later, on the way home, as the fireworks light up the sky behind us and with me strapped in the back seat of the car like an overgrown baby, I listen as my mother gently snores, her hat quivering on her lap, her fingers clutching the official programme.

Major Dad clears his throat. "Tough day for you, old man?"

I sit up in surprise. Was this sympathy and

understanding? Was this my father, Mr Frank Cosgrove, military administrator for Defence Estates for over twenty years and probable inventor of the term "stiff upper lip"? The same father who has never kicked a ball in the garden with me, never made me a meal, or offered one word of encouragement in any direction other than the military? Who remarked, when I won the coveted school art prize, that painting was an "officer's wife's sort of hobby"?

I say nothing. It has indeed been a tough day. I am never going to do what they need me to do. I have failed in life and I am not even eighteen yet.

"This is a dream come true for your mother."

I nod pointlessly. He can't see me in the gloom of the back seat.

"There's still a chance you can put things right," says Dad firmly, and I sink back into the seat.

"Knuckle down at college, get your As, and who knows, Sandhurst may accept you after all if you show how you've learned from your mistakes. Plenty of officers have been expelled from school." He looks at me. "Even ones who have messed up as much as you."

I can't help a groan escaping from my gut. The entente cordiale was brief. Dad was just softening me up before he went in for the kill.

"It's not going to happen," I say softly, hardly believing I am daring to say it out loud.

"Yes it is," says Dad, his eyes never leaving the road,

his knuckles whitening on the steering wheel. "I'm not going to let you throw your life away."

The hum of the car is very loud. I feel light-headed. It occurs to me I could open the door and fall out to meet my maker. There may be a soft verge. Then I remember the child lock. I'm trapped.

"It's my life," I say with false bravado as Dad eyeballs me through the rear-view mirror.

Mother coughs in her sleep.

"This has been the best day of my life," she murmurs.

I cover my head with my arms.

Keeper's Cottage

The sun was already high in the clear blue sky above the moor. The forecast warned of dangerous heat. Alex stood in the doorway of Keeper's Cottage watching three wild ponies graze by the outhouse.

He lived with Tim, his dad, in the cottage, which stood in a small copse of silver birch trees up a long, battered track. Keeper's Cottage wasn't a big place, just two up and two down and a back garden where the grass and nettles rampaged. The back room had space only for a vast sofa along the wall, a TV and a log burner which they always kept lit, apart from days like today, when it was so hot the slate floor was sweating. The kitchen had a small table and cracked wooden chairs. The only decoration was an old picture of a pheasant above the mantelpiece, which had been there when the family had moved in, fifteen years ago. Alex stepped into the hallway to the stair cupboard and opened the door. A tall, grey metal cabinet was screwed into the wall. He took out a small key and fitted it in the lock. The door squeaked as it opened.

Inside the cabinet was a row of gleaming guns. In contrast to the house, they smelled of oil and polish. There was not a speck of mud on the handles and the barrels shone where Tim had polished them.

"You have to keep your weapons clean," he said. "Or they might misfire."

Alex ran his finger over the guns. There were five altogether. Tim's 5.6mm air rifle, a Beretta Silver Pigeon shotgun, a 7mm Mauser deer rifle, an ancient stun bolt gun inherited from Alex's granddad, and his own Crosman, a 4.5mm gas-sprung air rifle, given to him on his twelfth birthday.

Every now and then the police would come round and check the firearms on their list against the weapons in the cupboard. They checked the licences were up to date and that the gun cupboard was kept locked.

Alex took down the shotgun, felt the weight of it in his hands. He lifted it to his shoulder and aimed along the corridor and out of the open front door. It wasn't loaded. Tim was obsessive about gun safety. Through the sights Alex could see the moors, humping up in a blue-purple mass ahead of him. Lowering the gun, he saw woodland and meadow and a couple of wood pigeons flying across the sky.

"You have a brain," Mr Goulders, his school history teacher had told him before he had left, over a year ago now. "You must use it. You don't want to spend your life in this backwater, do you? You'd die of boredom. You could do anything with your life. You don't have to raise pheasants for the rest of your days. You'd do very well at university and from there, the sky is the limit."

Alex hadn't replied. How could he say that raising birds and working out in the fresh air at Stonebridge was all he did want? And it wasn't the same all the time. Like winter, the shooting season, they were flat out, and in summer it was all about rearing up the young birds and keeping them safe. Not to mention the hedging and field work he did.

What did he want with university?

He felt a cold nose in his palm as his dog, Gaffer, a black spaniel, arrived at his heels. Gaffer was an old dog now, nearly sixteen, and too old to come out for long walks on the moors with him or go out on the shoots. Alex pinched a flea from the dog's broad old back and popped it dead between his nails.

"Fancy a rabbit, Gaffer, me old pal? You fleabag hound." Alex scratched the dog's neck and the dog grunted with pleasure. They used to be inseparable. Everywhere Alex went, Gaffer went too. Alex had spent his whole childhood roaming around the estate and the moors with his dog.

Stonebridge was a vast estate with over five hundred acres of moor and farmland. The owner, Tony Delaney, lived abroad most of year apart from the shooting season, and it was left to the farm manager, Jason Slaker, and Alex's dad to run the place. Jason farmed the sheep and Tim ran the game farm. They farmed pheasants, grouse and partridge. And in the winter, the guns came for the shooting. Stonebridge house, a big serious-looking place down by the river, was hired out in the summer for weddings and conferences and in the winter Delany came home and took up residence and hosted the shoots. Alex and his dad were flat out then, arranging the shoot days, sorting out the beaters, looking after the guns and their dogs and delivering huge meals, twice a day, for everyone. Alex loved it all, but a year after leaving school his dad had made him go to college in Hammerton to do his A-levels. Tim said if Alex didn't do them now, he never would. Now Alex only had a year to go but he couldn't wait to leave. At least college was different to school. There was much less swaggering and bullying, but he looked forward to finishing. Then he'd be free to get on with his life up here. Why he needed geography, maths and technology A-levels he had no idea.

"Happy birthday!" His father stood in the doorway, a smear of engine oil on his cheek. He grinned at his son. "Eighteen at last."

"Cheers," said Alex. He'd already had his present. It was a second-hand Apache quad bike, now sitting out in the shed. It was bloody fantastic.

"Want some bacon to celebrate?" asked Tim.

Alex shook his head. Tim removed his boots and went to the sink to wash his hands. His father was a tall, lean man, with close-cropped grey hair and friendly eyes.

"Shouldn't you be in college?" he asked. "You've got biology first, haven't you? And I thought there was a geography outing today."

"It's only a research trip," Alex said. "It's not worth going in. They want us to stand on the flyover and count cars."

He'd been much too freaked out to tell Tim about the terrifying incident with the soldiers in Golden Combe.

You're dead.

Alex kept imagining what could have happened. If the soldier had hurt him, no one would have found him in the tree. Alex hadn't told Tim because he knew his dad would be intrigued and would want him to tell the story over and over, and as likely as not, the tale would resurface in The Miner's Arms over a pint of ale. Soon enough, everyone in the valley would know that Alex Jebb, the gamekeeper's son, had hidden in a hollow tree from a crying soldier who had committed the ultimate crime of losing his gun.

"Come on," said Tim. "I'll give you a lift. You don't want to miss out."

Alex let out a deep sigh.

"Your mother would kill me if I didn't make you get your qualifications," said his dad apologetically.

Alex thought this was highly unlikely, as his mother had been dead for nearly thirteen years.

"That reminds me," said Tim. He went to the kitchen

drawer, took out a pale blue envelope and handed it over. "The last one," he said, and had to look away.

This wasn't just any old birthday card; it was written by Alex's mother. She had written thirteen cards just before she'd died. Every birthday, there would be an envelope, a different colour and shape each year, with the familiar neat handwriting addressed to Alexander Jebb. Dad had them all stashed away, ready to roll out each one every year.

Alex put the card in his pocket. He'd open it later. Each card always contained a letter from his mother. Alex wasn't up to reading this one now, especially as he knew it was the last one. Tim had told him that Helena had only had the idea right before she'd died, and didn't have the strength to write beyond Alex's eighteenth birthday.

"Come on, old man," said Tim, interrupting his thoughts. "Time to mingle."

Alex locked away the gun, reluctantly turning the key.

"Don't you want to see your mates?" asked Tim. "How's Levi?"

"Fine." Alex nodded.

"There must be some nice girls at college?" fished Tim.

"There are some lovely girls at college," replied Alex. He grinned. "But none of them think I'm very lovely."

"You might be surprised," Tim said. "You've inherited my good looks."

Alex stripped off his T-shirt and washed himself at the sink. He dried himself with a tea towel and dragged a clean T-shirt from the string over the fireplace. At least he'd get to see Sasha today. Not that she'd notice him.

"All right," he said. "I'll go."

Levi

The bus shelter is a cliché of graffiti (I did it myself two years ago), aroma of urine (I don't *think* this was me) and discarded sweet wrappers (these are universal, are they not? They cover the surface of the earth like big flakes of dust). I pull my trilby hat low over my brow and adjust my earphones. I'm listening to hip hop. Nothing else is worthy of mine ears.

Ah ain't gonna bite you / Don't want to fight you
I ain't damaged and don't need to be managed
I'm not meek but I ain't a freak / Just let me
groove, yeah
Without getting rude. . .

The beat makes me nod like I'm having a fit. At 180 BPM this is my finest track. It's called "Let Me Groove" and it's like rapping over a jackhammer. Me and Gerry Fisher recorded it at home on my computer with my beatbox and the unfeasibly cool microphone I'd requested for Christmas. I'd been in the process of getting a group together at school when I was expelled. It's a bummer because I need Gerry to work the music program on my computer (I haven't got round to reading the manual – I'm the artist, I leave all the menial details to him) and I haven't seen him for over a month.

The bus pulls up and lets out my neighbour from hell, Mrs Simmons, who despises me for boyish crimes committed in prehistory and likes to pretend I don't exist. I climb on board and present my brand new pass to the surly driver. I hope he's sober; he holds my life in his hands. There are no seats at the front so I have to walk past everyone. I pass two teenage girls in the front seats, a mum with a snotty toddler two seats back and Old Father Time who may or may not be about to wake up. I think they are all frightened of me because they are all trying hard not to look. My new shoes, black patent and very pointed, like an elf at a wedding, are pinching my heels. They look cool, though. I swing gratefully into an empty space, shuffle my bony bum over to the window and lean into the glass. I turn up my device. There's a big fat man sitting behind me. I can feel his obese eyes boring into the back of my neck. I pull my collar up so he doesn't telepathically bruise my skin.

It's midday. Benji, Francisco and Gerry will be tucking into their school lunch. The chow at The Risings is surprisingly disgusting considering the "astronomical" fees my parents used to pay. Not any more. I'm saving them thousands of pounds now I've gone "state". They should at least be grateful for that. I stare out of the window, pretending to be preoccupied with the moor, looming up behind the hills like a headache. I think the girls in the front seats are whispering about me. I wonder if they go to Hammerton College. I hate enclosed spaces like this bus. Everyone is pretending that they aren't watching everyone else. We're like a box of wasps trying to relax. I'm feeling as twitchy as hell. I'd pull a moony if it wasn't for the ogre behind me.

Last month, when it all happened, I hoped I might earn some kudos from being the first boy to be expelled from The Risings for five years, but it hasn't been that way. Instead it feels like all my friends are shrinking further and further away from me. It's like I'm being left behind. Strange, when you're on the inside, stuck in a classroom, you can't wait to get out and see what the world is all about. But when you're on the outside, it's all grey. Being expelled is a fool's paradise.

I'm trying to stay out of Mother's way as my presence irritates her. At first she was either crying or cross, or both, and would lay into me without warning about what a disappointment I am. However, since the Commissioning Ball and Simon's passing out parade, she's all buzzed up. She's decorating again, and the house is awash with smug builders and dusty plasterers and crazed electricians, and the noise of banging and scraping and builders' eclectic conversation invades every space. There's nowhere to hide. Thank God the tech has amazingly agreed to take me on despite my high-risk track record. Dad must have bribed the principal. I've been there two days and haven't made any friends yet. No one wants to talk to me (do they all know about me already?). This is OK. It means I can watch and assess. I can plan my next moves.

The Risings School is only two miles from home. Me and Simon used to ride together down the narrow, leafy lanes, racing side by side on our mountain bikes. Now I have to take the bus down twelve miles of busy road before we reach the thrilling market town of Hammerton. I've been demoted in every way.

Finally, we arrive outside the squat, grey college buildings. I traverse the pavement, stepping carefully behind a gaggle of girl-humans, clad in bright, tight clothes and slick with lipstick and perfume. I'm not wearing the right gear. Funny again (ha ha) how, when at school – proper school that was, not tech – I'd despised my silk tie and blue blazer. I'd scorned my ironed white shirts and my black trousers with a central crease hanging over my polished loafers. (Mum did it all.) But I know instantly that my new baggy-bottom jeans are the wrong sort for this crowd and my trainers are way too fly. My shirt is tight, pink striped and very fashionable. I'd be the coolest kid around in some London college. But here, in a small town on the edge of North Dartmoor, I look like a twerp.

"Sasha Tavey is back at college all day," chirps a short dumpy female creature in zebra-striped trousers.

"What's happening with her baby?" answers her pal, a shapely blonde in a phlegm-coloured jumper.

"Her mum's looking after it," replies Zebra.

"She won't be the same," warns Sexy Phlegm wisely. "No more parties for Sasha. It will be all big saggy boobs and bibs."

The girls snigger nastily.

All this is new too. This sounds like someone other than me also has shame, though this was tech shame, not in the same league as my Risings shame.

Zebra clocks me ear-wigging so I hang back, clacking my patent beetle-black shoes on the paving stones. I put on my coma-face as I pass a group of lads sitting on the wall in front of the college building. They fall silent as I pass. I don't make eye contact so I'm less likely to engage the enemy. I haven't spent my childhood milling around on military peripheries not to learn something.

Dad went apocalyptic when I got expelled.

I was, he shouted, beyond disappointment. He said my behaviour was *demonic* and I was extremely lucky not to be slammed up in a psychiatric prison. I'd let it roll over me, pretty sure he'd cool down, like he usually does. But this time he just got hotter and hotter, like a dodgy nuclear reactor, and then he decided to personally arrange my punishment. I'm not going to go over that now or I'll never make it through these paint-chipped swinging doors.

*

I'm inside. I'm making definite progress over the ploughed carpet.

I'm not supposed to be here. I want to shout it out. I want to tell that mousy girl in the blue shorts, and the small human with the snappable plant-stem neck reading the noticeboard, and the hairy librarian woman, roaming down the corridor like a queen, that I OUGHT to be touring SOUTH AFRICA with the first eleven. I should be sipping iced lemonade and fretting myself about the sweat patches on my whites.

There is a crunch of bone as I kick the brick wall very hard.

No one has noticed except for mouse-girl, who twitches her whiskers and scurries off down the corridor. Now my foot hurts. I move on, limping. I hope I look like John Wayne, hot for battle after a hundred miles in the saddle.

The pain slices into my toes but it clears my head and in a funny way it makes me feel better. I have made it into college for the third day running. No one has tried to murder me or offer me extra tuition. No one has attempted to mug me or hug me or. . .

"Max Cosgrove." A chunky black lad with a serious haircut stands squarely in front of me. He's grinning like he's my adored nephew. "I *thought* I saw you here yesterday. Now you're here again. Why is that?"

I halt, and as I am a man of manners, I take out my earphones. I have no idea who this interloper is. He doesn't look aggressive; he has a friendly, open face. But how does he know my name?

HOW DOES HE KNOW MY NAME?

What else does he know?

The boy fills in the silence.

"I'm Levi Jones. We met five years ago at army cadets. You only came for one week, but we were partners on the high wall. You were scared of heights. You, like, froze." The boy does a little dramatic pose. "I talked you down. Remember?"

Yes, I remember the sick fear of falling and the humiliation that danced alongside. Someone had talked to me over all the shouting and yelling and had coaxed me out of my faint and got me off that horrendous wall. It wasn't the instructor; he'd scared the pants off me. This must be the guy who calmed me down.

Fantastic. More humiliation.

"You didn't come back," Levi goes on happily. "I was only there another month, and then I fell off the same wall and broke my arm in three places, see." He holds up his right arm and it crooks backwards like a boomerang. "So my mum banned me."

Levi has an inoffensive West Country accent and stocky, muscular arms. He's wearing a grey T-shirt, blue jeans and battered trainers. Not a dandy then.

"So?" asks Levi. "Why are you here? Don't you go to The Risings?"

WHAT DOES HE KNOW?

"I never forget a face," says Levi helpfully. "Especially if I've saved their life."

"I got expelled," I say. I may as well say it now. He probably knows anyway.

"Fantastic," says Levi, clearly delighted. "What did you do?"

I look at Levi carefully. I don't want to spoil our little tête-à-tête.

"You don't have to tell me," says Levi, cocking his head. "Must have been bad."

"I stole food," I try experimentally. "uite a lot of it."

"Oh." Levi's eyes narrow and he has to look away to bounce the lie into the corner. "And you got expelled for that?"

"I stole more than once," I explain, getting into the swing of the thing. "It got to be a bit of a habit, I'm afraid. I went into the kitchens and took food from the cupboards. I got loads of warnings, but I couldn't stop myself. I'd sworn an oath on the school shield not to do it again, so they had no choice."

"You must have been hungry," says Levi, scratching his nose. He can look at me again now. He's beginning to work out what sort of man I am. A. Liar.

"I'm always hungry," I say. "Look how skinny I am. I've got a hyper metabolism." I hold up my own weedy arm for inspection.

Levi nods. "Was that all you stole?"

Nope. My brain has thrown a blank. My lips are all empty. Nothing is coming. Levi may as well have asked me to calculate a solar quadratic equation.

To my relief Levi lets the cross-examination go and

checks his phone instead. I guess a sociable chap like him is going to have friends who are going to be sending him messages, unlike me.

"Whatever. I've got geography in two minutes. Where are you going?"

"Geography," I say with utmost confidence. "I understand there's a field trip?"

"Follow me," says Levi, like he's some kind of cult leader.

We cross concrete steps, rubbery floors and corridors strewn with bad art. Levi elbows through the crowd, clearing a path for me.

The truth will come out eventually, but at least I have bought myself some time. It gives me a chance to work out what angle I should take.

What next?

First Blood

This is one of those humiliating situations that unfathomably occur every now and then in education: fifteen students with fluffy-cornered clipboards counting cars like rabid traffic wardens. Every one of us is clad in fluorescent yellow tabards.

I'm billeted on the Hammerton flyover with Levi and a tall, rangy lad with a seriously serious face. In addition to the tabard, he's wearing a faded black T-shirt with holes in the shoulders, scruffy combats with a coil of orange string poking out of a pocket, and dirty steel-toe-capped boots. He looks like the third sinister son of an elite pig farmer. His eldest brother is the heir, the second, the spare and this one is the psychopath.

"Max, this is Alex," says Levi like he's hosting a cocktail party. "Don't be fooled by the innocent exterior. This guy is deadly. He can blast the head off a pheasant at a thousand paces."

I knew it!

Alex's face twitches almost imperceptibly. He's got the sort of darkish looks foolish girls would probably go for. He has grey eyes and a needle chin. However, he doesn't appear to be able to talk.

"And this is Max Cosgrove, hungry dude and ex-employee of The Risings," Levi continues. Alex raises an eyebrow a quarter of a centimetre. I wait for him to ask what happened, but he doesn't say anything. Whoa! The ice man cometh.

"Hold on to your lunch," Levi advises Alex. "From what he's just told me, when Max gets hungry, he'd eat his starving grandmother's breakfast."

I feel an annoying blush bloom up my neck and flood my face. I hadn't expected my little lie to be paraded quite so soon. I curse my liar's cheeks. Simon is also a terrible blusher so it must be genetic. My brother pinks up if any female except Andrea or our mother speaks to him. It's funny how someone that sensitive is now a trained killer.

"Do you have brothers?" I enquire playfully.

"No," says Alex. He returns his manly attention to his clipboard.

I lean on the railings of the bridge. Below us are allotments and the cycle path leading into town. On the other side the fields stretch up to a belt of woodland and beyond that, the cursed moor. I watch Alex out of the corner of my eye as he scores the traffic. He's not a talker, but it's all right, because Levi can't stop. He's like a man who has drunk a thousand coffees. And in the TWO HOURS we are marooned on the bridge, Levi covers:

Girls in the geography class.

Girls in his maths class.

Girls in his chemistry class.

The forthcoming match between Barcelona and Chelsea.

The curious formation of the geography tutor's chin.

Interracial marriage.

The time he played football against The Risings School and scored the winning goal.

The time he pulled a nineteen-year-old girl at the Hammerton Tech disco.

How he is technically not a virgin.

How bananas can stop you from pooing.

Why his mother still believes in God.

How his dad was the first black man to run Hammerton Fire Station.

The relative merits of Mars versus Snickers.

Why the internet will soon be wired into our brains at birth.

Divorce.

The city of Lincoln.

The time he went potholing in Hammerton sewer and found a wedding ring.

After two hours of this I feel I know more about Levi than I do about any of my so-called friends back at The Risings. But as the day heats up, even Levi's talk dries up and we fan ourselves with our clipboards and start making up the numbers as the traffic slows to a near standstill. I am making up a poem entitled "I Felt

Like a God on Hammerton Bridge" when I notice an army truck beginning to crest the hill. It's an old dark-green vehicle, like something from another age. There's nowhere to hide. As it crawls past, wedged like a giant toad in the line of traffic, I see ten or so lads sitting in the back. I suddenly find the composition of the allotments utterly riveting, my clipboard clasped to my chest like a shield. Then something small and silver flies through the air and slaps Levi in the face, slicing his cheek open. It's a foil sachet of food.

"Have lunch on us," calls a gurning face from the rear.

"Look at that!" Levi shows us a palmful of blood from his cheek. "Morons," he yells after them and I hear laughter from the truck. Up to this point I have been valiantly keeping my head down, but I can't help roaring after them, "GO AND GET YOUR HEADS BLOWN OFF."

The soldiers begin hooting and Levi and Alex look at me with puzzled faces.

But this only spurs me on.

"WHEN ARE YOU LOT GOING TO START WINNING?"

This remark causes some lively responses from the soldiers as the traffic moves on.

"LOSERS."

"Shut up, Max." Levi grabs my arm. "You're well out of order."

I notice Alex is watching the departing soldiers intently.

"Oh dear. Were they friends of yours?" I ask as the truck finally vanishes over the bridge.

"No, no," says Alex hurriedly. He looks at Levi. "Are you OK?"

"Direct hit," says Levi, gesturing to the package on the ground. He looks slightly shell-shocked. He picks it up and reads, "Carrots, potatoes and meat stew."

He drops the package, spits on his fingers and tries to clean his cheek, but the blood keeps coming.

"Have you got a beef with those guys?" Levi asks me.

"They assaulted you," I squeak. "Was my response inappropriate?"

"Yes," says Levi. "I don't need that sort of backup."

"Oh, my brother is in the army," I say cheerfully. "Take it from me, these guys love a bit of grief."

"Well, I don't," says Levi. He turns his back on me and paws at his face.

"Hey," I say. "Is that the cold shoulder I see?"

Levi can't resist my charm and chuckles. "You're mad."

"So I've been told," I reply.

Only ten minutes to go. I doodle all over my survey. Levi seems deflated, like when he was cut all his pep ran out along with his blood. We decide to give up and rejoin the rest of the class. As we're walking single file down the flyover bridge, a navy-blue minibus with gold lettering turns off the roundabout and edges up towards us.

I swear and pull my hat over my brow. It's the Risings school minibus.

Now the traffic is stopping altogether. What is this? Is it Destroy Max Cosgrove Day? I throw a punch into the sky, hoping it hits Jesus, or the Fates, or whoever else is in charge. I scan the bus under my eyelids. There are six lads inside this time. No one has noticed me yet; they're all looking out of the window at something on the other side. There's Ben Robinson and Frodo Tomms, and sitting at the back laughing, as usual, is Francisco Lennox. Three weeks ago I was doing a joint art project with him. We were the best artists in the school. It was a massive project, a vast mural in the school foyer with a picture of every kid in the school. It was the finest thing I've ever done. My talent really showed. I wonder if someone else has finished it.

The bus is stopping right opposite us. Everyone inside could give me away. My face is beginning to heat up again. I look over the bridge. It's too far to jump. I'd be jam, and although the allotments below look good and soft I don't want to be impaled on a bean pole.

"Look, you can just make out the red flag."

I turn to Alex in astonishment. This is the longest sentence I have heard him utter.

"Look," Alex urges. He points to the moors, to the horizon. I gratefully look out at the moor. I don't focus. I'm just relieved to have a legitimate reason to look away from the road.

"Can you see the Live Fire flags?" asks Alex. "Do you know about the Army Range flags?"

"Yes," I say wearily. The bus engine roars. The sound

makes me feel schoolsick. I've sat in that very bus a gazillion times, off to some match or other. The bus has an instantly recognizable *chugga chugga*, a deep sound unlike other vehicles. We call it the Boom Wagon. And this lot would be off on the art trip to St Ives.

"Have you seen the flag?" Alex demands.

"No," I mutter.

"Over there," Alex points. And sure enough, in the far distance, I think I might see the flutter of a military flag.

"When you see that you don't go on the moors," says Alex. "It means there is live fire. The soldiers hoist the flags so civilians don't get caught in the crossfire." He pauses. "You get red lamps at night and red flags during the day. Remember that. It might save your life."

I know all this, of course. I've lived next to the moors for two years and am better versed in army ways than most. All the same, I'm grateful for the diversion because now the Boom Wagon, with its treacherous occupants, is moving on.

But as I look at my clipboard the doodles and numbers seemed to blur as a shout comes from the departing bus. There's a thump as six big lads break from their belts to gawp at me from the back window.

"MAX MAX MAX MAX MAX."

"HE'S STALKING US!"

"PLEASE DON'T KILL US, MAX!"

"GET IN, GET IN!"

"THE RISINGS TERRORIST STRIKES AGAIN!"

I hurl my clipboard at their smug monkey faces but the bus suddenly accelerates away and the papers flap instead into the windscreen of an old lady's Punto, making her lean on her horn in outrage.

Levi takes hold of my elbow and walks me down the pavement. Alex brings up the rear, breathing down my neck.

"I tried," muttered Alex.

"I know," said Levi. He looks at me. "My, you're a live wire."

"I have my moments," I reply, taking my tabard off. In a moment of supreme self restraint I do not throw it, or anything else, off the bridge.

"Dare I ask what they were on about?" Levi asks.

I shrug. "Just Risings humour."

We walk off the flyover and walk over the grass verge back to town. The others have stopped trying to keep me out of mischief and walk on ahead. I watch Alex. He helped me back then. He worked out that I was unhappy about the Boom Wagon and deliberately gave me an excuse to look away. Why did he do that for me? It's not like we're mates.

Whatever. Alex gets a tick. I owe him.

Sasha

Alex should have been at college, analysing population statistics, but he wasn't going in. He couldn't sit indoors on a day like this. There was a soft breeze and a blue sky all over and no way he could broil in a stuffy classroom that smelled of farts and cheap perfume, with wafts of chips blowing in through the air conditioning from the cafeteria.

Dad was at work in the game pens. The young chicks were kept in a series of vast pens in a paddock just beyond the cottage.

Alex walked up the track that ran up past the cottage through a tunnel of beech and ash and oak and bramble with Gaffer sniffing at his heels. His new quad bike had sprung an oil leak and Jason was fixing it down at Stonebridge Farm, so Alex had to walk if he wanted to get anywhere.

"Think you can keep up, you old has-been?" Alex tickled the dog.

The birds sang around him. It took Alex twenty minutes to reach the top. Here the trees thinned and he reached a pasture full of Swaledales and their lambs, now stocky and dozing in the sun. Alex remembered back in March, in the bitter cold, when these little creatures were being born at a rate of fifty a day down at the farm in the valley, and were sent within hours of their birth up to these perishing fields. That was the problem with the estate. Tony Delaney, the owner, hadn't updated the agricultural buildings; he was only interested in the pheasants.

Alex hummed, happy that he had escaped a day of drudgery. He had his gun on his back and was on the lookout for rooks. Gaffer had never liked gunfire, which was a problem considering he was supposed to be a gun dog. But over the years he'd got used to it. He could cope with the tinny bang of an air gun but still shivered if anything more powerful was fired. Alex suspected this was because the old dog was going deaf. He swore he did all his listening by lip reading.

There were no red flags today. Alex decided he would therefore take the long walk over to Belstone Hill, checking the corvid traps on the way. It was such a clear day, he'd be able to see for miles and miles.

This was the way he liked things, just him, Gaffer and his gun. No bloody college. He just wasn't interested. Alex had stopped looking at the TV years ago and wasn't bothered about reading Dad's paper. He wasn't interested in the wars overseas, or the rate of income tax, or how many schools were being closed down.

All he wanted was to be left in peace, and to get on with his work. No wonder Dad called him "old man".

He had his birthday letter in his pocket. He'd read it three or four times since his birthday. They were always bittersweet, these birthday letters. His mother would write about Tim, and what she thought he, Alex, might be doing. She told him stories from her past. And always, in every letter, she wrote again and again how much she loved him.

He sat on a lump of granite as Gaffer wagged through the gorse, sniffing and panting, and unfolded the letter. It was three pages long, with jokes, a recipe for lemon cake (an explanatory note said it would impress girls) and then there came the bit which he had read over and over again.

Your dad always laughed at me about my thing for hares, but they are magic. When I was first diagnosed, three years ago, the doctors gave me six months to live. You were only two years old. I went for a long walk on my own and I saw a hare, down in Golden Combe. It came close to me, and I swear time stood still. I swear the wind stopped blowing and the birds fell silent. It felt like a spell. I asked the hare out loud for more time, in that frozen moment, and I believe, in a crazy sort of way, that I am able to write to you now, three years later, because of that hare. Because he granted my wish. And I have lived long enough for you to remember me and that is a gift.

Alex grunted and Gaffer cocked a deaf ear. He was only five when his mother had died. He remembered her, but sometimes he couldn't work out if his memories were actually made up of photographs and letters and stories that his dad talked about. She was twenty-eight when she died. She had cancer of the lungs, even though she'd never smoked. There was a photo album that lived in the drawer in the sitting room. This had pictures of Mum inside. She would be forever young. Alex drew in his breath. He'd got over it, hadn't he? He thought he did pretty well, most of the time, but he did know that every day, every hour, there was a shadow of sadness hanging over him. Some days it was darker and colder than others. He refolded the letter, put it away. This eighteenth birthday letter was the last she had managed to write. She was too unwell to write any more. There would be nothing new from her now. She had really gone. Now Alex was really on his own.

"Do you remember your mother?" Alex asked Gaffer. The dog gave a low woof.

"I'll take that as a yes," said Alex. He aimed his gun at a black shadow in the sky and fired. He missed. As the rook flew right over his head, Alex uncocked his gun and walked on. He didn't mind. His heart wasn't in it.

He'd been walking for maybe an hour when he saw a small white car going along the metalled lane above him. The car pulled over to a picnic spot and he watched as a couple of figures got out. Usually, if he saw walkers or tourists, he'd just melt away into the moor, but the car park was directly in his path and he couldn't be bothered to make a lengthy detour. Alex set his jaw, zipped up the air gun in its pouch and put it on his back. As he got closer he saw the picnickers were two women and one of them was holding a baby. The other waved.

"Hey, Alex, is that you?"

Alex paused, then waved back. It was Sasha, from his geography class. She'd had a baby (this must be it). She must be skiving college too. He hadn't spoken to her much, though she was good friends with Levi. She was the sort of girl you couldn't help looking at.

And now Alex had no choice but to say hello.

"All right?" grinned Sasha as he approached. "This is my mum, and THIS –" she took the baby from her mother and held it proudly aloft "– is Sammy-Joe." The baby was wearing a blue suit and a huge sun hat.

"Cute," nodded Alex. He didn't know what you were supposed to say about babies. He prayed that she didn't make him hold it. Sasha was wearing a brown skirt which blew about in the breeze and a close-fitting yellow T-shirt. She had a pretty, freckled face and strong-looking legs.

"Why aren't you in class?" she asked teasingly. She had a million freckles and wide eyes.

Alex shrugged. "Couldn't face it," he said.

Sasha laughed. "That's no excuse. We had to take Sammy-Joe for his eight-month check this morning.

Then we thought we'd come up here for a breath of fresh air as it's such a nice day." Sasha held the baby up to the sky and he giggled at her.

"Want to hold him?" asked Sasha.

Alex froze.

"Leave the lad alone," said her mother. Alex smiled at her gratefully. Sasha's mother looked a lot like Sasha. She also had freckles and a bright look about her. She was wearing jeans and trainers and her hair was tied up in a ponytail. She couldn't have been more than thirty-five years old herself.

"Sorry," muttered Sasha. "I always think everyone must find him as irresistible as I do."

"You don't seem to find him irresistible at three in the morning, Sasha Tavey," said her mother, unscrewing a Thermos. "Coffee?" She offered Alex a cup.

Alex shook his head. "No, thanks." He remembered what Levi had said about Sasha: that she had had the baby at seventeen, that the dad wasn't involved and that her parents helped look after the baby so Sasha could go to college. Levi was sweet on her. She had this kind of vitality about her, her skin glowed and, like Levi, she couldn't stop talking. He wondered what it must be like for her, having a baby so young.

"Cute dog," said Sasha, watching Gaffer sniff the car wheels. "Though I'd have thought you would have owned a pack of bloodhounds."

"They're at home, eating raw baby deer," said Alex, deadpan.

Sasha's mother smiled and looked away.

"What are you up to, anyway?" asked Sasha. "Are you stalking something? Are you looking for a fluffy beast to string up on your gibbet?"

"Shooting crows," said Alex. He wondered what she would make of that. Girls like her didn't like the idea of guns and killing, he was sure of it.

"Ohh, have you got a gun? Is that it?" She pointed to his air gun. "Can I have a go?"

Alex chuckled. He'd better not: she wasn't licensed, and you didn't handle guns around small children.

"She's only joking," said her mother.

"No, I'm not," said Sasha. "Never mind. Another time."

"Do you live round here?" asked Sasha's mother.

"Yeah," said Alex. "About five miles in that direction." He pointed down the valley.

"Don't you get lonely?" she asked. "There's nothing for a lad your age to do up here, is there?"

"I like it here," said Alex.

"I love it up here," sighed Sasha, smoothing her hair behind her ear. She grinned at Alex. "What do you make of the new boy, Max? I call him Mad Max. I think he's a bit loopy."

Alex shrugged. He thought Max was beyond loopy but he didn't like to say so.

"Want a sandwich?" asked Sasha. "We've got more than we need."

"No, thanks," said Alex, and his stomach growled.

"Go on," said Sasha. "We've got ham, cheese or

disgusting hummus. The baby likes them. Don't you, my evil one." She kissed the baby, scrabbled in a box and brought out a sandwich in one movement. "Here's ham. You look like a flesh eater."

Alex was about to refuse again, when he thought, why not?

He took the sandwich and bit into it.

"Why can't we move out here, Mum?" asked Sasha. "Somewhere like that." She pointed to an isolated farmstead buried deep in the next valley.

"You wouldn't want to live there; that's Strangeways," said Alex.

"Why not?"

"It belongs to the army now. They use it for their training exercises. It used to be a working farm up to about twenty years ago. But the farmers went bankrupt and sold the whole place to the military."

"You know a lot about it," said Sasha, setting the baby down and watching him toddle through the heather.

"It used to be my grandparents' farm," said Alex, surprising himself. He wasn't used to talking about it.

"That's sad," said Sasha.

Three sandwiches, a slice of cake and a plastic cup of coffee later, as Alex continued his walk up to the tor he heard Sasha's mother say, "Ooh, Sash, he's gorgeous."

He made a face as he walked. Tim would kill himself laughing. Twenty minutes later, standing on Rowtor, with the wind blowing under his clothes and into his face, he saw their white van retrace its path down the hill. It couldn't be easy to be Sasha, to be a mother so young, and yet, she always looked like she was loving life, even if she often looked more tired than the other girls.

The moor rolled away from him, the peaks and valleys stretching as far as he could see. The hills were a dull purple and brown, and a line of red flags fluttered in the distance. From the next valley came the rumble and bang of the army guns.

Friday

We're watching girls, Levi and I. We're sitting on the wall outside the college, sipping Cokes and chilling. Against all odds I think I may have gained a friend. This is good. I was beginning to think there must be something wrong with me, especially as Gerry, my former henchman, has been avoiding my calls. At first I thought me and Levi had little in common. Levi says he lives with his mum in a small boxy house on the outskirts of town. He's been in council education all his life. He's popular, always texting someone or high-fiving people in the corridors. His mother phones him very frequently. Levi doesn't appear to be embarrassed about this, he just says she is "a worrier because I am accident-prone". He likes football and talking about that girl, Sasha Tavey, who had a baby. He laughed out loud when I admitted that my mother owns a horse, and has just wrangled an invitation to come back and ride it sometime.

"Sure," I say. "But my parents are obnoxious."

I receive what I am beginning to recognize as a Searching Levi Look (SLL).

"In what way?"

"In all ways," I reply, swallowing my Coke. "My mother is an utter bitch."

Levi looks shocked, bless him. "You don't say that about your own mother. Where's your respect?"

"She doesn't respect me, so I don't respect her," I respond. "The sooner I can leave home, the better."

"Do they hit you?" Levi asks gently.

"No, no, of course not." I laugh at the idea of it.

"Ignore you?"

"No."

"Do you get enough to eat?"

"Yeah, look, it's not like that."

"I can see cash isn't the issue," says Levi, eyeing my gold trainers, iPod and has-been designer T-shirt.

"Yeah, they give me blood money."

"So what is it? Mental cruelty? They tell you you're crap?"

"Not in so many ways. They sometimes imply I'm not trying hard enough. . ."

Levi looks thoughtful. "So does my mother, but I'd never call her a bitch."

"They just don't understand me, or even like me. I'm this huge disappointment to them."

"Have they said that?"

"Yes!" At last I am on firmer ground.

"They've paid for you to go to private school all your life, right?"

I nod. This is true.

"Motorbike, piano lessons, ski trips, cool clothes, the latest tech. You look like you've been given it all."

I don't like where this is going.

"And then you got expelled from this school, threw it all back in their faces, for repeatedly stealing biscuits! Man, if you were my son, I'd be pretty bloody disappointed in you myself," says Levi.

I ought to belt him for that but instead I laugh in a slightly manic way to show that I can take it. Can I take it? Levi touches my shoulder and I flinch, muttering something about not being into body contact.

"I'm sorry. I don't know the facts. I'm not trying to get at you. I'm just trying to see where you're coming from." He gives me another SLL. "Hey, chill! It's OK! I've just got a big mouth. My mum says I call a spade a spade and I should learn some charm."

He looks worried. I ought to be cool about someone being honest with me. I decide to forgive him.

"It's all right," I say eventually. "You're probably right."

I smile innocently at Levi. "My mother's still a bitch, though."

Levi rolls his eyes. "Come out on Friday," he says. "A gang of us can hit the town."

I hesitate. Levi is all right, but none of his friends have exactly warmed to me.

"It's cool," says Levi, reading my thoughts. "I admit I have ulterior motives. I'm going to ask the lovely mini-mum Sasha to come too, but I don't want to scare her off, so I need a group of us, yeah?"

"Sure," I say. "I'll be your foil." I don't see anything in Sasha myself: she's quite noisy and annoying, and worst of all, she has a baby! Personally, I'd run a million miles before getting involved with someone like that.

"There's Alex, I'm going to ask him too," says Levi, slipping off the wall. "He looks like he could do with some fun."

I scratch my head. I don't get Alex. Levi is a straightforward, smooth-running sort of man, but there is something watchful about Alex, like he's got a devious hidden agenda. Despite the lifebelt he threw me on Hammerton Bridge the other day, I don't think I like him very much. For one thing, he doesn't know basic manners. He never smiles and rarely makes eye contact. Maybe he's just shy. I shift on the wall. Or maybe Alex doesn't like me either.

His reflection was distorted in the kitchen tap; his nose looked huge. Alex rubbed at the chrome to wipe the grime away. There wasn't a mirror in the house.

"What are you doing?" Tim asked him, a note of amusement in his voice.

Alex rubbed at his eyes. "I'm going out with some mates." He gave up trying to see his reflection. What did it matter what he looked like? He couldn't do anything about it. As long he had a clean face and clean teeth and clean clothes. He frowned. Clothes. What should he wear to a pub on a Friday night? He hadn't wanted to say yes when Levi had asked, but he'd been persistent. Besides, Alex liked Levi. And when he'd gone on to mention Sasha was going to come, he thought, why not? Usually he'd rather sit in a cold river than spend a Friday night out in Hammerton, but he supposed he ought to make some kind of effort for Levi.

"Anyone I know?" asked his dad, lightly. They both knew this wasn't like Alex at all.

"Levi and a kid called Max," said Alex. He knew his dad was hoping he was going to say a girl's name.

"Who's Max?" asked Tim. He opened the freezer compartment of the fridge and brought out two frozen dinners.

"He's in my geography class. I don't know him really; he's only just started."

Alex didn't tell his dad about Max being expelled from The Risings.

Tim removed the cellophane from the fish dinners and popped them in the oven.

"It's just a drink," said Alex.

"Out on the town on a Friday night," said Tim in mock alarm. "You!"

"All right," said Alex. "Lay off."

"I'm sure Levi has asked you out with him before," said Tim. "Why now and not before?"

Alex thought again of Sasha.

"Why not?" he said. "Now go away and let me get ready."

Alex settled on a pair of jeans, some nearly clean trainers and a plain black T-shirt. He sucked in his breath, as the jeans, barely worn, were rather tight.

Dad came in from feeding the dog, looked at him and chuckled. "I never thought I'd see the day," he said. "I haven't seen you in those jeans for years. Do they still fit?"

Alex breathed out. "No," he said in a shrill voice, and they both laughed.

Half an hour later, with his usual moleskin trousers on, Alex wheeled his bike out of the shed. Dad came out to say goodbye and held out a tenner.

"That should buy your mate a drink," he said. "But be careful. It can be a jungle in Hammerton on a Friday night."

As if Alex needed reminding.

Mother pulls over at the bus station.

"Dad will pick you up at eleven. Don't get into any trouble, will you." She admires her lipstick in the rear-view mirror. It doesn't make her look any better. She's always saying, "Ooh, I can't step out of the house without my lipstick!" I once suggested she could if she put a paper bag over her head. This little joke didn't go down very well.

"Who are you meeting?"

"Levi," I say.

"Isn't that a brand of jeans?"

"I'm not having a drink with a pair of jeans."

"Only joking. But it is a funny kind of name, isn't it?"

"Any name is funny if you say it often enough," I answer. "Take your name, for example. Jill. Jill. Jill. Jill. Jill. Jill. Jill. Jill. Jill. Ji . . ."

Mother slaps the steering wheel. "Why do you have to be like this?"

I pause. "Like what?"

She puts away her lipstick and shows me her witch face. "Why are you always so rude and sarcastic and aggressive?"

I consider, for this is an interesting question. "Well," I begin. "If it is nature, it's your fault because I have inherited your genes. If it is nurture, it is also your fault, because you brought me up, or bribed others to do so. Either way it is unequivocally your fault." I smile sweetly. "Happy, Mother?"

"Don't be late or spend your taxi money," she responds.

I open the car door, sling my slender legs to the pavement and ease myself out. A group of girls run by, chattering and giggling. I can feel nerves flood me. Why am I here? I'm wearing my sunglasses, my trademark hat, my white skinny jeans, an ironic Paris Hilton T-shirt and my trusty pointy shoes. I look insanely great, but I don't fit in this beef-town of a place.

"Bye, Max," calls my loving mother.

I nod and slam the door. Mother drives very carefully, easing her way out into the road, with indicators flaring.

Too late I realize I'm too cowardly to walk into O'Malley's pub on my own. I'm not eighteen for another month. What if they don't let me through the door? I have Simon's ID, but don't know if it will work this time. I scrunch the false ID into my pocket and step in the pub.

O'Malley's smells of beer and disinfectant, a classy joint. I peer through the gloom to see if I can spy Levi. It's very dark with my shades on but I am not man enough to remove them. Mock-Tudor black beams zigzag the white walls along with rusty metal adverts for Guinness and soap. Levi must be running late. I slide into a chair with my back to the barman and sit there for a little while trying to summon up some courage. I'm not good in places like this. I don't know what to do with my hands. Eventually I feel more embarrassed just sitting there than actually doing something, so I rise and swagger over to the bar.

The barman has a long black ponytail, sideburns like topiary and pale, muscled forearms. He looks like an ancient Gallic chieftain and I think he wants my head on a rope, swinging from his horse. This is not a person I would naturally gravitate towards. What shall I order? Vodka and orange? That would make me look like an experienced drinker, but I'm obviously not. Lager and lime? Sounds disgusting. Besides, lager makes me burp.

A pint of Guinness? Francisco once told me if you drink too much Guinness you get black poo with a white tip. I don't need that complication.

"Yes?" says Chieftain Bar Lord, eyeing my neck. I bet he's wondering how easily he could remove my head. I bet he has a collection of skulls belonging to underage drinkers in his cellar.

"A Coke, please," I say meekly.

Chieftain operates the Coke siphon with his mighty arms. He adds ice, then pops in a pink striped straw. Was that deliberate? Maybe it was a secret signal to all the other bar staff not to serve me alcohol.

I pay my money and return to my seat. No one is going to believe this is rum and Coke with a straw in it. I feel so fearful! I've turned into the cowardly lion. A few months ago I breezed into this place with a gang from The Risings and I didn't worry in the slightest. I brandished the fake ID and bought myself and Gerry Fisher a pint. Now here I am shivering over my fizzy drink, scared as anything. What has happened to me?

A blast of cool air hits my neck as the door swings open. I look through the reflection in the picture in the opposite wall to get a clear view of the door. Through this screen I watch three men troop in. From their very short hair, overpowering man perfume and clean, pressed clothes, I suspect they are soldiers from the barracks. They are of a type, instantly recognizable: a close-knit group of young men, healthy, smart and aged roughly eighteen to twenty. There's lots of laddish banter with loud, confident voices. They're soldiers, all right. I wonder what Simon is doing right now. He's supposed to be coming home tomorrow.

The soldiers invade the bar and I make myself invisible. This is a trick I developed at The Risings: if you make eye contact with no one, looking fixedly at some point in the distance and just assuming no one can see you, then very often no one does. I've become a bit too good at being invisible; sometimes I find myself muttering to myself, assuming no one will hear.

I don't mutter now; instead I drain my glass, but I've lost all nerve to go up and order another.

I could just wait outside for the others, or maybe I'll just go home.

After what happened at The Risings, Dad called me an idiot and a coward. I run my finger over my mouth.

"An idiot and a coward," I say softly. There, I knew it, I'm talking to myself. That's what happens when you let down your guard. I'm turning into a mad old woman, looking for her knitting. I will leave this hellish place just as soon as the soldiers at the bar take their drinks and sit down. I don't want to risk walking past them.

The door opens again and here at last is someone I know. Now it would look odd if I left. Alex the mountain man stands dazed and blinking, but looking pretty sharp for Alex, all in black.

"Over here," I say in a croaky voice, not wanting to draw attention to myself. Alex isn't much of a conversationalist but it is better than being alone. To my surprise, Alex smiles as he heads my way. I didn't think he possessed the necessary facial muscles to do this. Oh. Now I see why he's smiling: Sasha-the-girl-mother is just behind him.

I nod at her. Where has she put the baby?

Alex pulls a chair out for her.

"Levi's always late," says Sasha. She's wearing a green T-shirt and jeans. The T-shirt is a bit tight though admittedly she has great boobs. Her stomach sticks out a little bit. That must be the result of having the baby. My own stomach is always concave no matter how much food I put into it. Apart from Dad, who is built like a prize-winning turnip, the rest of the family are all thin. Simon is your typical beanpole and Mother has been on diets ever since I can remember. She has a fear of fat like it is a poisonous substance. She deeply scorns and pities lardy women (but oddly enough, not flubbery men). Mum gets kicks out of not eating very much, like she's got an imaginary giant sticker chart and every time she turns down a muffin she awards herself a virtual gold star. When Dad's in a playful mood he calls her "chub" just to wind her up. It works a treat even though he has pounds more fat on him than she does.

The soldiers, mercifully, ignore me. All the same, I can't stop watching them.

"This place smells of wee," announces Sasha loudly as Alex goes to the bar. "It's not you, is it, Max?" She grins. My, she's a wit as well as fertile.

So this is a single mother. This is a subject my parents go on and on about. They pretty much blame single mothers for the fact the country is going to the dogs.

Apparently it's something to do with them getting all the flats (the mothers, not the dogs). I'm finding it hard to look Sasha in the eye knowing she must have Done IT at least once in order to make the baby.

"Did you get a council flat?" I ask conversationally.

"No," says Sasha managing to draw out the word into two syllables.

Hah! That's one in the eye for the old ones. Next time they are on this particular rant I will be able to inform them that I know a single mother who did NOT get a flat.

"Do you go to the dogs?" I ask sweetly (I need more information).

"I don't approve of gambling," says Sasha. "Or idiots," she adds.

I swallow. What to say? What to say? There were no women at The Risings bar Matron, and she had hairy palms. I have had precious little practice.

I decide to take the bull by the horns.

"So you've actually had a baby!" I say, folding my hands behind my head. "Did it hurt?"

Sasha's face clouds over. Have I taken this too far? Is this something only females are supposed to mention?

"Because my father says childbirth is to women, what war is to men," I say brightly.

Sasha leans forward and I get a glimpse of a rather sexy cleavage.

Oh god, has the baby, does the baby . . . does it. . .?

"Has your father been through childbirth?" asks Sasha, colouring up.

"Not yet," I reply.

"And I've never been to war. But as far as I'm aware, childbirth is about giving birth; war is about killing people. I don't recognize the comparison. Maybe if I had a council flat, I could stage the debate there. But I don't because I'm not a freeloader. So I suggest we all shut up."

Oufff. She's touchy! Women! Mercifully, Alex returns (I never thought I'd think that). He carries two Cokes and three bags of crisps. I watch, fascinated, as Sasha tears into hers. No wonder she's a bit fat. Mother never eats crisps.

"So tell me, Alex," Sasha says turning to him after her crisps fest. "How much wildlife have you murdered since we last met?"

He's not going to like that. But Alex merely smiles. (That's twice in five minutes!)

"I only shoot or trap wildlife that is likely to harm the chicks – like crows, for example; they pick off the young birds. And ravens, they come over in massive flocks from Wales at lambing time to prey on weak lambs." He pauses (he's unused to all this talking, I can tell). "I can tell you, if you've ever seen a lamb being eaten alive by a fox, you might be inclined to do some murdering of your own."

"I love lambs," says Sasha. "When I was pregnant with Sammy-Joe I could have eaten them alive. I craved blood."

"Then I would have had to trap you," says Alex, deadpan.

Are they flirting? Please, no!

At the far end of the bar, the soldiers' laughter is getting louder. There always seems to be one or another of them at the bar, buying rounds of pints. But my shades are doing the trick and they are taking no notice of me.

"How is Sammy-Joe?" asks Alex in his straightforward voice.

Why didn't I say something like that rather than go on about flats and dogs? I could be in there. She's obviously (ahem) easy.

"Nuts," says Sasha. "He ate a handful of cat meat this morning before anyone could stop him."

Alex laughs. He has good teeth. "Maybe he doesn't think much of your cooking."

I am marvelling at this transformation. At college Alex barely says a word and now he's the life and soul of the party.

"Cheeky," says Sasha. She's showing him a picture of the baby on her phone when the door swings open, banging the wall, and Levi wobbles in.

"The party has arrived," he smiles, clearly tipsy. He is followed by three lads and two girls. I recognize them from college but don't know them. I budge up to let them sit down, relieved to put distance between me and Sasha.

For the next hour, I try to have a good time. It should have been fine. I like Levi and everyone is in high spirits. The girls are quite pretty and are dressed up to the nines, with short skirts and lipstick, but seeing how I crashed and burned with Sasha, I can't think what to say to them. I feel a pang for my mates at The Risings. It was effortless to have a laugh with Gerry or Francisco. But now my stream of wit has dried up. I have no opinion on the football talk at Levi's end of the table and I'm not interested in the techie talk going on next to me: they're talking about downloads and buzz technology. Sasha, it seems, is into her gadgets. She's going on about the future of digital music and although I'm certain Alex doesn't have a clue what she's on about, he's lapping up every word like she's Bill Gates. I watch as Levi clocks the pair. He catches my eye and looks away.

Right, that's it. I'm going in. I start talking to the girls sitting over the table, asking them if they like hip hop and telling them about my music, but it is clear they are distracted. They keep eyeballing the soldiers across the room and muttering and sniggering to each other. A blond soldier with a tatoo keeps looking back, winking and making them laugh.

Is that all it takes? A wink? No wonder we've had a patriarchal society for millennia. One wink and the entire female species submits to a lifetime of oppression.

I'm about to give up and go home when I feel a hand on my shoulder.

"Come on, bro." Levi grins blearily down at me. "It's time for a proper drink."

Second Blood

Alex clocked Saul first. Apart from the clean civilian clothes and the lack of warpaint, he looked pretty much as he had down by the river. The others, however, were transformed, and it was only when Alex spotted the tattoo on the blond soldier's wrist that he finally worked out who they were. Baz, in an immaculate pale blue shirt with a gold chain and with a tanned, laughing face, was almost unrecognizable as the wild, hysterical soldier Alex had seen on the moors. And Riley, in a striped polo tucked into chinos, sipping beer and twinkling at the girls, was utterly unlike his furious, aggressive brother. Alex turned his back firmly on the group, a nervous tension in his stomach. Baz might recognize him, but the interior of the beech tree had been as black as night, so it would have been difficult to see much. Alex wanted to leave and go home, now. But how could he to do so without drawing attention? He'd only been in the pub for half an hour. He wondered what had happened that day when the soldiers had finally got back to the barracks. Had the Lance Corporal covered it up, seeing as they had retrieved the weapon? From what he heard, losing your gun just was not done in the army.

Now he could hear them chattering behind him. They were laughing about a game called "Pound a Pig". Apparently each of them had put five pounds in the kitty and the one who got off with the ugliest girl won the money.

And there was Max, now guzzling back the beers like a hardened drinker. He was getting increasingly loud, trying to impress the girls. Alex tried to distract himself by listening to Sasha. She didn't seem to know the other girls. They smiled politely at each other but that was all. And when the girls left, they didn't even bother to say goodbye.

"My mates have all left college," she said, reading his mind. "I had to take a year out when I had the baby."

"So you're. . .?"

"Nineteen at Christmas. I had Sammy when I was nearly seventeen. It's great being here," she went on. "I don't get out much. Sammy doesn't like it. And Mum and Dad have been so brilliant I don't want to take advantage, you know?"

Clearly Alex didn't, but he nodded anyway. He noticed Levi watching them. Careful, thought Alex. He saw that all Levi's other male friends, apart from Max, who was at the bar, had also left. They must have gone with the girls. He'd been too busy talking to Sasha and keeping an eye on the soldiers to notice.

"How's your training going?" Sasha called over to Levi.

"Steady," said Levi. "I walked ten miles at the weekend."

"Levi wants to walk the whole south-west coastal path this summer," Sasha told Alex. "It's five hundred miles and will take about a month. Is that right?"

Levi nodded, suddenly looking shy. This is the stuff we don't hear about, thought Alex. The sort of stuff he'd tell his girl.

Was Sasha Levi's girl?

"I'd do it myself if it wasn't for Sammy-Joe," said Sasha.

"Bring him along," said Levi. "Seriously."

But then there was a commotion going on at the other end of the room and everyone stopped talking. Max was at the bar and one of the soldiers, Baz, was shouting at him. Max had drunk three pints of lager in the last half hour and his face was flushed. Alex grimaced. He really didn't want to get involved.

Levi, however, pushed back his chair and stormed up to the bar. Sasha exchanged glances with Alex.

"What's going on?" Levi asked.

"Your pal spilled his drink all over me," snarled Baz. He'd gelled his short blond hair up into spikes. His trousers were also wet all over the crotch and thigh.

"He pushed me," said Max, his eyes slitty and glistening. "I nearly fell over."

Levi put a hand on Max's shoulder. "Come sit down."

Alex watched as Riley stood behind his brother. Baz put a hand in the air, as if to keep him there.

"I know his face," said Baz. "It's bugging me."

"You're bugging me," said Max.

"Shut up," said Riley. "And buy my brother another pint."

They'd all had way too much to drink.

"No way." Max turned his back on the soldiers and made a comic face at Alex and Sasha.

"Come and sit down, Max," repeated Levi, taking his arm.

Now the barman was looming over them. "Any more trouble, and you can leave."

Alex sat, waited. It wouldn't do any good to wade in right now. He'd just be another angry bloke. Better just to sit back and wait.

"I recognize you," said Riley, ignoring the barman. "You're the joker on the bridge."

"Is it?" asked Saul, who had just returned from the toilets.

Max said nothing as Levi dragged him back to the table.

"Chill, flab-head, I'm not getting bashed for you," snapped Levi.

"Mercenary typhoons," muttered Max. "Batten down the hatches."

Sometimes Alex really wondered what was going on in Max's head. He watched as the soldiers argued at the bar, staring over at them.

The barman crossed the room to their table.

"Leave, please, guys," he said, aware of the charged atmosphere. "I'm not having any trouble."

Max started to argue with him but Levi hauled him up and propelled him towards the door. Alex looked at Sasha and they both followed.

"Calm down, Rambo," Levi was saying.

But Max spun round. "What about him, chief?" he yelled, pointing back at Baz. "He started it, him and his baldy boyfriend."

"You can come back when you can behave like a big boy. Now clear off," said the barman.

The door swung shut and Max thumped the window so hard Alex thought it might crack. The barman rushed outside and Max ran off down the street, shouting, "DON'T DRINK IN O'MALLEY'S. HE'S AN EVIL DRUID, HE'LL HAVE YOUR HEAD!"

"I'll follow him," said Levi and he pelted after Max.

Alex and Sasha wavered in the street. The night smelled of beer and traffic fumes. There were the usual triplets of drunken girls, snogging couples and violently swaying single blokes. Alex really wanted to go home. This was his first night out on the town and he'd been on the edge of a fight. But he couldn't abandon Sasha.

"I hate things like that," said Sasha shakily. "What is it with blokes and booze?" She looked at him. "Blokes are much nicer when they haven't been drinking. Look at you! You're being lovely."

"I think you're nice too," said Alex, and felt like a tit. If his dad could hear him, he'd kill himself laughing. Alex's amazing chat-up line – *I think you're nice too*.

"They will have gone to the Green Café," said Sasha. "It's open all hours. But I need to get home. It's not far."

Alex cleared his throat. "I can walk you home, if you like. If I can just fetch my bike first."

Sasha nodded. "Yes, please. It's aggressive tonight." She looked down the high street at the lit pubs and noisy crowds.

"How well do you know Max?" she asked.

Alex told her that he had only known him for a couple of weeks, and that he had been expelled from The Risings.

"Do you know what he did?" asked Sasha.

"Levi said Max kept stealing food," said Alex.

"That's odd."

"So's Max," replied Alex.

They turned off the high street towards the river and the din of the night receded. Alex listened as Sasha told him about the baby and then about the baby's dad, Charlie, who was now at university in Scotland and with whom she'd had a massive fight before the baby was born.

"I never want to see him again," she said. "He's been a nightmare. He wanted me to, you know, get rid of it. But I couldn't do that in a million years." Her voice broke. "And when Sammy-Joe was born, he never even sent a card. Charlie's mum did, though. She sent a hand-knitted jumper for Sammy-Joe and a bunch of flowers for me. So we visit her sometimes. It wouldn't be right to cut her out."

Alex was silent. All this was a world away from the stuff he knew. He wondered what he would do if he found out he was going to be a dad. He sighed. It was unlikely to be the sort of problem he would have to face for a long time. If ever. He was relieved to see his bike was still on the railings by the river. He'd be glad to get home. There was something charged about the air, like each air particle was fizzing with intent.

"Levi isn't answering his mobile," said Sasha, putting her phone in her bag.

Alex twisted his key and pulled his bike out of the rack. Levi could look after himself, he was sure of that. Max was another matter.

"Oh hell," said Sasha. "I've left my bag in the pub."

Back in the town centre Alex glanced over the parade to the yellow-red windows, gloomy with people-shadows.

"I'm such an idiot," Sasha said, beginning to cross the road. "You can tell I'm sleep deprived, can't you? Blame it on the baby."

"Don't go in there on your own," said Alex, running with his bike to join her. "They'll all be as drunk as skunks."

The windows of O'Malley's were steamed up and condensation ran down the inside, distorting the people within.

"I left it under the table," said Sasha.

"I'll get it," said Alex, peering through the window. He stiffened as he watched Riley and Baz downing drinks through long glass vials. It was a scene that he had only seen before on TV.

"Thanks," said Sasha. "Since I had Sammy-Joe I'm not keen on crowds." Alex stepped through the doors into the crowded pub. Through the fug the barman frowned at him.

"Lost bag," mouthed Alex.

"Hurry up," replied the barman.

Alex began by checking the coat racks: nothing. And there was no sign of it on the floor.

"HELLO," roared Baz, looking over his drink. "Somebody has lost his pals."

Alex thought he could be out of here in less than five seconds.

Then he spotted the bag. It was white with a buckle, and sat just under their old table. The problem was the soldiers were now sitting there. The bag was just by Baz's feet. He could hardly just sidle over and pick it up. What if Baz recognized him? But then he saw Sasha, pressing her nose up against the window. She pointed at herself. "SHALL I COME IN?" she mouthed. Alex shook his head. It was loud, hot and horrible in here. He had an image of Sasha, standing on the moor in her brown skirt, holding her baby, with the sunlight making her hair gold.

He swallowed and walked over to the men.

"Hello, chum," said Saul. The group seemed to be in better spirits than before.

"Is there a bag under there?" said Alex. "My friend left it there."

Baz looked under the table and scooped up the bag.

He held it out to Alex, who reached for it, but Baz flicked his wrist and the bag swung away. Alex overbalanced and landed on his knuckles on the table. The table rocked and the drinks spilled and Alex found himself staring into Baz's eyes. In that instant he was back in the tree, being pressed in by the dead wood, and the panic rose in his throat.

"WATCH IT," snapped Riley.

The music stopped and there was a moment of quiet and Alex coughed. Baz blinked.

"Do I know you?" he asked, soft and dangerous.

"No," said Alex. "Can I have the bag, please?"

"Give him the bag, you muppet," said Saul.

"Not till he asks nicely," said Baz.

"He did ask nicely," hiccupped Saul.

Alex's heart was hammering. He wished he'd never come out.

"I'm sure I must have seen you somewhere before," said Baz. "All these familiar faces are coming out of the woodwork tonight."

Alex could feel all their eyes on him.

"Who are you, anyway?" asked Baz.

"What's it to you?" asked Alex. He held his hand out for the bag. Any minute he'd lose his nerve and be out of here.

"Your pal," said Baz. "We know him."

Alex shook his head. "It's none of my business," he said. He could feel another cough coming and had to fight to keep it down.

Baz passed him the bag and Alex took it.

"Suits you," grinned Baz.

He was about to leave when he noticed movement at the window. There was Levi, and Max. Why had they come back? The barman had made his way over to the table. He looked at the boys outside.

"Time to go, lads," he told the soldiers.

Riley protested. "We haven't done anything."

"I think they should stay in here," said Alex. But nobody listened so he shouldered through the swaying crowds and cleared the door. He'd made it.

Outside, Max and Levi were plastered. They had each got hold of a bottle of cider and were both three quarters of the way through. Max leaned back against a lamp post, taking deep gulps.

"We came to look for you," slurred Levi. "I wash worried 'bout Sasha."

He tried to put an arm round her but she shrugged him off.

"I only like you when you're sober," she said sternly.

"She likes me," he beamed at Max as Alex handed Sasha her bag. "I'll walk you home."

"No, thanks," said Sasha. "You need to get yourself home."

"I'll take her home," said Alex, and Levi gave him a hard look, his misty eyes suddenly fierce.

Watch yourself, thought Alex.

He looked at the door. "Let's go," he said as Saul, Riley and Baz stumbled out.

"Go," said Alex. He put his hand on Max's back, guiding him away from the pub. Glancing back, he saw Sasha holding Levi's hand (hell!), leading him out of trouble.

"Wash the rush?" mumbled Max, but he allowed himself to be hustled along. Alex didn't know where they were going. He just wanted to put as much distance between him and the soldiers as possible.

But then Max stopped.

"Need a piss," he said. He stepped away from Alex and crossed the road.

Hammerton High Street was divided by a small central plaza, complete with flower beds, a chipped iron bench and a war memorial: a large granite obelisk, topped with a statue of a praying soldier. Max wobbled up the first step, unbuttoned his trousers and peed against the plaque that named the dead soldiers.

The roar came up the street, growing louder and louder. Alex watched as Baz tore over the road and grabbed Max by the collar. Shouting and swearing, he yanked him backwards so he fell from the memorial on to the ground.

"Where's your RESPECT?" screamed Baz.

"Are you trying to look at my willy?" hiccupped Max from the flower bed. "What are you, a poof?"

"You don't piss on a memorial," shouted Baz. "These men died for you."

"I don't care," said Max, unsteadily getting to his feet. "It's history. History is dead. So will you be soon, I expect. Anyway, I heard your barracks are going to be closed down because you're all useless."

Now Riley had joined Baz, so Levi and Alex reluctantly crossed the road.

"You should be banged up," said Baz. "I know you. I know what you did. I know about your punishment. You're the school terrorist."

Max changed then. He gave Baz a look of pure hatred. "Shut your mouth," he said.

"I saw you coming out of the cooler," said Baz. "Is it true you cried like a girl?"

Without a word Max attacked Baz, flying at him and headbutting him in the stomach. Alex watched in horror as Baz buckled and fell, clutching his gut.

"Oi," shouted Riley and he ran at Max.

Alex went to help him but felt someone grab his arm and he swung round in alarm, but it was only Sasha. "Get out of it," she said. "Don't join in."

Alex watched as Riley and Max grappled, briefly,

ending with Max on the ground. Any minute Alex expected carnage, with the other soldiers wading in; he'd have to help Max.

"Run," he said to Sasha. "Sammy-Joe doesn't want his mum getting hurt."

Levi hurled himself at Baz, who kicked Max, now groaning on the floor.

"Get off," he yelled. But it was Riley and Saul who pulled Baz off.

"Baz, he's not worth it."

Alex found himself kneeling with Levi, both holding Max down. The boy was flailing and shouting and yelling curses like he was possessed. Heart thumping, Alex watched the men march Baz away. After a minute Levi nodded at him and they pulled Max to a sitting position. Blood poured from his nose and he was coughing like an old man. He was shaking and his pale skin glistened with sweat. Alex could smell the blood and sweat on him. He smelled like a fresh kill.

"CANNON FODDER," screamed Max after the departing soldiers. "MURDERING ROBOTS."

"Shut up," said Alex, grabbing Max's shirt. "THAT'S ENOUGH."

He dropped him, feeling anger coursing through him. "NOW GO HOME."

Purgatory

My right eye has swollen up so much I can barely see out of it. Three days after the fight it's puffy, yellow-blue and angry-looking. My eyeball is bloodshot and I have a fetching rim of purple etched into my upper cheek. I have a bruise on my back and on my bum. (I used mirrors to see.) I cannot remember much about the latter part of Friday night, but judging by these souvenirs I believe I may have said something inflammatory to a minotaur.

My mother, as usual, is bursting with maternal passion and refuses to look at me as she serves the shredded greens from the china bowl.

I wrinkle up my nose, pretending to be a rabbit as a mild protest at the refreshments, but no one notices. Dad is telling Andrea some dull tale about army pyrotechnics, Andrea is fervently listening, Mother is dispensing her vegetable matter and Simon, oh! He's looking at me. Result! I put my hands to my head and fashion a pair of rabbit ears, which I waggle.

Simon catches my eye (I only have one to catch) and twists his hand in the air, like he's turning off an invisible tap. So I obediently desist from all rabbit-like activity.

Before dinner, Simon, fresh from the battlefields of Surrey, had taken me outside to the camellia bush for A Private Talk. I walked slowly because quite a lot of my body hurts.

"I know everything," Simon had said. Even in his civvies he looked somehow military. He was spotless: hair trimmed, clean-shaven. His shoes were polished and his shirt was ironed. Softy old Simon stood straight-backed with shoulders squared. His voice had changed too; those public school vowels had softened. Maybe he was trying to get in with his men by aping their speech.

"It's all right, you're not on parade now," I growled.

"Madison's brother is posted here in Hammerton," he said. "He said you peed on the war memorial and insulted a couple of Toms in town on Friday night. He said you attacked them."

The army was rife with gossip. Simon probably knew about the fight minutes after it happened.

Simon lowered his voice. "Max, you can't do stuff like this any more. You've had your last chance. If you carry on like this, you will get banged up."

"Don't tell," I said, sounding about six years old, even to my own ears. "They think I fell over after having had a drink."

"Of course I won't tell," said Simon. "But I bet Dad will hear about it eventually." He looked at me. "Max.

You need to get a grip. I'm really, really worried about you. You're acting like you are out of control again."

"Control," I said. "Con-trol. If you split the word, you get two nasty words, con and troll. No wonder I'm no good at it. It freaks me out. Every time I try to be good, I worry that the nasty Con-Troll is going to come and lick me with his long frogspawny tongue."

"Shut up, Max," said Simon. "This is me you are talking to. I don't want to hear this crap."

I felt a pressure under my eyes. "But you used to love this crap," I said. "You used to roll around the floor laughing at this crap."

"You've got to learn to turn it off," said Simon. "You've got to stop being so aggressive and rude and antisocial or I swear you'll end up being sectioned."

Silence. I looked at the dead brown flowers fallen under the bush. Time passed. The wind blew. Elsewhere in the world, things died.

"The soldier knew about me." My voice wobbled. "He knew what I did at The Risings and he knew about Dad's punishment." Thinking about Dad's punishment is like looking into a bottomless black pit. I felt an arm around my shoulders. Simon is the only male person I'd allow to do this.

"I didn't want him mouthing off to my mates," I said. I touched my eye gently. It felt like a hot bag of pus.

Then Mother was calling us in for dinner.

"Don't say anything," I pleaded.

*

Of course it isn't Simon who dobs me in. Big, loyal Simon has been cleaning up and thoroughly disinfecting my messes for years. Andrea, however, has a new agenda.

I sit at the white cotton tablecloth and view with dismay the spotless plates and well-cooked hot food. The napkins are folded into quarters and are set, with military precision, just a quarter of an inch above the dessert spoons. Each spoon points left. Each wine glass sparkles. The floor beneath me is spotless pale yellow carpet. The flowers stand white and yellow with no blemishes on the leaves.

Simon sits, now incongruous in his jeans, with his slender, glowing girlfriend, resplendent in lilac, her small feet tucked into proper women's shoes.

I crouch in the midst of all this splendour like an oozing toad. I know Mother would love to sweep me up with her dustpan and brush and drop me in the bin. Then she could scrub the spot where I'd squatted and spray round the air-freshener. Then the room would be perfect!

(Again, Simon catches my solitary eye, trying to make meaningful contact, but there's nothing but static in here today.)

And here's Dad, carving the meat, dad-like, cuffs folded back, sky-blue shirt ironed, socks fragrant and nostril hairs trimmed. He's in terrifying faux-jovial mode, beating to death a joke about a three-legged horse.

"The reason you don't get three-legged horses is if you tried to shoe them, they'd fall over," he guffaws.

I eye Andrea. She looks luscious in that horrible dress. It is the sort of dress that completely covers her chest, but the material is so thin you can make out everything that is going on behind it. She has very clear skin and a big mouth which she rarely keeps shut. Like now she's yakking on to Mother about something or other. She's pretty ugly, really, but very sexy. Her hair's so straight and shiny you could eat your dinner off it. I imagine throwing the plate of cloud-fluffy mashed potato into her hair, imagine watching it slide off in potato-poo dollops all over her big, squashy chest.

"You look very thoughtful," says Mother, butting in. "Do share."

Dad shoots her a look. "Really?" he says.

"I was looking at Andrea's t—" Simon intercepts with brotherly telepathy. We dock and he guides me to the shore.

"I was looking at Andrea's teeth," I say. "I wish I had teeth like that."

"My teeth?" Andrea touches her lips.

"Are magnificent," I say. (The Con-Troll has me in his webbed toes.)

A pause and the conversation turns.

Like me, my dinner isn't behaving. Peas shoot out over the table, potato gravitates to the floor and the meat will not cut. I saw at it, chicken-elbowed, and my knife scrapes against the plate, earning myself a reproving glance from Mother. Again I attack the overcooked flesh but I slip and a knot of carrot fires over the table and ends up floating in the gravy boat.

"Max," snaps Mother.

I renew my assault. Over my head, the talk is of commissions, operations and foreign tours. I absolutely do not want to think of Simon in Afghanistan, or Iraq, or anywhere where there is danger. In my mind, I see Simon, aged eight, with blond fluffy hair and red shorts, stuck halfway between the uppermost branches of the camellia tree and the open window of our mother's bedroom. Safe on the ground, unable to scale such heights, the fear I had felt for my brother had made me wet myself. In the event, Simon climbed down to safety and I had been sent to my room for wet trouser crimes. And now, with talk of training and accommodation, I feel the familiar old fear rise up in my chest.

My hands are shaking and I feel hot.

"Are you all right, Max?" asks my mother from far away.

"Fine," I swallow. "Just need the bog." I get up in a hurry and knock my glass over; luckily it is empty. I rush from the room like Cinderella and lock myself in the downstairs bathroom. Is the room spinning? Am I going to freak out in there? My eye hurts and now, blast it, it is beginning to weep. I splash cold water on my face and feel a bit better.

When I rejoin the bosom of my family Andrea is droning on about her university course and "the next logical step" and I can see Mother is all ears.

"Of course, after the wedding, we'll move into family accommodation," Andrea says.

I drop my fork with a clatter. Wedding? What have I missed? I look wildly at Simon, sending our old distress signal, a humble wink, time and time again, but all previous channels seemed to be closed as my brother gazes fondly at his hawk-nosed, soft-chested beloved.

Now I'm all ears and I gradually glean that Simon really is going to marry Andrea in a year's time.

"No one told me!" I blurt out. To his credit Simon looks genuinely upset.

"I was going to," he says. "I was waiting for the right moment." He gives Andrea a reproachful look. "I was going to ask you to be my best man."

I puff up with pride. "Wouldn't you rather have one of your officer pals?"

"Of course not," smiles Simon. "You're my brother."

"It's traditional, I suppose," says Mother, the cow.

"But no drinking for this one, hey!" smiles Andrea. "I don't want any fights at MY wedding, thank you very much."

There is a long, nasty silence, during which the fires in my father's eyes light up.

"What fight are we talking about?" he asks in a light, clear voice, like the thinnest and keenest blade. "Max?"

Andrea laughs girlishly. I think she must be a devil in disguise. Underneath those boobs and those legs there's a nasty, laughing, twisted elf.

"Surely you've noticed his eye!" she says. "Oh no."

She claps her hand over her mouth in mock horror. "Have I let the cat out of the bag? What did he tell you? That he bumped into a door?"

Through my one good eye I notice that Simon, the swine, is sending Andrea OUR signal, the eye wink. He's gone and told Andrea OUR signal. Traitor!

"Max?" Dad asks again in his Good Cop voice.

The expectant breathing of my family washes over me. Outside, an aircraft drones through the sky. How am I going to get out of this? Do I need to pull a spectacular stunt? I can't just give them all the information on a plate. It would be like giving your enemy a load of guns to fire at you.

"Personally I wouldn't take on a gang of squaddies myself," supplies Andrea, shooting me a mocking look. "But at least he's brave, wouldn't you say?"

"Do elaborate," says Dad. God, how I hate him.

Should I accidentally set my hair on fire? Could I pretend to have urgent intestinal issues? Or stage an epileptic fit?

"What have you done now?" asks Mother bitterly.

I decide then and there to tell her the truth, because that is what will hurt her the most.

"I got into a scuffle in town," I say. "I besmirched the memory of our glorious forefathers with my bodily fluids and I headbutted a soldier." I sit back, push my plate away and fold my hands.

"Any questions?"

College

Alex emptied the feed pellets into the hoppers and the young birds crowded round. Altogether they had about five thousand birds, ranged in various pens in the long field next to the cottage. Most of the pens were covered with netting, to stop predator birds like rooks and buzzards attacking the young birds.

"We lost eight last night," sighed Tim, filling up the water urns. "I just found them dead." Alex looked at the limp brown bodies outside the pens. He'd bury them later.

"Rats?" he suggested. "The cold?"

"It's hardly cold." Tim moved on to the next hopper. "I was hoping to turn this batch out next week."

"Let's do some ratting," said Alex. "I'm sure there's a nest under the feed bins. We could borrow Sparky." Sparky was Jason the farmer's terrier. He had an unquenchable thirst for rat blood and could despatch forty or fifty in a couple of hours.

"Haven't you got college today?" Tim watched his

son pick feathers out of the feed hoppers. "You should be out with your mates, not killing vermin."

Alex shrugged. After last Friday, he wasn't keen to hang out with "his mates" at all. Max had gone berserk! Alex had never shouted at anyone like that before. As he'd grabbed Max by the shirt he'd felt an incredible and slightly scary flood of anger, but it had worked. Max had allowed himself to be poured into a taxi, get strapped in, and be driven away. Afterwards Sasha had been in a rush to get home.

"Sammy always wakes up at midnight," she'd said, pounding the pavement. "He'll go nuts if I'm not back."

It was hardly romantic. Not that he had had any hopes, of course.

"I don't have to be in until the afternoon," said Alex. It was a fine summer morning with a light haze settling over the trees. Later this would lift and it would be boiling again.

"Why don't you invite some of your friends up here," suggested Tim, wiping his wet hands on his jeans. "We could get the traps out and shoot some clays. Do you think your mates would like that?"

Alex considered. Levi would probably love it, and Max too, though he wasn't sure about Sasha. But did he want them here?

"How about next Saturday?" asked Tim. "I'm not doing anything in the afternoon."

Alex knew his dad was desperate for him to be more sociable. When he'd left school Alex had stayed at home for a year and, apart from Levi, had lost contact with the few lads he used to hang around with.

"All right," said Alex. "I'll ask them."

The room smelt of dust and floor polish and stale breath. The sunlight showed every smear and patch on the windows. Alex was late into class, but there were plenty of empty seats. He reckoned nearly a third of the class was missing. It was the sunshine tax; no one wanted to sit in a stuffy classroom on a day like this. But there was Sasha, sitting at the front of the class, her bright hair falling over her books. Behind her sat Levi, who was concentrating on his mobile phone. Max stared out of the grimy windows. That was some black eye. Alex slid into a seat at the back of the class and tried to concentrate. If he was going to be stuck in this classroom, he may as well make it worth his while.

He watched as Levi twitched and fidgeted through the class. He tapped his feet and rubbed his face; the boy couldn't keep still for a minute. Alex watched him flex his biceps, again and again. Almost imperceptibly, Levi rose up in his seat, then sank again, doubtless exercising his gluteus maximus.

After class, queuing for coffee in the canteen, Alex asked Levi if he'd like to come up to the farm on Saturday, and his face exploded with pleasure.

"Like it? Bruv, I'd love it. Are you going to let me get my hands on a real gun? Fan-tastic."

Max too nodded through his bruises, though Alex

wished he'd said no. He felt shy around Max today. He had a hell of a temper. His eye looked even worse close up. Alex was itching to ask what the soldier had meant, the thing he'd said about Max being the school terrorist. But Max obviously wanted to keep it hidden. Everyone was entitled to secrets.

Levi had no such qualms.

"Dude," he said. "What made you kick off on Friday night, if you don't mind me asking?"

Max froze, his coffee cup midway between the table and his mouth. Hanging. For a moment he looked like he wanted to empty it over Levi's head.

"He was annoying me," he said.

"But all that stuff about terrorism?" said Levi. He glanced at Alex, who willed him to shut up. "Or can't you remember?"

"You must have heard wrong," said Max. "They were just a bunch of Vikings. One of them knew my brother, so they think that gives them the right to have a go at me." He frowned. "The army is like that."

"But – oh hang on." Levi's phone rang and he began a hurried conversation.

"I'm fine, Mum. Yeah, I'll be back at six. Chill, woman!" He rolled his eyes as he put the phone away.

"Is she OK?" asked Alex, sitting at a table.

"She's anxious," said Levi. "I am her one and only number-one son. Dad is in Lincoln so I'm all she's got. She's always worried that something terrible will happen to me." He sighed. "I humour her. I'll probably be the same when I have kids. Speaking of which—" He spied Sasha through the glass partition, hurrying along the corridor and waved.

"Oh, she's lovely, isn't she," remarked Levi.

Alex nodded, trying not to seem too enthusiastic.

"Do you like her?" asked Levi carefully.

Alex hesitated. "Everyone likes Sasha," he said. "Including me."

"Have you met her kid?" asked Levi. "I have. He's quite funny, actually." He sighed. "Do you know if she ever sees the dad?"

"I don't think so," said Alex. He looked at his watch. Two minutes until biology. Then he could go home.

"Have you invited her to your little shooting party?" asked Levi.

"No," said Alex, and Levi seemed relieved. Alex hadn't asked Sasha because he didn't want to annoy Levi. And he wasn't sure he wanted her to come anyway. He couldn't quite imagine her with a gun on her shoulder, though that was probably sexist of him.

"Oh well, count me in for Saturday," said Levi. "It will just be us, the three musketeers."

Strangeways Farm

"This place is awesome." Levi blinked in the sunshine as they sat on a broad stone, surrounded by rocks and scree, demolishing a packet of biscuits. The moor spread out before them, miles and miles of broad, brown-backed hills. Alex and Levi had ridden up on Alex's quad, now fixed.

"It's called Golden Combe," said Alex. "There are loads of stories about it. My mum said it was magic."

"Your mum died when you were a baby, right?" Levi wiped the biscuit crumbs from his shorts.

"When I was five," said Alex. "Cancer."

"That's terrible," sighed Levi. "Where is she buried?"

Alex breathed in abruptly. No one ever asked him questions like this. "She was cremated," he said. "Her ashes were spread up on Cosdon Tor, behind us." Alex pointed.

"Beautiful," said Levi, gazing up. "It's good to have a place where you can connect."

Alex gave him a look.

"I want my ashes scattered on the pitch at Chelsea football club," said Levi. "Just so you know."

Alex laughed. "OK, I'll remember that."

It was Saturday morning and Max hadn't turned up. This was a good thing because Tim wouldn't be able to organize the clay shoot after all. Jason the farmer said he needed him with the sheep shearing.

"Sorry, lads, we'll rearrange for next week," he'd called, waving to Levi as he drove out of the yard. "I know you'd be sensible, but I can't let you do it unsupervised."

Earlier, on his mobile, Levi had said he wanted to come up anyway.

"My mum brought me up single-handed," said Levi. "My dad lives in Lincoln now. But before that he lived with us until I was about seven. He didn't like it down here."

Alex looked at him in surprise. "Why?"

"He felt exposed, being the only black man in town. He said it was mostly all right, but every now and then he'd get some comment or other. He said he didn't want to feel like an outsider in his own home."

"But there are other black people around," said Alex pointlessly.

"There weren't then," said Levi.

Alex hadn't known that racist stuff still went on. "So he felt he was driven out."

"No," smiled Levi. "My mum did that. Anyway, he's got a new woman, Emma, and now I've got two half-brothers up in Lincoln who I hardly ever see apart from two weeks in the summer holidays and alternate Christmases."

"Do you miss him?" asked Alex, offering him another biscuit.

"Course I do," said Levi, snapping the biscuit in half. "I miss him like hell. He's a lovely bloke, funny as anything. Only my mum didn't think so."

"Sounds complicated," said Alex.

"It's not really. I just mostly live with my mum. She works in the supermarket, fends off her boss and worries about me. Life is uncomplicated." Levi lowered himself on to the scrub and cleared his throat. "What do think is going on with Max?"

"He probably didn't want to get out of bed," said Alex, unable to disguise the edge to his voice.

"No, there's more to it," said Levi, shading his eyes to watch the crows at the bottom of the valley. "I think he's avoiding us. I think he lied to us about why he was really expelled. All that stuff about food is crap. I reckon he did something really bad. I mean, you've seen what he can be like. And why did that bloke call him The School Terrorist?"

"What do you think he's done?"

"I'll find out." Levi got up. "So what is there to do around here?"

Alex thought. On a day like this, if Levi wasn't here, he might climb Cosdon Tor and look out over Devon. Alternatively he might clean the bird droppings from the feeders, or fix the fence behind the garden, or take Gaffer down to the river and throw him some balls. He might go out on the quad and burn around the fields. He might go and inspect the badger holes to see if they'd moved back. He could check the traps for live crows, or just sit at the kitchen table and give the guns a thorough clean. If he was in the mood he might go out with his gun, hunting crows, before checking the fat lambs in the high fields. Later, he would write his geography essay and slice some onions for a cheese and onion pie. He'd chop some logs for the stove. He'd wash some of his clothes so he'd have something clean to wear to college next week.

"There's nothing to do out here, is there?" said Levi.

"We could ride out even further?" suggested Alex. Somehow he didn't think Levi would appreciate cleaning out the bird feeders, or clearing the traps for the mice in the feed bins, or burning the poisoned rats in the grain hoppers.

"Time to let me drive," grinned Levi, getting up.

At the summit of Belstone Tor (they'd had to leave the quad on the track, a little way down) Alex pointed out the landmarks: Brown's bog – gleaming purple-yellow – the old tin mine, pockmarking the slopes, and the distant blur of Hammerton. He didn't know if Levi was really listening or not as he stood gazing out over the moor.

"What's happening over there?" Levi pointed as a jeep drove up a rough track and stopped by a pair of red flags. As they watched, a tiny figure got out and took down the flags.

"They're always practising," said Alex. "There's a firing range over there. Sometimes it's bang bang bang all day. People round here can get quite annoyed, especially the walkers and the tourists."

"And what's happening down there?" Levi pointed as a column of army vehicles the size of dinky toys drove up a farm drive.

"That's Strangeways," said Alex. "It's an old farm that was bought up by the army. There are quite a lot of outbuildings and a big old farmhouse and about twenty acres of land. The army use it in their training. We go down there sometimes to sort out the pigeons."

"What sort of training?" asked Levi.

"All sorts," said Alex. "I think they use it sometimes as a checkpoint and storage area when they are on an exercise on the moors, but also they use it for fighting operations, practising clearing the enemy from buildings and built-up areas. I sometimes watch them running in and out of the buildings and they use blank ammunition and simulated grenades, all sorts."

"Fantastic." Levi's eyes gleamed. "I'd love to see it."

"Better not," said Alex, watching the vehicles crawl away. "It's fenced-off army property."

"But we could take a closer look," said Levi. "I'd like to see where they do their training." He watched the line of vehicles. "Ever thought about joining up yourself?"

"Yes," said Alex. "But I'd rather be a gamekeeper. I get to use guns but if I shoot something, it doesn't try to shoot me back."

Levi laughed. "That would teach you, a badger with a twelve bore."

"What about you?" asked Alex.

"I'd like the training and the travel." Levi stretched and flexed his arms. "But every time I mention it, my mum goes nuts. She's a real peacenik, you know, ban the bomb and all that. She'd go mad if I joined up. She says it's signing your life away. And when it came down to war, I could never actually kill someone. Could you?"

"No," said Alex. "No way."

Levi got up. "Come on, I want a closer look at that farm. How long do you think it would take to get there?"

"We could probably get most of the way on the quad. But we'll have to walk when we get to the bog," replied Alex.

Even on the quad, it was slow going, and it was twenty minutes before they reached the edge of the marsh in the valley. The lads clambered off the bike and continued on foot.

Alex checked his bag. His bottle of water was running low, but there was a spring over the next hill. He hadn't been down this way for some time. His work at the game farm had got busier and busier, and college ate into his time. Still, the sheep paths were the same, etched into the heather. They followed the trail as it wound down the hill. Levi was pretty quiet, for Levi, but Alex was impressed how fit he was. Alex himself was hot and panting, but Levi wasn't even out of breath. Levi was at least a head shorter than Alex, but he had bigger biceps. Alex knew he was strong, but he was wiry, rather than stocky like Levi. As they walked the gorse popped and a heat wobble rose over the hill ahead.

A barbed-wire fence stood a little way off. The whole twenty or so acres of Strangeways was fenced but the fields were left to rot. No one wanted their sheep in those fields; there might be unexploded ordnance and bits of shot. Alex thought of them as dead fields. The only animals that lived there were the rabbits, and sometimes the rats. Levi wanted to go right up to the fence. Alex thought there was probably no harm in it as there was no one there and they were still on public land. Before they reached the fence, Alex filled his bottle from the brook that ran over the scrub. He'd been drinking moor water all his life so he reckoned he'd developed an immunity to any bugs. Levi didn't care about bugs. When he reached the water, he scooped it all over his face and into his mouth.

"We are well and truly in the middle of nowhere," he said, sitting back.

"Yep," Alex agreed. "The nearest proper road is about three miles away. The closest house is in the next valley and that's a holiday let. No one even walks here much cos it's not as pretty as other places, and because of Strangeways."

Levi got up and picked his way through the heather to the fence. It was topped with barbed wire and stood at least ten feet tall. They could barely see the old farmhouse and outbuildings, as elder, nettles, brambles and scrubby trees had grown up in the paddocks around the farmyard. Only the grey-slate roofs rose out of the greenery.

"Wish we could go in," said Levi.

"We can't," said Alex firmly.

"We could," said Levi. He pointed. "Look at that." A short way along the fence was a small hole, all grown over with grass but just about big enough for a man to slide through. "Why isn't it all barbed wire and security cameras?" asked Levi.

"Because we are in the middle of Dartmoor and all there is are some old buildings. There's nothing to protect. Who would want to walk into an army training zone?"

"Me," said Levi. "This is just so interesting."

"I'm not going in," said Alex.

Levi cocked his head. "There's no one here. I only want a look round."

"Not with me," said Alex. "But you can get a better view from over here." He led Levi round the fence to a small copse of trees. Here the land fell steeply away and they could clearly see the old farmhouse. The render was falling off the shot-marked walls and all the windows were battened with metal shutters. The garden was waist high with weeds and litter flitted in the breeze like butterflies. A horseshoe of farm buildings stood round a trampled, empty farmyard.

"They've trashed it," said Levi.

"I think that's the point," said Alex. "Think of war zones you see on TV. Places where people actually live. Bombed houses, ruins, sniper fire, soldiers fighting to secure positions. This is a place where they practise doing it." He shivered. Strangeways had changed so much.

There were signs on the fence.

MOD PROPERTY. LIVE FIRING. TRESPASSERS WILL BE PROSECUTED.

Someone had scribbled out the word PROSECUTED and written SHOT!

"I still wish we could go and look round," said Levi longingly.

"There's nothing to see," said Alex gruffly. "It's just a sad old burnt-out place." He sighed. "It was my grandparents'. My dad was born there. But small farms like these don't make enough money. My granddad kept going until he was bankrupt. The receivers sold the whole place to the MOD. Funny to think there used to be kids living in that house." He pointed. "That top window was my dad's bedroom."

Levi's eyes widened. "Let's go see. There's no one here."

"No way," said Alex. He leaned on the fence. He had

a dream that one day the army would move out and the place would be put up for sale. Somehow he'd have enough money to buy it back. As soon as the papers were signed, he'd go down there and light all the fires in the damp old fireplaces; he'd get smoke coming out of every chimney. Then he'd fix up the walls and repair the roof. He'd unscrew the metal shutters and putty glass back in the windows. He'd walk every inch of the place, scouring the ground with a metal detector to remove every scrap of ordnance and military debris. He'd dig over the garden and roll new turf over it. Then he'd move in, maybe with his family (a brief vision of Sasha and her baby came into his mind). He'd farm sheep, grow veg. Shoot. He could even manage Delaney's estate shoot from here. That was his dream.

"Does it make you mad?" asked Levi.

Alex smiled. He liked Levi's bluntness. "Yeah," he said. "I found an old boot in the hedge here. I took it home. It could have been my granddad's boot. I didn't want the army mucking around with it."

But Levi was walking off, following the fence, banging a stick on the links like a little boy. "Look." He picked up an exploded shell case.

"It's a blank," said Alex. "You see the traces of powder here." He traced the serrated edge of the metal capsule. "There's stuff like this everywhere. It's left behind from the training sessions."

"I want to see more," said Levi.

Now they were in the trees and the grass was long

and wispy and the nettles stung through Alex's trousers.

"What's this?" Levi gestured at a small derelict wooden barn just the other side of the fence. It was separated from the main farm buildings by two paddocks and a wild, overgrown copse of trees and was almost hidden by the thorns and brambles that had grown up around it. The roof bowed nearly to the ground at one end and the pillars leaned in crazy directions.

"It's inside the fence," said Alex. "So it's army property."

"They obviously don't use it," said Levi. "Come on, I just want a quick look inside."

Before Alex could stop him, Levi had run back along the fence and was squeezing through the hole. Alex dithered.

"What are you afraid of?" asked Levi from the other side. "There's no one here.

"There's nothing to see. It's just an old barn."

Levi just nodded and scampered over the tussocky, uneven ground to the building. He was unstoppable. Alex looked around. There really didn't seem to be anyone about. Growling under his breath, he followed his friend.

When they reached the barn, a couple of rabbits shot out.

Levi looked inside. Then he glanced at the tin roof. "If it's held this long, I expect it'll last another five minutes," he said, ducking under the bowing pitch. Alex did not want to go in the rickety old building at all, but Levi was so unconcerned he told himself he was being a coward and followed Levi into the darkness.

A wooden pillar had collapsed in one corner and the roof dipped to the ground. A substantial sycamore tree grew up through the roof and the ground was a mess of mud and weeds and dead grass. A low shelf ran along one of the more stable walls, capped with flat stones.

"There's nothing here," said Alex, as his eyes got used to the light. "Let's leave before we get buried alive." He didn't like the feel of the place and was horribly aware that they were trespassing on military property.

But Levi was scrabbling away in a corner.

"What are you doing?" asked Alex.

There was a pile of bricks roughly piled against the side; they were all topsy-turvy, like they'd been dumped in a hurry.

"Just having a poke about," said Levi.

The dark and shadows were spooking Alex. Big, heavy cracked beams ran above his head. One of those would squash them both dead if it came away from its mooring. The place was held together with ivy and dead wood.

"I want a souvenir too," said Levi. "Like your granddad's boot. Sasha loves stories. I want something for her."

"A slate?" suggested Alex. He eyed the treacherous

roof and could see daylight coming through the holes. "Or a dent in your skull?

Levi moved one brick to the ground and then another. They made a gentle chocking sound, like a tree being felled.

"Maybe we could fix up this place," he said. "We could sleep out in it, make a fire. We could spy on the army boys playing their war games. They'd never know we were here. Look, it's like a swamp back here."

"Don't step there," said Alex. "You might sink altogether. Bogs don't stand still; they creep over the ground through the years. This one has started to swallow the building."

"It looks like something has been digging in it," said Levi. "See how the ground is disturbed." He got a stick and rammed it into the mud in the corner of the barn. The stick went down and down and Levi ended up kneeling, with his hand flat on the ground. "It went all the way down," he said. "I could drown in this barn." He yanked at the stick but the mud held it fast.

"Let's go," said Alex. "We shouldn't be here."

But Levi pulled and pulled and at last the stick flew out, making a wet, sucking noise. Levi gasped. Something else had come with it up out of the mud, long and thin, wrapped in plastic and tied up tightly with string. Alex felt an unexplained ripple of fear in his stomach. Levi pulled and pulled and the object came up out of the mud. He pulled at the plastic and uncovered stiff oily canvas, also bundled in string.

"Put it back," said Alex suddenly. There was something sinister about it. The canvas looked like skin.

"Hold on." Levi knelt and pulled at the bundle, tearing at the string that criss-crossed the canvas. Finally he pulled it off and unfolded the greasy canvas.

There was a rifle inside, smothered in oil.

Cache

A fine mist had stolen over the moor and settled in the valley. Inside the ruined barn the ground was growing damp. The boys had lost all sense of the time. Alex had found a metal bar and Levi was digging with a spade with a broken off handle. With these makeshift tools the boys pulled gun after gun out of the mud. They'd piled the weapons on one side of the barn, dozens of long-barrelled rifles, each carefully sealed in oilskins and plastic. And they were still coming. The boys weren't bothering to unpack them from their plastic any more as there were so many. Levi was ecstatic, whooping each time they unearthed another, but Alex was biting back sheer panic.

There were two makes of weapons: AK-47 assault rifles, Kalashnikovs, used by armies around the world. The other rifles were SA80's. They were in astonishingly good condition, save the marks of wear and tear, a missing handle here, a scratch, a dented barrel, a missing safety catch. But for the most part, Alex reckoned, after a good clean, they were completely serviceable.

They were deadly.

Still Levi dug more and more weapons out of the mud and now Alex was standing by, just watching.

"Maybe they are part of some army training exercise," said Levi, tugging the string as another bundled weapon was sucked out of the mire. "Strange, though."

"I think they've been put here recently," said Alex. "The ground is all churned up. But they've been wrapped up for years; see how the string is rotting in places?"

If they were part of an army manoeuvre, why had they been left out here? Strangeways wasn't secure. It could be catastrophic.

"We don't know for sure they've been put here recently," said Levi. "They might have been here for donkey's years and have been forgotten about."

Alex thought differently. He thought they had been buried in the last couple of months and someone hadn't forgotten about them.

"Maybe they've been thrown away?" suggested Levi. "Here's another – come on, give me a hand." But Alex was getting more and more uncomfortable about even touching them. They had over thirty guns now. Thirty! He unwrapped a bundle and took out a heavy gun, black with grime and oil. Another Kalashnikov. He felt the weight of it in his palm and it seemed like his fingers were tingling. He opened it and was shocked to find live bullets in the magazine. Levi watched, biting his lip, as Alex carefully emptied the ammunition on the floor, his hands shaking. Jesus! A loaded weapon. What the hell was going on here?

"We should stop," he said. "This is dangerous."

"But that's thirty-eight guns," panted Levi. He was kneeling in the mud, his face smeared and his hands thick with dirt. "And there's more, loads more." He prodded deep in the bog with his stick. "I can feel them." Alex looked at the pile of weapons. The walls of the barn seemed more rickety than ever and the roof seemed to wobble. He sank to his haunches.

"We've got to put them back," he said. "More of them could be live. They might go off by accident. Don't dig out any more." Levi obviously had no idea how dangerous these weapons were.

Levi stared at him, incredulous. "Put them back? You must be joking. I've just spent ages digging them all out."

"But what would we do with them?" asked Alex.

Levi shrugged. "I haven't got that far yet, but they must be worth a fortune. Are they? You know about guns."

Alex shrugged. "My dad bought a comparable second-hand rifle recently, an Enfield 48, for two thousand quid."

Levi's eyes widened. "Oh. My. God."

"But these aren't ours," said Alex. "They must belong to the army."

"But they've been abandoned, forgotten, maybe even thrown away," said Levi, wiping the mud from his face.

"Or deliberately hidden," said Alex. He looked outside at the swaying trees and the grey blue sky. He felt jumpy. What if there was someone outside, right now? He needed air. He bent himself out of the barn and straightened up, gratefully breathing in the fresh air. Out here the world was still and empty. There were no madmen searching for their guns, just trees, mist, marsh grass and sky. He did not know what to do.

Back in the ruined barn, Levi had dug up two more guns. He wiped the mud from the barrel.

"Careful," snapped Alex. "Always, *always* point the muzzle of the gun away from you. Or anyone else," he added. Could these guns belong to some kind of terrorist group? He wondered why they were buried at Strangeways. He shivered. Had there been a big plan that had gone wrong? Some evil plot against the army that had backfired, leaving these weapons to sink in the mud?

"We have to put these back, and then we have to tell the police, or the Commanding Officer at Hammerton barracks," Alex said.

Levi stopped digging. "Then they'll know that we were here. You saw the sign. It said TRESPASSERS WILL BE PROSECUTED. We don't have to do anything. And anyway," he continued, "finders keepers."

"Not when you find guns," said Alex. "Not in a place like this. We can't just leave them here like this." He indicated the pile. "Someone might find them. These are dangerous weapons, Levi. One of these guns could blow your head off."

"No," said Levi, with a hard-faced expression Alex hadn't seen before. "Not yet. There's money here, Alex, loads of it."

Alex felt a rush of anger. "Oh for God's sake, how are you going to sell them? You're just a kid, not an arms dealer."

"EBay," said Levi stubbornly.

"You can buy pellets on eBay, but not guns."

Levi stared at him and his expression softened. "I know this is crazy, but let's think about this before we go to the authorities," he begged. "This is a once in a lifetime opportunity. Just let's have a think about it."

"What for?" Alex was seriously unnerved now. All sorts of scenarios played in his head. Whoever had got them here was obviously very powerful. This was a bad place for them to be. And the guns themselves, cold and abandoned, just felt wrong somehow. These were not guns for target practice, guns for taking down carrion crows, rogue foxes or sick deer. These weren't guns for shooting clays or bullseyes. These guns were meant for death. They smelled of damp metal, which smelled of blood. The guns smelled of death. Alex felt a rush of heat in his head and a ringing in his ears. The ground seemed to heave and he had to steady himself on Levi's shoulder.

"To work out the best thing to do," said Levi. He looked suddenly angry. "My mum is desperate for money. She hasn't got a penny, her manager is a perv. . ."

"These weapons can take away life," interrupted Alex. "This isn't a game. They should be locked away, at once."

"But no one's going to find them here," said Levi. "This is private property, military land."

"We did," replied Alex.

A noise outside, like the crack of a whip, cleared his head. He glanced at Levi, who knelt, cradling a dirty rifle in one hand.

"For God's sake, BE CAREFUL," whispered Alex.

"What was that?" mouthed Levi, looking uncharacteristically nervous.

Alex listened. Outside the barn, leaves were cracking, like someone was walking over them. Alex put his finger to his lips and walked carefully to the entrance, where the mist seemed to swirl in lazy circles. He took a breath and crept round the ruined barn. A shape fluttered out of a tangle of brambles and nettles and he took a step back and let out a gasp. But it was only a crow, its beady eyes gleaming. Alex waved his arms and it flew off, settling on a low branch, and, when Alex returned to the entrance of the barn, it landed nearby with a hop, utterly unafraid.

"Let's go," said Alex. He felt jittery, like he'd drunk too much coffee, and he wanted to be gone as quickly as possible. He picked up the nearest gun and dumped it back in the bog. Levi started to protest, then seemed to change his mind.

"I guess it would be like stealing," he said. Reluctantly he started putting the guns back into the muddy crater he had excavated.

"Be careful," repeated Alex. "Remember these things are designed to kill humans."

Levi rolled his eyes.

"I'm serious," snapped Alex.

"Where does your dad buy his guns?" asked Levi.

"There's a gun shop in Plymouth," replied Alex. "Anyone buying a gun is carefully vetted, and you have to have a licence."

"Would they buy these guns off us?"

"Not in a million years," said Alex. As they worked, he felt himself growing more and more afraid. The walls seemed to lean in, compressing him. Who really owned these weapons? There, that was all. He and Levi shovelled mud over them and pulled an old tarp, dark with dust, over the site.

"Come on," he said to Levi. Levi took a last longing look at the back of the barn before following Alex out into the daylight. Alex felt exposed, walking home. It felt like someone might be watching them from behind every boulder, every tree.

"I don't think we should go running to the army yet," Levi repeated. "The guns could be part of an official exercise. If we go back, they might all be gone. Anyway, I don't want to be involved with them. They'll want to know why we were trespassing in the first place."

Alex didn't want to go back, not ever. He realized that he was angry as well as scared, angry that someone would bring danger like this to his part of the world. It was supposed to be safe up here.

"Are you going to tell your dad?" asked Levi.

"I don't know."

"I think we should leave them alone," said Levi.

"I thought you wanted to sell them?" Alex shot a sideways look at his friend.

"That was stupid; let's just forget about them." Levi lowered his head and marched on to the track where they'd left the quad.

The boys were tired and hungry by the time they reached Keeper's Cottage. The lights were on in the lower windows and the radio blared out, playing some mindless song. Alex sighed out his relief, kicked his boots off at the doorstep and went in. Levi followed, grazing his head on the low doorway. Tim stood at the sink, cutting up lengths of potatoes with his penknife. Alex started at the knife. Should he tell Tim? His dad would be horrified to hear they had gone on to military land. Ale watched as he scraped the chips into the hot fat. All this was normal: Dad's hammer thumb (split almost in two when a gun backfired), the smell of chips, the new rat traps stacked in the corner, and Gaffer, one ear cocked, snoring by the Rayburn. All was normal and safe.

He couldn't risk it. Tim looked up and grinned.

"I was just about to send out the search party. Your mum phoned, Levi, and I said I'd give you a lift home." He looked at Alex and his face changed. "Are you OK?"

"Yeah," muttered Alex, his voice sounding thick.

Later, when Tim was turning the truck round in the yard, Alex touched Levi's shoulder.

"I'll say nothing to Dad," he said. "But you mustn't tell anyone either. Guns are dangerous, right? We can't possibly have them falling into the wrong hands."

"Chill out," said Levi. "I'm not going to do anything stupid."

Breakfast Tune

I spy on Father as he pulls out of the drive, the royal blue Saab purring over the gravel. Every morning it is the same. At eight a.m. sharp he opens the front door, crosses the yard to his car and places his noble brown briefcase embossed with his initials in the boot. Like an automaton he climbs in the driver's seat, checks his reflection in the rear-view mirror, licks his finger, smoothes his wayward eyebrows and drives away. The routine never changes. Watching Dad do this makes me want to press the pause button. Just once, just once, couldn't he turn left at the end of the drive, instead of right? Or why couldn't he stop, put down his briefcase, kick off his shoes and run over the dewy grass on his bare old man's feet?

But Father does not deviate from his routine, and when the last puffs of exhaust have polluted the air, I hear, like clockwork, the chiming computer muzak as Mother switches the machine on. She will now spend two hours surfing internet chat rooms, though she pretends otherwise. Father does not understand the internet. He says it is "reducing everything to banality".

Consequently Mother leaves the switching on of the computer until her masterful husband is one hundred per cent off the property.

Dad says I can get a lift into college with him but there is no way I will ever get into that car with him again. The last time was four weeks ago, when he drove me, against my will, to Hammerton Barracks. When I finally got out of that place, I ran over the moors into the town and stayed the night in the bus shelter. I got the bus home two days later, having spent the now fabled "Max's Missing Forty-Eight Hours" mainly hiding behind the chip shop, sitting in the dumpster, eating cold chips and reading out-of-date tabloids, pretty much my perfect day apart from the fact I couldn't stop shaking.

I swear I will never ride anywhere with Dad again.

Dad obviously thought he was doing the best for his youngest son when he betrayed me and destroyed my life. I must think to the future. I must think of my new almost friends, and the day when I walk out of this twisted house and never look back. I've got to stop thinking about Dad. It makes me feeling like my brains are rotting and turning to vinegar, generating all these foul-smelling twisted thoughts.

Think of something else, Mr Max Cosgrove. I'm like a Buddhist monk, trying to train my mind. Pow!

In the canteen yesterday I overheard Sasha asking Alex (Alex! The silent one!) if he wanted to go on a picnic with her and her smelly baby. Levi was not pleased when I reported it.

"They're free agents, man," Levi said unconvincingly. "What's it to me?"

I think Levi and Alex are up to something sinister. They've been having tiffs, and muffled conversations out on the grass. I am afraid that they have found out about me and what I am. They go quiet when I approach. It's a dead giveaway.

Mother lady-hollers from downstairs.

"YOU'RE LATE ALREADY! GET UP!"

I tsk and step out of my room, ready to run the breakfast gauntlet.

"Have you done your homework?" Mother looks at me over her screen.

"What are you reading?" I ask, ignoring the question.

"Only the news," trills my mother. She's lying, of course. She'll be reading about celebrity breast implants, talking to her virtual friends, or scrolling through online designer clothes stores.

I fetch myself a bowl of cornflakes and work my way through them. They make me think of large flakes of crusty dead skin. And I'm eating them!

"I do worry you won't get *any* exams."

Chew, swallow, chew, swallow. I'll be out of here in forty seconds. I thump my fist on the table to the beat of my chewing jaws.

Chew, swallow, chew, swallow (yeah yeah)
Swallow (hey)

"Frank thinks we should withdraw your allowance until you start showing some application."

Gettin' thru meals / Old lady on my back
It's like nag nag nag / Always under attack
"I see you are wearing THAT *damn hat."*
I ain't misbehaving / At least not now
Get off my back / You mothering cow

"You've spilled cornflakes down your top. MAX. You're like a child."

Treat me like a child / S'no wonder I wild
And ahm wild, girl (oh yeah oh yeah)
I'm WILD, girl (swallow, swallow, chew, chew, swallow)

"Could you stop banging the table?"

Look at me like I'm some kind of ***BUM***
Where's all the love, man, you're s'posed to be my ***MUM***
Chew swallow, chew, chew, swallow.

Wahey! I'm feeling the buzz of excitement I get when a new tune arrives, fully formed in my head, like a gift! It's been ages since this has happened. Trauma has suppressed my creative gifts. I have to get Gerry round to help me record it, like today. I still haven't got to grips with the powerful computer Dad bought me a couple of years ago. The technology is pretty dense, and reading the online manual drags me out of my creative flow.

"Your college bag is very heavy."

"Heavy with drugs, porn and library books," I snap. I hate being interrupted when I'm on a musical bender. "You should know that, don't you check it every night?"

Mother is looking especially odd today. I watch her take my empty bowl and carry it to the sink. Her face has been powdered white by pixies with fluffy puffs and her skirt matches her top, an edgy kind of lime green. When she walks, her legs rub together, and her tights make a noise that sets my teeth on edge, like she's firing static rays out of her hosiery.

"You hate me," she says quietly.

I look up, startled. "Wha?"

"You heard me."

I feel a tingle of perverse excitement. At last events are taking some kind of turn. All the same, I take refuge in the universal boy response.

"What you on about?"

"Please try and grow up, just a little, Max," says Mother wearily.

I *do* hate her, but not all the time. But this is because she despises *me.* My parents wish I had never been born. They know I am never going to be another Simon.

Then Mother unexpectedly offers me a lift to college,

a motherly-style deed to gloss over her little emotional leakage. I accept the lift (it was not she who drove me into hell last month). But my arms and legs are dragging, like I haven't got enough juice to power them.

I would very much like to rip this house apart. I would get a lot of pleasure out of breaking everything. And I wouldn't just stop when I'd smashed the furniture, the cups and the pictures. I'd take a sledgehammer to the walls. I'd smash the windows into smithereens and then I'd crack the roof open like an egg.

Being Six

Alex couldn't sleep, and when the clock told him it was four-thirty a.m., he gave up and got out of bed. After pulling on his clothes, he paused outside Tim's bedroom and listened to his father's soft breathing before creeping down the stairs. He gulped from the tap and splashed his face and hair.

Gaffer wagged his tail.

And now, out in the morning, with the sun turning the sky orange and nobody else awake, Alex fired up his quad and made for the moor.

Levi had phoned him three times last night. The excitement and worry was obvious in his voice and Alex couldn't get a word in.

"What are we gonna do, bruv?"

"I'm worried someone else is going to get to them first."

"We can't do nothing? Can we?"

Levi talked about the guns like this was some exciting escapade. He couldn't see the menace that hung all around them. Alex wished they had never found them. His instincts were screaming at him not to get involved in any way.

Alex drove as fast as he could, wheels bouncing over the rocks and spinning in the dust. The world was beginning to wake up around him; ponies grazed in the distance, flowers opened their petals. He roared on up the track, past the stone hedges and the high marshes, now covered with pale pink orchids. He flew past the stone row, startling Jason's beef cows and followed the path round Cosdon, passing the mire and stone circle and wheeling into the deep valley. He abandoned the quad in the leat at the foot of Belstone and ran hard up the Irishman's wall, his breath tearing at his lungs and the muscles in his legs burning. At the top of the tor Alex felt like he could see the whole world. The wind blew gently through his clothes. He looked at the silver line of the horizon, far off to the south, and closer still, the squat brown buildings of Hammerton Barracks. In the day the place was full of bustle, vehicles moving, coming from the town, men out running, on manoeuvres. Alex pictured the soldiers sleeping in their barracks, though likely as not, they were off on some exercise or other. There was a line of huge buildings at the back of the camp. These vast barns housed all kinds of amazing machines like armoured vehicles, people carriers, trucks and motorbikes.

Alex turned away from the barracks and looked over the long reaches of the moor. There was Strangeways, buried deep in the moor, empty and dead, and beside it, the smudge of trees that hid the barn.

The gun barn.

It stank of danger. And the guns frightened him. Something very odd and sinister was going on. He knew the army would not leave such a cache of weapons buried where someone might stumble upon them. The public footpath ran not forty yards away, following the stream. It was a mad place to hide them.

But why hadn't he told his father about them? These days Alex had few secrets from Tim, but he didn't want his dad involved with this. Tim got along in his own way. He reared the pheasants, organized the shoots. He was immersed in his world. Stuff like this, this reminder of darker things, might throw him off track completely. Alex wasn't prepared to go through that again.

There was a time soon after Alex's mother had died, a few months after the funeral, when his dad had almost closed down. He put food on Alex's plate and gave him lifts to school, but everything was skewed. Tim never really looked at Alex, or hugged him, or asked him anything. Every meal might be the same for a week; baked beans mixed with sweet corn. Alex's bed sheets would be rumpled and unwashed, smelling of urine. The bread in his lunchtime sandwiches might have a bloom of blue mould in the corner. He would arrive at school at eight in the morning, spend the hour before everyone else arrived swinging on the bars and greeting the caretaker. He got flea bites all up his legs where the dog had become infested (he slept in Alex's bed) and he would scratch his bites until the blood ran down into his school socks and they dried stiff and knobbly.

Alex himself had lice in his hair and worms in his bum. His teeth, unbrushed, began to ache, and he developed a greasy sheen on his skin, a result of too-few baths with no soap. Tim picked him up from school, fed him, took him shooting, parked him in front of the TV, but he barely said a word. At home Alex spoke only to Gaffer. He named the dog as his best friend in a school essay. The house was always quiet; there might be a brief rumble of speech from Tim, but then it would sink back into silence. The creak of the beams, the rustle of mice in the walls, those were the nosiest things in the place. After school Alex used to walk out to the moor to seek out some noise. On the moor, the wind blew, and the buzzards keened in the sky. Out on the moor he could shout and yell if he wanted to. No one raised their voice at home, and the silence was heavy and frightening.

Then all at once, everything changed. It was Alex's eighth birthday. He'd come down to breakfast early, woken by an unfamiliar noise, a loud chugging that made the house shudder. And stepping into the kitchen, he had been struck by four things. One, the washing machine was going. (He'd thought it was broken.) Two, there was a hot plate of scrambled egg and soft white bread steaming gently on his breakfast plate. Three, his annual birthday card and letter had no envelope (and therefore must have been read) but sat by his plate, and four, a new air rifle leaned against his chair.

"Happy birthday," said Tim, and he had hugged him, like he hadn't done for years. And after that, things had improved. Tim gradually lost his faraway look and started talking more to Alex, asking him questions about his day, his friends. Laundry was processed, albeit in an ad hoc fashion. Fresh food sat in the fridge. Dad finally filled in the right forms and Alex was able to catch the school bus, now arriving at school just five minutes early, within a swirl of other children. Hot baths, metal combs and chalky pink medicine, and all his little parasites were banished. Six months later, Tim met Amy, and things improved again. She brought books, hot water bottles, fruit and cough medicine into the house. Things got cleaned. Bedtimes were supervised, at least sometimes. (Ten years on, Tim and Amy were still an item, though he had never been able to persuade her to move up to Keeper's Cottage, and she had never convinced him he should live in Plymouth.)

Alex knew his memories must be distorted. How could he really remember, that far back? But he could remember the smell of dirty, wet trousers, left to bake in the sun. A sandwich crust, fossil-hard from months at the bottom of a school bag. A tower of orange shotgun cartridges, gun smudges coming off in his fingers. The acrid smell of a fire made from a slosh of diesel, glossy paper and damp wood. But most of all, he remembered the silence.

All these things made him six years old again. And when he was six, he was sad.

And so was Tim. And now, here was this. These guns! And with them, more than a whiff of something terrifying. This was the stuff of nightmares. It seemed to Alex that, at a flick of a switch, things could revert to those dark, lonely days; days of early mornings and a silent, grim-faced father driving him to school. Swinging on the sun-hot bars, waiting for the caretaker to arrive. Plates of wet, tepid food that left your tongue curling and your stomach sickly hungry. The days of furred teeth and endless black nights. And worst of all, a memory of watching Tim go out into the darkness with his gun, and wondering if he would ever come back.

Maybe that was why Alex hadn't said anything. Tim would go blazing down there with shovels and metal detectors. The place would be full of police and reporters. There would be a spotlight on the place, and he, Tim and Levi would be at the centre. It would upset the balance of things. It was better to stay quiet, keep his head down, and get through. The guns could sink back into the ground. Maybe this time they would stay there for ever.

Quartermaster Sergeant Furzey

Alex awoke to the sound of rain drumming on the roof. He knew this might put a kibosh on the picnic with Sasha. The rain ran in brown rivers down the track, washing off the dust that had coated everything for the last few weeks. Alex looked at the parched grass and imagined it soaking up the wet, drinking it in like a thirsty man. If the picnic was cancelled, he would most likely go with Tim to Somerset to pick up some poults.

He heard the phone ring downstairs. Tim answered.

"Just come up anyway. It might clear up later."

That must be Sasha. Not cancelling.

Last night, Dad had raised his eyebrows so high his forehead was a mass of lines when Alex had told him about Sasha's picnic.

"Good lord, have you got a girlfriend?"

"No," said Alex. He grinned. "Not yet."

He told Tim about Sasha. Told her she was just a friend. Then he mentioned Sammy-Joe.

"A baby?" Tim was uncharacteristically stunned. "What do you know about babies?"

Alex shrugged. "He bit me the other day. Sasha said he only does that to people he likes."

Tim shook his head. "You really are smitten."

Alex snorted. "Don't be soft."

"Sasha and Sammy-Joe," marvelled Tim. "You've got the whole package."

Alex told Tim about the time Sasha had stood on the canteen tables to rescue a martin that had strayed into the classroom. He told him about her theory that fat women sing better and that mind control is as real as microwaves.

"She sounds like more fun than pheasant poults," Tim said.

Downstairs, Alex looked around anxiously, trying to see the place through Sasha's eyes. Was it him or was the place dirtier than usual? There was mud smeared over the doors and dog marks on the walls. The corners were dusty and a spider metropolis hung from the ceilings. Should he clean up? Alex threw an old can of dog food, thick with fluffy mould, into the bin. Then he washed up the breakfast things and opened the kitchen window to alleviate the smell of dog farts and gamekeepers' armpits.

Then he went outside in the rain to take Gaffer for a run.

Sasha's Fiesta drew up into the yard at eleven a.m., the rain bouncing off the bonnet. Alex watched through the window as Sasha ran to the house, holding Sammy-Joe under her arm like a rugby ball. Alex opened the door. She was wearing a purple jumper and jeans and her hair clung damply to her head.

"It's not picnic weather," he said. "But I can do tea."

And now here she was, sitting in the kitchen sipping scalding tea, as the baby fooled around on the floor with a newspaper and ratty string.

Alex had been worried he wouldn't know what to say but Sasha chatted on easily. Any gaps were filled by Sammy-Joe, who was hell-bent on exploring the kitchen. He got in the log basket, in the dog's bed, pulled open the cupboard door and smashed a couple of plates before Sasha could get to him.

"Oh shit, I'm so sorry," said Sasha. "Look, I'll pay for them."

"Don't worry." Tim appeared at the door, rain dripping off his hat. "We've got lots of plates we never use."

Alex made the introductions and Sammy-Joe shambled over to Tim and grabbed his leg, pulling himself up and gazing at him. The baby raised his arms and squeaked, demanding to be picked up. Tim shrugged off his coat and lifted him up. The baby slapped him in the face and they both laughed.

"Showing me who's boss?" said Tim, delighted. "You were just like this when you were this age, Alex, smashing things up, thumping people, then coming over all sweet and innocent."

"Really?" Alex watched with some bemusement. Tim never talked about when Alex was small. Alex supposed this was because he couldn't bear to think about Helena, his mother, and what was happening to her at the time.

Sammy-Joe leaned in and hugged Tim, who fished a bit of chocolate out of his pocket and fed it to the baby.

Then he looked at Sasha. "Oh God," he said. "I suppose that wasn't allowed."

"Just this once," said Sasha. "And you've got a friend for life now."

It was very strange to see his dad there, holding a baby.

Tim sat down and kicked off his boots. "I know all about babies, more than most men my age," he told Sasha. "When Alex was this little, his ma wasn't very well, so I had to do most of it."

This was news to Alex.

"What did we do? I remember, porridge in the morning, then I had you strapped to my back most of the day so I could get things done. Your mother said it was why you didn't walk until you were nearly two. Not enough practice." The baby wriggled and Tim put him on the floor. Then he opened the drawer in the table and pulled out a velvet box containing silver spoons. These spoons had languished in the drawer for as long as Alex remembered. He supposed they were valuable, and that was why his dad had hung on to them. They didn't like to eat with them as the spoons left an acidic tang in the mouth.

Tim set the spoons down and Sammy-Joe crowed in delight as he thundered towards them, removing one at a time, replacing them and starting all over again.

"You played with these for hours," Tim told Alex. "I'd leave you here with these and I knew I'd have enough time to get your mother out of bed, dressed and fed before you got tired of them." Once again, Alex reeled at this information. Dad didn't talk like this. Just five minutes with Sasha's baby and it was like he had unlocked himself.

"It must have been hard," said Sasha gently. Alex gripped the table, embarrassed.

"Not really," said Tim, handing Sammy-Joe back a spoon. "I was too busy to think about it. I don't mind work." He paused. "It was only hard once she had gone."

Alex let out a long breath. He was fascinated by all this, of course. But it was all coming too soon, and was so unexpected.

The wind rattled the windows and the door blew open. A draught of cold wet air flew in and Alex closed it firmly.

"Maybe we should have the picnic here," he said.

Sasha nodded. "I've only got peanut butter sandwiches and apples anyway. What have you got?"

Alex had a bar of chocolate.

"I'd better get going," said Dad. "These birds won't fly themselves here." He nodded at Sasha.

"Come back on a sunny day," he said. "We'll show you the farms."

"Cool," smiled Sasha.

Tim tickled Sammy-Joe on the chin and the baby glared at him, outraged.

"Nice to meet you, Sammy-Joe." He went out into the rain.

"Cool dad," said Sasha.

"He liked you too," said Alex, still blown away by all the revelations. "Come on, let's eat."

When Sasha went along the corridor to the loo, she asked Alex to keep an eye on the baby.

"Sure," said Alex, panicking. He hadn't looked at the downstairs loo this morning. It was probably disgusting, but it was too late now. She was halfway there. He watched as the baby thundered towards the log burner.

"Hot," said Alex. He'd lit it for the first time in weeks because of the rain. The baby took no notice. Alex lunged and grabbed him just as he was about to put a fat hand on the hot metal.

"Head case," said Alex.

There was a thumping on the door. Alex peered out of the steamed-up window, clutching the baby. There was a military truck with a daub of orange paint on its bonnet standing in the yard. He tensed, suddenly afraid.

This had to be about the guns. Damn, why, oh why had he let Levi talk him into going through the fence?

Alex heard a cough from the other side of the door.

He knew it was Furzey, the Quartermaster Sergeant at the barracks. He turned up every now and then if he wanted work done at Strangeways or to find out about the winter pheasant shooting schedules, or if he just wanted a chat with Tim. He'd been around forever.

The hammering on the door got louder.

Reluctantly, Alex opened it.

Furzey was a tall man in his early fifties. He had greying brown hair and crow's feet were deeply etched around his eyes. He was wearing military uniform of green jumper, army trousers and black boots. Rain dripped from his beret.

He stared at the baby, momentarily bewildered.

"Not yours, I hope?" he asked gruffly.

"No," said Alex. "Come in."

The Quartermaster Sergeant sat at the table and accepted Alex's offer of a cup of tea.

"Your father not at home?"

"No," said Alex, and he whisked the baby away just as he made a grab for the Quartermaster Sergeant's beret.

Furzey cleared his throat. "We've had reports of intruders at Strangeways," he said, looking at Alex keenly. "Have you or your dad seen anything on your rounds?"

Alex felt his face tightening. He must mean him and Levi. Hell! He mustn't say anything.

"No," he managed to say.

"I've had reports that the perimeter fence looks tampered with."

Alex shook his head to indicate he knew nothing about it. He couldn't help thinking that Furzey, for all his polite conversation, knew everything already.

"It's extremely dangerous to trespass on military land," said Furzey, leaning forward and folding his big grey hands. "We sometimes have live firing down there, and very often we're using the place to practise manoeuvres. We have mortars, grenades, lasers. Even if we're using blank ammunition, it is absolutely no place for a civilian."

"Sure," said Alex. "Was there any damage?" God, Furzey must be able to tell he was bluffing. Alex was a useless liar.

Furzey sat back. "It's probably only badgers," he said in a lighter tone. He sipped his tea. "They caused a major security scare a few years ago, digging a hole under the fence. In the end we had to put a concrete tube in for them."

Sasha came back and took the wriggling baby from him. She gave a half smile to the Quartermaster Sergeant, who watched as she sat in the old armchair by the log burner.

"Alex, you're always roaming around. Are you sure you haven't noticed anything or anyone unusual?" Alex felt a booming in his stomach. This was awful. Should he tell after all? Furzey sounded like he knew it was Alex.

Alex shook his head, not trusting himself to speak.

He felt himself looked at.

"You realize breaking and entering Her Majesty's property is a serious crime, don't you?" said Furzey gently.

Alex nodded, his mouth firmly closed. He glanced at Sasha, who looked completely confused and a bit scared at the sudden arrival of this large, serious, uniformed soldier. He couldn't mention the guns. He didn't want Sasha mixed up in it in any way, and she was the sort of girl who would want to know everything.

Furzey suddenly clapped his hands and made them both jump.

"Let me know if you have any bright ideas," he said. He reached into his pocket, drew out a pad and wrote down a number.

"This is my direct line," he said. "I'm dealing with this one personally."

Alex took the piece of paper and folded it in half, hoping he would never have to use it. He was a bit scared of Furzey. The first time he had met him was at a barracks open day when he was about twelve. Every year the barracks opened to the public, to let them look around. The idea, Tim said, was to improve community relations, so hopefully locals wouldn't get cross about the firing zones and red flag days.

Tim had got talking with someone so Alex had wandered off, looking at the rows of armoured vehicles, the military fire engine and the ambulance. He'd stepped away from the crowds and come across a huge barn-like building with the panel doors hanging open. Alex peered inside.

In the gloomy room there was a big jeep with a curtained roof and metal hoops. The thing looked ancient. The wheels were big and thin with balding treads. He twisted the door handle.

"This area is NOT open to the PUBLIC, trespassers will be PROSECUTED," roared a voice, and Alex had nearly wet himself, as standing in the entrance, in shadow, was Quartermaster Sergeant Furzey himself.

"Oh," said the Quartermaster Sergeant when he realized Alex was just a boy. His voice softened. "I thought you were a lad from the town who's been winding me up all morning."

Alex said nothing, but fled.

He never told his dad; he was too ashamed. But he steered clear of the Quartermaster Sergeant for a long time. It was several years before he realized that Furzey was all right, that he must have caught him at a bad time. In fact, today was the first time he had actually spoken to him. The Quartermaster Sergeant had a good reputation in the town. He was well-liked. And when his wife left him, giving up everything to live by herself in Plymouth, everyone was shocked.

In his kitchen, with the rain pouring outside, Alex remembered his humiliation in the jeep shed.

"I've seen nothing," said Alex, and swallowed.

Furzey nodded and looked at Sasha. "I don't believe we've met," he said.

"I'm Kate Denison," she said politely, before Alex could speak.

"Is that your vehicle? The Fiat?"

"Am I being interrogated?" asked Sasha.

The Quartermaster Sergeant laughed. He had one tooth missing at the side. "I'm sorry."

"I guess so," smiled Sasha. "Well, yes, that's my car."

"Poo," said Sammy-Joe tugging at his trousers.

"That's my cue," said Sasha. She scooped up the baby and walked into the next room.

The men watched her go. "Have you known her long?" asked the Quartermaster Sergeant.

"Ages," said Alex, firmly.

After the Quartermaster Sergeant left, Alex apologized to Sasha for the interruption.

"I've been through childbirth," said Sasha. "I'm not scared of anything now."

"But why did you say your name was Kate Denison?" Alex had to know.

Sasha sighed. "Was that terrible of me? I don't give my name out to men I don't know, even important ones wearing uniforms. Anyway, my name *is* Kate Denison. Or it could be. It's my clone name, you know; everyone has one. It's my second name, Kate, married up with my mother's maiden name, Denison. So I'm Kate Dension. I wheel her out sometimes when I'm in need of backup. She's like a super me. She's the part of me that doesn't take any crap from anyone and is fearless. She's been useful over the last year or so, hasn't she,

Sammy?" She pinched the baby's fat pink cheek. "If I get comments about Sammy, I call on the mighty Kate." She looked up at Alex. "I suppose you think I'm a madwoman now?"

"No," said Alex, thinking that he was finally seeing just a hint of the difficulties Sasha must have faced having Sammy. She was usually full of bravado.

"So what's your clone name?" asked Sasha.

"Edward Sands," said Alex. He smiled. He made more tea and they watched as Sammy-Joe tore around, upending piles of newspapers and toppling boots. But Sasha was quieter than usual and when the food had all been eaten she seemed to be in a hurry to leave.

"It's great to see your place," she said. "It's lovely out here. But I need to get Sammy home for his nap." They left soon after.

Alex looked at the tyre tracks in the yard from her car. She really was gone, but her perfume lingered in the kitchen, and the mayhem from Sammy was still evident. There were squashed raisins on the floor, a chewed-up tissue, dirty plates in the sink. Alex cleared up slowly, reluctant to remove the evidence of Sasha but at the same time worrying about Quartermaster Sergeant Furzey.

He couldn't help thinking that if he and Levi hadn't been the intruders Furzey was talking about, then who was?

Levi's Bed

I'm with Levi in his back garden. It's crammed with pots of flowers and has grape vines climbing the fence. There's a statue of some Greek hero posing buck naked on his plinth, smack bang in the middle. We're hanging on out stripy deckchairs, drinking iced lemonade, our trousers rolled up to the knee. Sunday's rain has cleared up and the day is as blazing hot as ever. One of our classes, history, got cancelled at the last minute and amazingly Levi invited sketchy old me back to his house for an hour or two before our geography seminar.

I think I said YES far too quickly because he smiled a little smile. Still, I'm here now and nothing has gone wrong.

"How can I make her love me?" sighs Levi.

He's talking about Sasha. Of course.

"She has everything: brains, looks, humour. . ."

"A baby. . ." I say.

"Is that a problem?" asks Levi, sitting up.

I suck up the last of my lemonade. "It would be for me. Who needs that responsibility? There's thousands of girls out there."

"Alex doesn't seem to think so," says Levi darkly. He touches my arm and I look at his hand. I'm so not into physical contact.

"Do you think I'm out of the running? Should I bow out gracefully or keep at it?"

I really can't see the appeal. Sasha is mouthy and her hair was greasy this morning.

"Alex won't tell me what he's up to with Sasha," moans Levi. "He just gives his shrug and says 'search me'. He's keeping his cards close to his chest."

"The Gamekeeper." I lie back, causing Levi's hand to fall away. "Alex is like a sinister cartoon comic strip character. It's a good name for him."

Levi frowns, doesn't take the bait.

"I say, Mellors," I mutter. "Off with the plus fours and into the shrubbery for some rumpy."

"What's that?" Levi asks.

"Haven't you read *Lady Chatterley's Lover*?"

A copy was passed round my class a year or so ago, the rude bits underlined in green felt pen. When my teacher, Mr Browne, found out, instead of confiscating the book, he was ecstatic. He said he was delighted that a class of sixteen-year-old twenty-first-century digital natives could still be titillated by sixty-year-old mild erotica. It gave him faith, he said, in the eternal innocence of youth. Then he made the whole class read the book and write a review on it by Monday morning.

"I think The Gamekeeper has set his sights on your

woman," I say slyly. "Right now he's building a snare for her. . ."

"I'm not into nicknames," says Levi. "They can sometimes come across as a bit nasty, y'know?"

"Right." I'm surprised. At The Risings, everyone has a nickname. Mine used to be Toad, I don't know why. Just before I was booted out, I was given a new nickname. It's pretty nasty and wouldn't look good on my CV. I decide to keep quiet about it. Levi can be irritatingly loyal and noble at times. It's no fun. And anyway, he's not himself today. He's touchy and snappy like a stranded crab.

"What would you do if you had loads of money?" asks Levi suddenly. "I mean loads, like ten thousand pounds."

Ha! I'm forgiven for my mean little jokes. I think about money a lot. Everyone does. I even have a little tune about it.

How can I get some money / get some money?
Shoot the loot / shoot it over my head
Get showered in lolly / wanna swim in the bread
Wanna flash the cash / wanna big God-wad
But the dough is rising slow, man
And this poverty bringing me low, man.

I eye Levi speculatively. Should I share? The next few lines totally kick butt and, if Levi likes my tunes, maybe he could become my new partner in rhyme.

"I'd buy my mum a camper van," Levi is saying.

"She's always wanted one of those with the pop-up roof and the built-in bog. Then I'd get me a crash course in driving lessons (no pun intended) and a silver Porsche convertible. And I'd take Sasha for a ride."

"No room for a baby seat in a Porsche," I say.

Oops, he doesn't like that at all. "You would bring that up."

"Just saying," I reply.

There's a crashing sound from the kitchen. Should I be startled?

"That would be my number one woman," says Levi.

Oh no, is Sasha coming round?

"Hi, Mum," says Levi, rolling out of his deckchair on to the grass as a short, dumpy mumsy-woman steps into the yard.

"Hello," she beams.

Levi's mother is white. This surprises me a little, as Levi is brown. I'd expected her to be a similar hue. She has messy hair cut into a short bob, smiley-tired eyes and massive boobs. She's wearing the livery of the local supermarket. Oh dear, she looks vaguely familiar. I so hope I have not been rude to her in the past. I'm not too good in supermarkets. All the bright lights take me into another realm.

Levi does the introductions. His mother's name is Sarah. She kisses Levi fondly on the cheek, leaving a damp mark of mum-spit, and drops a cherry Bakewell in his lap. Then she turns to me.

"Have you been admiring Adonis?" she says,

gesturing to the nudie statue. "He's the only souvenir from my classics degree in Manchester." She pauses. "Well, him and Levi." Ah! A wit!

She turns back to her beloved son and starts hassling him, asking about his day, asking why he was home, telling him what was for dinner, all the stuff that my own mother would say. The sort of stuff that irritates the hell out of me.

Askin' me 'bout every effing hour
Making damn sure you hold all the power. . .
I don't have to justify my day
Cut the baby cord witch, let me get away. . .

Levi, however, chatters on Levi-like, telling his mother about the cancelled history lesson, about his lunch, the homeless man he spotted wandering into the college canteen with a pigeon, and about little me. Then he asks her about the supermarket.

"Get any grief from Jim?"

His mother sighs. "Nothing I can't handle."

"I don't know why you put up with it," says Levi, honestly cross. "You should jack in the job, you're overqualified."

"Soon, soon," soothes his mother. "Anyone want another drink?"

"Don't all those questions drive you crazy?" I ask now we are safely ensconced in Levi's boy-bedroom.

"Why should it?" He's genuinely surprised. "She loves me, man."

Levi's room is painted sky blue, oh how his mother loves him! There are glo-stars on the ceiling and a space rocket clock on the wall. There the childishness ends. Three posters, each depicting a luscious female clad only in very small pants, are taped over the bed. I can't take my eyes from the six meaty breasts. This is sensory overload and my eyes are whirling around like bluebottles, unable to settle.

"Doesn't your mum mind?" I point at the buxom sirens in case he doesn't know what I'm talking about. My mother would go *septic* if I had porn on my walls, not least because the sticky tape would rip the wallpaper.

"She thinks I'm just going through a phase," says Levi. "She calls them my 'wives'." He breathes in. "Max, your brother is in the army, right?"

I nod wearily.

Levi scratches his head. He wants to spit out some controversial words but is nervous about doing so.

"What?" I say. Then I think bad things, like he's asking about the army because he KNOWS. "What?"

"Nothing," says Levi. He looks at me. "Max, you weren't really expelled from school for stealing food, were you?"

Ouch, a sucker punch. Where did that come from? I feel myself getting nervous.

"Come on," said Levi. "I'm a big boy. I can take it."

Now I feel better. Levi does NOT know about me. He is just ASTUTE. I glance at his "wives". And maybe, just maybe, if he did know what I did, he might not freak out. Not everyone is a ramrod Cosgrove. Or a fee-paying Risings parent, gunning their darlings for Oxbridge.

"Did you steal food?" Levi persists.

"NO," I say loudly. There, I am liberated from my fodder lie. I fold my arms and lean back against the wall, sinking into Levi's carpet. We listen to his space rocket clock tick away the seconds.

Levi nods. "Thanks, Max. I appreciate your honesty." He sounds like a social worker at circle time and I feel a smidgeon of annoyance dart through me. He gives me a sideways look. "Going to tell me the whole truth some day?"

"Probably not," I reply.

"Good. I need to talk to someone who can keep quiet about things. You're good at that. Can you keep a secret?" Man, he's really looking at me.

"Mostly," I say. What is going on here? Am I about to be admitted into the inner circle of Hammerton Tech?

"Look at this." Levi kneels by his bed and reaches underneath. He draws out a long object wrapped in a blanket. He places it on the bed and draws back the blanket. I feel the inside of my cheeks suck in, like I am eating lemons.

Inside lies a rifle.

Oh my! I feel my skin prickle. Now this really is

something. I look at the weapon and feel drawn to it, like a vampire after a virgin.

"Is it yours?"

Levi doesn't answer.

The rifle is black with grease. I run a finger along the barrel. It feels magic. "Does it work?" I ask softly. This must be how Gollum feels about the ring.

"We think so," says Levi. He's watching me carefully. "There's more, Max, loads more."

And then he tells me a story about him and Alex and the moors and some old barn and loads of rifles just like these. I'm so excited I'm having trouble listening to the details. This is *brilliant*. This is proper madness. Levi says he cycled up to the moor last night, walked to the spot and recovered one of the weapons as a souvenir. He says Alex is refusing to have anything more to do with them, but that he really thinks they should call the police.

"And what do you think?" I ask silkily.

"We've looked them up on the internet," answers Levi. "Alex reckons they are worth from five hundred pounds each to two thousand pounds, depending on their condition. And there are at least a hundred guns down there."

Levi sighs. "I'd love to get my mum out of that bloody job. There's this manager at work who . . . well, never mind, anyway. The money would be good."

"The money would be great," I say. "But apart from that, this is really cool." My eyes narrow. "I want one."

I wouldn't *use* it, of course. It would just make me feel so much better if I knew I had a gun. Simple.

Levi frowns, bless him. "They're not toys. I wondered if your brother had any contacts, you know, being in the army. Someone who might buy them."

"So you're setting yourself up as an arms dealer?"

Levi's face falls. "No, probably not. That doesn't sound so good."

'So what shall we do with them?"

Levi sighs and, to my disappointment, wraps up the gun.

"Alex is scared. He says we should do nothing. He's probably right." He looks at me. Concern is making the corner of his mouth twitch like a dying mouse.

"To be honest, I'm a bit scared now, Max. Last night I dug in a different place and found this, all wrapped up in oilskins and cloth." Levi pulls a silver metal case out from under his bed. It's about the size of two shoeboxes. He unclips the fastenings and opens it to reveal a padding of thick black foam.

"Oh my!" I say again.

Inside is some kind of exciting electronic device: a plain flattish black box dotted with docking points, a silver cylinder with an optic disc at the end, a kind of numbered control box, and lots of bundles of wire.

Levi breathes in. "I tried to look it up on the internet. I think it's parts for some kind of laser guidance system."

"Oh my God!" I say. I feel drunk and wobly.

"There's more stuff like it," says Levi. "Lots more." He

lowers his voice. "I think it has all been buried really recently. The ground is all churned up, and there's no way it has been down there for long. I got so freaked out in the barn last night, I just grabbed this stuff and ran."

I am silenced, but my eyes flicker all over the equipment.

"Look, forget it. Forget I told you. I shouldn't have, only it was driving me crazy. I couldn't sleep at all last night. I'm not like you, I'm rubbish at keeping my mouth shut." Now I notice Levi has dark circles under his eyes and a crop of tiny spots have erupted round his mouth.

But I feel like a billion tiny lights have lit up inside me.

"I want to see everything," I say.

Tony Delaney

A killer got into the pullet pen last night. Nearly forty of the young birds were dead. Some had no visible marks, some had blood on their backs where they had been bitten, and some had been decapitated. It looked like the work of a fox. Tim hadn't shot any for some time and Alex had seen a family of cubs playing in the lower fields in the spring. He wished the foxes wouldn't do this. If they sneaked in and just took a bird or two, or ate rabbits, then they wouldn't have to shoot them, but foxes could be cat-like; sometimes they killed for sheer pleasure.

Tim climbed into the pen and handed Alex a sack. As they collected the stiff, cold bodies they looked around for signs of a break-in, but there was nothing. Maybe there had been a power cut and the electric fence was down.

It was odd that Alex hadn't heard anything. He was usually a light sleeper. They were only halfway through the job when a sleek black long-wheelbased Land Rover Defender pulled into the yard.

"What timing," muttered Tim.

"Trouble?" A tall grey-haired man, dressed in jeans and a leather jacket with a sheepskin ruff, eased himself out of the vehicle.

"Hello, Tony," said Tim. He put down his sack and reached for an empty one.

"Jesus," the man swore as he looked upon the carnage. He stepped into the pen and picked up a dead bird. "How the hell did this happen?"

Alex bit his lip. It was the worst possible moment for the owner of the estate, Tony Delaney, to make an appearance. Usually at this time of year he stayed in London, where he worked in sports television. Stonebridge House was let over the summer for weddings and conferences. Delaney took up residence in the winter to host the shooting parties.

"Alex and I were just discussing it," said Tim. "It looks like a fox."

Tony threw his hands up. "What about my shoots? I've got them all booked already. I can't have a shoot without any birds."

"There will be plenty of birds," said Tim quietly. "There always are. This has happened before."

"It's got to stop," snapped Tony. "What do I pay you for?"

There was an uncomfortable silence. They all knew that without Tim raising the birds, organizing the shoots, growing the suitable ground cover, recruiting the beaters, maintaining all the equipment and organizing the meals, Tony's shoot would never have gained the reputation of being one of the best drives in the West Country. Tony had owned the estate for years, but he was dependent on Jason to run the farm and Tim to run the shoots. He also paid them both a salary well below the minimum wage.

Tony breathed out. One of the better things about him was that he was never angry for long.

"Sorry," he said. "It's just a shock, you know, to come out here and see all my birds dead."

"There's thousands more still alive," butted in Alex.

"We don't like it either," said Tim, shooting Alex a look that said *shut up*. "We'll go out lamping tonight."

Tony nodded.

Tim looked at Alex. "Shouldn't you be at college?"

"Yeah," Alex sighed.

"I'll see you later, then."

Reluctantly, Alex went into the house to wash the smears of blood and other things from his hands. He heard Tim telephone the local police station. If he planned any night shooting, he had to let the local constabulary know so they didn't freak out over the gunshots. Not that anyone did round here, reflected Alex. There were guns and bangs all the time these days. The red flags were flying over Taw Marsh today. There would be no peace.

Alex collected his bike from the shed and rode past the pheasant pens, where Delaney was still stalking about and talking into his phone. He'd be gone soon; he never stayed long. It took Alex thirty-five minutes to cycle the five miles into Hammerton. He knew, with a feeling of dread, that as soon as he got to college, Levi would be on at him about the rifles. But Alex was beginning to think they should tip off the police anonymously. That way, none of them would be connected to the guns. That way, they could stay out of danger.

Ten past ten and Alex couldn't stop fidgeting. He stretched out his legs, then folded them again. Alex imagined invisible glue holding him on to his chair. Storm hydrographs and river discharge did not interest him.

Levi was trying to make Sasha laugh, dancing his fingers over the desk, a silly face drawn on his knuckles. And there was Max, in his stupid hat, glowering and farting in the background like a bad dream. The teacher droned on and on.

Alex had no intention of hanging around after the lesson, but as soon as it finished he felt a hand on his shoulder. Levi looked at him and there was something guilty in his face.

"We need to talk," he said. "Things have moved on."

Alex knew immediately what this was about. They walked through the hot corridor and clattered down the echoing concrete steps to the outside green.

Max sidled, smiling knowingly.

"You've not told him?" said Alex.

Levi looked guilty. "I've told him everything." He looked around to check no one else was listening and whispered, "You kept avoiding the issue. I needed to talk to someone."

Alex couldn't believe that Levi had told Max of all people.

"Look, this could be really cool," broke in Max. "I bet there's some way of selling these guns."

"What? You are seventeen years old, Max. Your mum gives you dinner money. You're not an international arms dealer."

"There's always the future," said Max. "We just need to move the guns somewhere else."

"What?" Alex felt a kind of blind panic. "This has got nothing to do with you." He didn't want Max involved at all.

"If we move all the guns to a new hiding place, we can work out what to do," said Max. "We might not do anything with them for years, right? But the point is, one day, we will do something, and make all of us a shedload of money."

"But these are guns," protested Alex. "They are made to maim and kill. They're not toys you can sell on eBay. Who are you going to sell them to?"

"That doesn't matter at this stage," said Max.

"Yes, it does," said Alex.

"What does matter is that we need to hide them," continued Max. "Someone knows where they are, so they're not safe."

"But they don't belong to you," hissed Alex. "Or had you forgotten?" He looked at Sasha, who was sitting on a wall, drinking water and watching them. "Don't tell me you've got her involved as well?"

"She knows nothing, I swear it," said Levi solemnly.

"I'm having nothing to do with this," said Alex. "Don't you realize those guns could belong to some nutter? Or terrorist? Or the army itself? People who are deadly! That's why we've done nothing. We should just steer clear and pretend we've never even seen them. You don't get involved with it, right?" He turned to Max.

"I already am involved," said Max. "It's too good an opportunity to miss. Levi says those rifles are worth loads of money. There's hundreds down there. And as for the laser system. . ."

"Max." Levi shook his head. "Please."

Alex froze, shocked to his core.

"Laser system. Levi?" He looked at his friend, wild-eyed.

"There's more stuff down there, Alex," said Levi. "Much much more. I went back. I found. . ." He swallowed. "I found some really odd things."

Alex clamped his hands to his head. This was becoming nightmarish.

"I'm sorry," said Levi miserably.

Alex didn't know what to think. His legs felt wobbly and he sat on the grass.

"Don't go back there," he said.

"Why are you the one giving the orders all of a sudden?" demanded Max.

Alex clenched his fists. Max was so difficult. And now he was wide-eyed with excitement. He was actually enjoying all this.

Levi looked uncomfortable. "Look, sorry, mate, for going behind your back. I so wish I hadn't now."

Sasha had noticed the raised voices. Alex watched as she started to make her way to them.

"Let's talk somewhere else," said Alex. "Come on."

Levi and Max looked at each other and followed. Just next to the college was a large graveyard surrounded by bushes and trees. Without giving Sasha a chance to catch up, Alex led the others out of college through the gates and walked up to a big old tomb with wide flat steps. A stone angel with chipped wings stood on top.

"I've been looking on the internet," said Alex. "Guess what sort of weapons the Argentine army used in the Falklands?"

"Our guns?" said Levi. "It stands to reason. But why are they here and not in a gun museum in Buenos Aires?"

"After the Falklands War, the Argentinean soldiers were made to give up their weapons," Alex told him. "The official line is they were all thrown in the sea or otherwise destroyed."

"Only these floated over here," said Levi. "Wow."

Alex scratched his head. "So these guns and maybe the other things have either come here via the British army, or by some other way. Whatever, someone has hidden them on public land, in an isolated place, near an army base. What does that say to you?"

"The soldiers hid them?" asked Levi. "But forgot to come back for them?"

"One man or thirty, who knows." Alex did not want to say this out loud. It was too horrible. But the others had to understand the magnitude of what they were getting into. "They might belong to some group or other that meant to harm the army, and they were buried nearby as part of a planned attack. Maybe on the army base itself. Or they were just hidden here by some cell of terrorists. We don't bloody know," he fumed. "But either way, they have NOTHING TO DO WITH US."

He slammed his hand against the wall. Levi looked startled. "I think you're both bloody crazy," Alex said.

"It's too late," said Levi quietly.

"What?" Alex felt a buzz grow in his ears, a buzz of sheer panic. "What have you done?"

Levi wouldn't meet his eye. "I've already moved some stuff."

"What?"

"I went out there, on my own last night. Dude, you were, like, static! I wasn't getting anywhere with you. I just wanted to have another look."

Alex leaned against the wall as a bloom of sweat broke out over his body. It had come back, that feeling he'd had in the ruined barn, the dark, sinister fear. The sense of something very bad.

"Where is it now?" He looked at the pair standing before him. "You haven't taken it home, have you? How many did you move?"

"I only took one," said Levi. "And the box of laser equipment. It was heavy." He said this with some surprise. "I just moved it somewhere temporary."

"Where?" asked Alex weakly.

Levi gestured to the grey college building, just showing through the trees.

"The box of laser equipment is still under my bed." He paused. "But the gun is in my locker."

Strangeways Again

Tim paused in the doorway gripping his travelling bag. His hair, newly washed, was still damp. "Are you sure you'll be all right?"

"Yes," said Alex, and he swallowed the dregs of his third cup of coffee.

"You've been odd the last few days. What's on your mind?"

"Nothing. Go."

"You'll water and feed the birds twice a day? Lock the office up?"

"Yes, yes."

Still Tim hovered. "We got the two foxes last night, but that doesn't mean there aren't more about. You'll check the charge on the fences last thing?"

"Relax. I'm on it."

"And you're all set for the ratting? You've got the key to the gate? The place isn't especially secure anyway."

"Yes, Dad. Go. Amy doesn't like to be kept waiting."

"Sparky is a good dog. He'll catch a hundred rats."

"I know, Dad, I've done it a thousand times."

"I know. You won't use the smoke, will you? It's a two man job if you use the smoke."

"I won't use the smoke."

"Maybe I should stay. Do the rat job with you. . ."

"Dad, Amy won't be impressed if you stand her up over a bunch of rats."

Tim rubbed the back of his neck and blew his cheeks out. "I've never been to Birmingham before. She's booked for us to go to this bloody concert and. . ."

"You'll love it," said Alex.

"Come too!" said Tim, brightening. "I'll get Jason to do the feeding. He's doing the morning work anyway. We can cancel the rats."

"Dad, I'll be fine," said Alex. "I do not want to come. No offence, but it's not my thing." He couldn't imagine anything worse than sitting on a cramped train for four hours travelling to an enormous city to mingle with thousands of people.

"All right." Tim looked hard at his son. He paused. "How's Sasha?"

Alex smiled. "She's great. Dad – vanish! I'm a big boy now." He could feel the caffeine from the coffee having its effect. He wanted to get going.

Still Tim was reluctant to leave. "Something is bugging you, though."

"You'll miss your train." Alex decided that if Tim wasn't going to leave, then he would. "I'm going to get things ready." He patted his dad on the back as he passed. He stepped out of the house and into the bright morning.

"I'll be back on Tuesday," called Tim.

When his dad had finally driven away, Alex breathed out.

There was so much to do. He passed the pens full of chirping pheasants and made for a tumbledown outbuilding they called the Rabbit Shed. No rabbits now; all it housed was broken furniture and Alex's collection of antlers. Alex crossed the dirt floor to an old carpet mouldering in the back. Underneath lay a large black bag.

Alex had insisted that he took the rifle home with him. He said there was no way Levi could have it in his locker. Even now, he felt himself go hot and cold at the thought of having weapons like this in college. Max had protested until Alex had threatened to call the police then and there and tell them everything unless the others agreed. He'd taken the gun into the loos and had opened it to check it was empty – it was – and then he'd taken it straight home, missing his afternoon seminar.

Alex hefted up the bag and took it out of the shed through the yard to Tim's old truck. He'd passed his driving test the day after his seventeenth birthday, though he'd been driving vehicles over the fields since he was about eight years old. He cycled to college because he liked it and because he didn't have much money for fuel. Sparky, Jason's terrier, waited for him, leaning out of the window and wagging his tail. Gaffer lounged on the back seats. He didn't mind being usurped from the top dog's position in the front; he wasn't that sort of dog. Alex hid the guns under Gaffer's dog blanket in the boot. Then he collected some plastic sacks, some thick gloves, a hammer and a spade.

Alex addressed the dogs. "All set, boys?"

Quartermaster Sergeant Furzey had phoned last night, requesting an urgent pest control visit down at Strangeways. He said the place was infested with rats and it was a health and safety requirement that they were got rid of. Tim had started to say that he couldn't do it for a few days, as he would be away, but Alex had intercepted. It was a perfect opportunity to return the rifle to the bog, and he'd been ratting since he was a boy. There was nothing to stop him doing the job. When he and Tim had been ratting at Strangeways the year before, they had been just left to it. No one from the barracks had bothered them. Even so, he was rattling with nerves.

He needed to shift, though, as the Quartermaster Sergeant said they had booked manoeuvres there later that afternoon, and it was nine o'clock already.

Alex rattled down the sun-dappled track. Sparky leaned into the windscreen, forepaws on the dash, like he was willing the old truck to keep going. Gaffer drooled and daydreamed in the back, like an old man on a pensioners' outing.

"We'll get us some rats, lads," said Alex. "Rats."

Sparky barked in excitement and even Gaffer pricked up his ears.

"I'll need your digging prowess, Sparky," said Alex. "We've got to dig under an old latrine. That is, a toilet. It's dirty work, but for a noble cause. RATS."

Sparky barked again, staring at Alex with intense concentration.

"The Quartermaster Sergeant is worried about Weil's disease, apparently," went on Alex, turning off into a small lane. "He doesn't want his men poisoned by rats' pee. By killing these rodents, we are helping to defend the realm." He beeped the horn at a sheep, dozing in the middle of the road.

"Out the way, wool-brains," shouted Alex. The sheep calmly got up and ambled off the road. As they drove past, Sparky stuck his head out of the window and barked at it.

"Save your energy for the real enemy, boys," said Alex. "Let's hit them hard."

The road wound along a ridge set above a river, then turned sharply uphill, climbing to the moor. Alex tapped his finger on the steering wheel as they reached a turn-off.

MOD PROPERTY. LIVE FIRING. TRESPASSERS WILL BE PROSECUTED.

The red flags were flying on the rise, but Alex knew the manoeuvres would not take place for hours. Apparently the health and safety report stated that leptospirosis was enough of a risk, given the infestation of rats, to cancel the training unless the rats were eradicated first.

There was a green jeep parked by the metal gate a little way down the road. A grey-haired soldier was sitting inside. Heart hammering, Alex pulled over, mindful of his sack on the back seat. He prayed his truck would not be searched. He recognized the man. It was Lance Corporal Reed. He lived in the town and was interested in hawks and birds of prey. He was often out on the moor with his binoculars.

"On your own?" he said, looking into the truck. Alex froze. Reed was looking directly at the bag.

"I've got these two," Alex replied, gesturing to the dogs.

Reed grinned. He seemed a decent bloke; he always waved at Alex and Tim when passing.

He stepped back, much to Alex's relief. "You've the key for the bottom gate, haven't you?"

Alex had.

"Seargeant Furzey is in command of today's operations. Report directly to him when you're done, OK? You've got his number?"

Alex could only nod.

"We're shifting operations to this evening. But you'll be long gone by then, won't you?"

Alex nodded again.

"You'll mark the position of any traps and poison on the chart?"

"I will," said Alex, patting the paper in his pocket.

"I'll let you get on, then." Reed waved and climbed into his truck. "Have fun."

Alex blew out his cheeks when he'd gone. That was way too close.

The track to Strangeways was maybe a mile long, and the truck bottomed out on the stones several times, making Alex worry that he might have damaged the exhaust. But as he drove, his spirits lifted. It should be easy enough to replace the gun. Then he and Sparky would deal with the rats' nest. Only when that was all done would he tackle the problem of the box of equipment under Levi's bed.

That was the plan anyway.

Strangeways. The track gently curved down the hillside, passing sheep, rocks and boulders. To the left, standing out on amongst the sun-browned grass, was a mound of grey, flat stones. This was known as "Beggar Boy", and was said to be a Bronze Age cist. The moor was full of prehistoric remains.

Alex drove through a copse of fir trees, then down into the farmyard. Strangeways was a series of low, old buildings, once whitewashed, now speckled with bullet holes. Slates were slipping from the roofs. There was the stable. (Tim had a photograph of his father leading a big white horse out of that very shed.) Over to the right was a low outbuilding where the turkeys had been kept. Most of the yard had been concreted, but the old cobbles peeped through at the edges. The farm was bordered on three sides by overgrown paddocks, now returning to marsh and bog. A stone barn was set a little way from the house. This was where lambs and calves were once born and where hay was stored for the winter. Now it housed a broken motorbike and an old creaking oil tank. The garden was bare earth, hard baked by the sun and worn to a flat, smooth sheen by the soldiers' boots. The small orchard to the right of the farmhouse still had a few fruit trees, some in full leaf and some dead. Here and there floated bits of rubbish: sweet wrappers, boot imprints, a trodden-in shell case, a wrap of plastic.

This was where they practised death. They practised clearing the enemy from the very rooms in which his grandparents had sat, read, cooked and slept. Now snipers trained their sights from window sills which used to house Alex's grandmother's trailing pots of geraniums. Explosives were set in the lambing sheds. Mock interrogations were staged in the kitchen. Radio checkpoints were set up in the old curing shed.

Alex looked up at the bedroom window where his father had apparently been born. Alex imagined Sasha in the orchard, sticking out her tongue. He added geese and maybe ducks crowding round her. He'd hire a digger and dig out the old pond, which had turned into a spreading swamp, now full of pink spotted orchids, yellow marsh flowers, green discs of fat leaves, speckled frogs and blue moths.

It would all get a hammering later today. Alex looked over at the periphery fence, beyond the paddocks and behind the overgrown trees. He could just make out part of the sagging roof of the old barn, black and bowing, like something out of a horror film. He'd go there in a minute and rebury the gun whilst there was no one about. Then he'd sort out the rats.

He realized he was sweating. He didn't want to go back into that barn. Never mind what was inside and how it made him feel, the roof wasn't safe. The whole structure could collapse at any minute. Alex backed the truck to an area of hardstanding behind the outbuildings. He got out and stood amongst towering clumps of ragwort and thistles. Lifting his binoculars to his eyes, he quickly scanned the surrounding hills. He saw nothing but scrub, stones and sheep. The place was deserted. Alex removed a hessian sack from the back seat and held it in one hand. This sack had formerly contained pheasant feed and was perfect for concealing the weapon. Alex had put some old rags in the sack to puff it up. He had his story straight. If challenged, he was going to say it was full of dead rats, and that he was burying it in the bog. And why would anyone want to look at dead rats?

Alex left the dogs in the truck and wound through the long grass and nettles of the paddocks. He crossed a stream bed, the water reduced to a trickle, and stepped into the copse surrounding the derelict barn. Now he had to fight through elder and brambles, but he noticed, here and there, a snapped branch or a trampled nettle. Levi would have come to the barn the way Alex had previously shown him, from the moor. So who had made this trail? A burning sensation in Alex's chest reminded him how scared he was. A bramble ripped into Alex's arm, dotting his skin with blood as his boot sank into a spongy dent of brown water. Even after this crazy hot summer, the marshes were still wet. Alex battled on, marsh birds shrill above him and a cold fear knotting his chest. There was the barn, leaning up against the fence. A few firm shoves and it looked like the whole thing would collapse.

Alex bent into the darkness of the barn. The place seemed smaller, the roof lower than ever. The rank, oppressive air stung his nostrils and limp, sunless weeds clung to his legs as he pushed through. He hurriedly untied the bag, fumbling with the knots, and gently placed the gun in the mess at the back of the barn. He did not want the owner of the guns to discover the sack, as it had HARRIS POULTRY FEEDS printed on it and he was paranoid about being traced. He found the broken spade and rapidly covered the gun with clods of turf and peat. He worked fast and sweat ran down his forehead and into his eyes, but it was already ten o'clock by the time he'd finished. A whole hour had passed since he had left Keeper's Cottage. He snatched handfuls of old, damp brown straw and scattered it about. That would have to do. Now he had to get out.

Back in the farmyard of Strangeways, Alex looked at the old farmhouse for reassurance. The red-brick battered chimney was beginning to crumble and the guttering was blocked with moss and stunted buddleia.

Thistledown floated in thousands of parachutes through the yard. The place was falling apart.

Sparky barked at him from the truck impatiently.

He'd done it.

It was nearly all over. Once the rats were sorted he'd call Levi and work out the best way of disposing of the remaining equipment.

Everything was OK.

Rats!

Sparky was itching to kill. He slavered as he sniffed around, tail wagging in anticipation. Gaffer was less possessed, but paced around, alert and excited.

"Rats?" hissed Alex, and the dogs barked. Alex felt trembly and hot after disposing of the gun. All he really wanted to do was to go home. But he had a job to do.

The old latrine block was situated in the field behind the stable. It had recently been replaced by a brick building with flushing toilets. The old latrines were basically two planks of wood over a deep pit in a wooden shack. There was no privacy for the user. There was no door in the rough wood wall and the tin roof was slipping off.

Leaving his air gun propped against the wall, Alex stepped inside. It smelt musty. He kicked off one of the planks and peered within. The stuff in the pit had set to the consistency of hard fudge. There was a solid crust on the surface, pitted and pocked like the surface of the moon. There were also several large holes, stuffed up with feathers and bits of dried grass.

Sparky jumped on the other plank, tail wagging, sniffing. Alex put on his gloves and reached for his spade. This was horrible, though Sparky plainly thought otherwise. The dog jumped down into the pit and started digging. Alex reassured himself that the stuff in here was not fresh. Straddling the pit, he plunged his spade into the nearest tunnel. The smell wasn't too bad; it was like the intense smell you get when a farmer is dung spreading. All the same, the thought of what he was digging into made Alex gag.

Suddenly a brown shape darted out of the hole, flew up the wall and over the plank. In an instant, Sparky was after it, cornering it and grabbing it by the neck. He shook and shook. The rat was dead in seconds.

"Good man," said Alex. He dug the spade in again. This time five or six large rats shot out. He should have brought more than one terrier. Alex brought his spade down heavily on a rat that scurried towards him, breaking its back and killing it instantly. Sparky, meanwhile, was going berserk, running here and there, biting and snapping and despatching rats, whilst old Gaffer barked and made tentative runs at the creatures, before shying away at the last minute.

Alex yelled as a very large rat ran right over his foot. "Sparky!"

He was so immersed he didn't register the shouting at first. It was all noise, barking, rats squealing, him whooping and jumping.

But there was shouting, really loud shouting coming from close by.

Breathing heavily, still clutching his spade, Alex stepped outside. He thought of the guns, lying in the freshly dug earth, and was gripped with fear.

But to his utter bemusement, Levi appeared at the gate of the paddock, followed by Max, and three soldiers.

Alex stood, sweating and confused, as the men approached. It was the soldiers from the river, the complete set: Saul, Riley and Baz. The very soldiers he'd least like to see. They were dressed in long camouflage trousers, green shirts and black regimental berets. He'd rather see ten Quartermaster Sergeant Furzeys than this lot.

"Who's this?" called Baz. "Not another trespasser." He stormed up to Alex. "Talk." Alex could say nothing. He remembered how he had seen this very man weep in the river, only a few weeks ago. He glanced at the others, Levi managing to look sheepish and defiant at the same time and Max pale-faced in his stupid pointy shoes.

What were they all doing here?

Saul followed close behind. "I'm Lance Corporal Saul Powers. What the bloody hell are you doing on army property?" He looked at Alex, saw the air gun on the floor, and his eyes widened.

Alex cleared his throat and forced himself to speak. "I'm supposed to be here," he said. "I'm clearing the vermin." He pointed to the latrines.

"So you're with the gamekeeper?" said Baz slowly, looking him over.

"I'm his son," said Alex, wondering what he was thinking. "I'm doing the job."

"And we're with him," said Max quickly.

"What's your name?" asked Baz, ignoring him.

Alex told him. He could see no reason to lie.

"And what exactly are you doing here?"

"Like I said. The army pays us to clear the rats. I've just spoken to Corporal Reed up the gate. He said there'd be nobody here until much later."

The soldiers exchanged looks.

"Reckon these are the intruders Q was talking about?" Riley muttered to Saul.

"What about these jokers? We found them digging around by the fence." Saul addressed him. "Are they looking for rats too?"

Baz shoved Max so hard he nearly fell over.

"No need for that," said Levi. "No bloody need for that."

Alex shot a look at his friends. They must be after the guns. He sighed. "They're with me. This is a paid job." He had no choice but to say it. But why were the soldiers here? Alex couldn't think.

"The manoeuvre isn't supposed to start until the evening," he said. "It's only ten in the morning."

"Hold on." Saul walked a little way off, talking into his radio.

"I recognize all of you from town," said Baz. He

looked at Max's face; the skin around his eye was still puffy and a deep yellow. "You just can't get enough of us, can you? The Risings Bomber strikes again. Did you have something in mind for here, too?"

"Shut up," said Max, going red.

"Boy Bomber," said Baz. "You disrupted a whole weekend with your sick antics."

Max was shaking, his face set.

"Did you know your mate was a terrorist?" Baz said to Levi.

"SHUT UP," screamed Max. "You're talking crap."

"What's this, Max?" Levi sounded friendly but curious. "What are they talking about?"

Alex said nothing. He watched as Max wound himself up, tighter and tighter. He was staring at the two soldiers like he wanted to kill them.

"So the boss gets a call at about eight in the morning, the day of my leave, I might add," said Baz conversationally. "Someone has rung the posh private school at Lydford. Says they've planted a series of bombs. The whole school is evacuated. Kids, teachers, cleaners, cooks, the lot. And who has completed his bomb disposal training? Muggins here. Eight of us comb the building until we find three hoax bombs, and a whole school full of terrified children."

"You?" Levi asked Max softly.

Max was blank-faced.

"So that's why you got expelled." Levi stepped back. "Christ, Max."

Max looked away, pulling at his ear.

"He hasn't told you the rest of it," said Baz. "This joker here didn't come forward until everyone in the school had been punished, so I hear. He only got caught when the headmaster played back the school security camera videos. The whole place was under a terrorist alert. We had Special Branch, M15 and the bloody home secretary at our heels." He shook his head. "Some of us looked pretty silly when it turned out to be a schoolboy hoax."

"I never heard about it," said Alex, amazed.

"I did," said Levi. "It was on the news."

"It was just a joke," Max protested. "It got blown up out of proportion."

"You don't ever joke about bombs," said Baz. He put his face very close to Max's. "From what I hear, you ought to have learned that by now. Maybe you need another lesson."

"SHUT UP," screamed Max, pushing him away. Alex knew he must take Max home. Never mind the bloody rats.

But Levi stepped over first. "Cool it, Max."

"Stupid kid," said Baz, stepping back. He looked at his brother. "What did he say he was doing here?"

"We're catching rats," said Alex, realizing how unconvincing this sounded.

"Show me how he catches rats," said Baz, pointing at Max. "Because I think he's just bloody trespassing. Q said there had been trespassers down here. That's why we're here. And now he's up to his sick little tricks again."

Max swore at him.

"Don't talk to me like that, you stupid little loser. God, your brother must be ashamed of you," said Baz. "Yes, I know exactly who you are."

"Where are the rats?" demanded Riley. He glanced over at the Lance Corporal, who was still speaking into his mouthpiece. Saul raised his hand and made a signal for "OK", then resumed his conversation.

"I don't see any rats," sneered Baz.

Alex raised his palms. "I'll show you," he suggested. His voice didn't sound like his own. He was desperate to know whether the soldiers knew about the guns.

The brothers looked at each other and Riley nodded.

"In here." Alex climbed into the latrine. "There's a nest down there. We were just digging it out."

The soldiers seemed to find this very funny.

"Show us," said Baz suddenly. "I want to see how you do this, boys. I want to watch you shovel shit."

"Clear off," said Max. "Go and play somewhere else."

"Get in there," roared Baz. "Do your job." Alex went to dig but Baz held him back. "Not you. I want to see Bomber Boy get to work."

Max took the spade from Alex, but instead of digging with it, he threw it at the soldier. It bounced off his shin, making him shout out in pain.

Levi put a hand on his shoulder. "No, Max."

But it was too late. Baz came barrelling towards them, knocking Max flat into the latrine pit.

"Like attracts like," said Baz. "Who's next?" But then

he turned and walked off. "You'd better be out of here in one hour," he called. "Otherwise I won't be held responsible. You'll get yourselves shot, or arrested for trespassing."

Alex went to help Max out of the latrine. Dried crusts of unmentionable substances feathered down his shoulders and in his hair and he coughed and spat like some had got in his mouth. Alex helped him out, then wiped his own hands on his trousers. Max leaned against the wall of the block, wiping himself down and swearing.

"Thanks for covering, man," whispered Levi.

"But what *are* you doing here?" whispered back Alex.

"I didn't want to, but Max said he was coming anyway. I had to keep an eye on him. You know what he's like."

Alex watched as the soldiers conferred in a group, a little way off. But when he turned round, Max had picked his air rifle up off the ground where Alex had left it and was idly stroking the barrel.

"You all right?" asked Alex.

"Is this thing loaded?" asked Max, aiming at the chimney of the farmhouse.

"Yeah," said Alex. "It's perfect for killing crows. Now put it down, will you?"

"OI," shouted Saul, spotting him. "DROP YOUR WEAPON, NOW."

Max froze.

"THE REST OF YOU, GET ON THE GROUND," yelled Saul.

"What?" Alex stood dumbfounded. He thought the trouble was over. Max was just messing around. It was only an air gun and. . .

"GET ON THE GROUND," screamed Saul.

"Jesus," said Baz. "He's at it again."

Max stood between the lads and the soldiers, gun on his shoulder.

"Go away," shouted Max, holding the gun up to his shoulder. He was panicking, Alex could see that.

Levi stepped behind him. "Don't be an asshole, Max. Put the gun down."

Alex blinked. The air gun really couldn't do much damage. But years of training had installed in him the rules: you never mess around with a gun, even an air gun. He shouldn't have left it on the ground.

"Put the gun down, lad," said Saul, calmer now. "Don't make this worse for yourself." He was standing tall, seemingly unafraid. Max, however, was shaking.

"Max, this isn't going to do any good," said Alex and he coughed.

For an instant, Baz took his eyes from Max and looked at Alex. His eyes widened in recognition.

"It was you, wasn't it?" he said. "By the river. You hid my bloody gun. GET ON THE GROUND."

Alex said nothing, but took a step back.

"Leave us alone," screamed a trembling Max.

Saul took a step closer. He was completely

unafraid. "What are you going to do with that thing? Tickle me?"

As he stepped towards Max, he suddenly lunged.

"GET ON THE GROUND," screamed Saul as the gun somehow fired and Riley let out a tearing howl.

It seemed like the world was operating in slow motion. Alex watched as Riley paddled at his eye, sinking to his knees. The eye was the worst place that Max could have hit him. Alex rushed to help.

"Get off me!" he screamed.

"Lie down," said Alex. He had no idea how bad the injury was because the soldier was clutching at his eye.

Baz stood gaping at his brother, unable to move and in total shock.

"Shit," he said. "He shot my brother." He started at the blood.

Saul shoved Alex aside. "Jesus," he said, lying the injured soldier flat.

"Levi, you've got a phone," shouted Alex in his friend's direction. "Call an ambulance. Levi? Levi?" He looked around.

But Levi and Max were running, hard, over the yard, to the fence.

Alex swore.

"I can't see," shouted Riley. There was blood everywhere. Saul lifted the injured man's hand from his face and winced. He caught Alex's eye and a look passed between them.

"I can drive him to hospital," said Alex. "It will be

quicker than calling an ambulance. They might get lost."

"I'll drive him," said Saul. He looked round for Max. "Where's the nutcase gone?"

Alex shrugged.

"I can't bloody see," said Riley, calmer now. "That kid, he's. . ."

"Can you walk?" Saul and Alex helped him to his feet. Alex took off his shirt and gave it to Saul, who held it to Riley's eye. Baz stood, staring dumbly.

"He's lost his eye," he said. Alex didn't want to look, but he couldn't help himself. There was a dark, bloody mass in the space where Riley's eye should have been.

"I'll just wear an eyepatch," he muttered. "I'll look like a pirate."

"Ladies love pirates," said Baz, kneeling to support his brother.

"I know," said Riley. "This was all part of the plan."

"You all right now, bro?" asked Baz.

"I will be when you pricks get me to hospital," said Riley.

"On our way," said Saul. He ran round to the farmyard and a few seconds later, Alex heard the roar of an engine firing up.

The blood was already stopping, though it pooled in the dusty ground.

"I'm going to kill him," said Baz, mopping his brother's face with a tissue.

"No, no," said Riley. "Don't do that. That's my job." He groaned. "OUCH."

Saul reversed an army truck rapidly over to them. The brakes screamed as he skidded to a halt. Alex helped Saul and Baz gather the injured squaddie into the back seat and helped him lie down. The smell of blood was very strong. Alex had the soldier's blood all over his trousers.

"I'm going to kill him," repeated Baz. "I'm going to catch that kid, and bloody kill him."

"Baz, cool, it, stay with your brother," said Saul.

"I'm OK," moaned Riley. His beret had come off and his bald head was streaked with blood.

Baz swore.

"I'm going to kill him," he said. Before anyone could stop him, he'd stooped to pick up Alex's air rifle and was running out of the yard after Levi and Max.

"Shit," said Saul. He spoke into his radio. "Q? Q?" He glanced at Alex, standing dumbly in the dust. "Was the weapon live?"

Alex nodded. He'd been using it to finish off rats.

The Lance Corporal swore again. "If you find those two idiots before Baz does, get them to come back and turn themselves in. You don't know Baz. He won't stop at anything. Stay out of his way."

"I never thought I'd get shot on British soil," Alex could hear Riley saying over the growl of the engine. "By a British lad, an officer's brother! Afghanistan, yes, Iraq, probably. But not at home in our own back yard."

"Kids today," said Saul. "They're crazy."

"Good shot, though," muttered Riley. "We should enlist him as a sniper."

"Snipers don't tend to fire at point-blank range," said Saul. "Try not to talk. Save your energy."

"These might be my last words," said Riley.

"These are not your last words," said Saul. "If they were I'd be listening."

"I ought to arrest you," Saul said, turning to Alex. "But for God's sake, you need to find your friends before Baz does. He won't stop at anything when he loses it." He slammed the door. "That's why he's in the army. Hurry up. Get them to the police station pronto. Do you know where they might have gone?"

"No," said Alex honestly. They might be lost already. He ran for the gate, Gaffer and Sparky panting at his heels.

"Stay out of Baz's way," Saul reminded him as he drove past. He abruptly stopped and threw a mobile phone into the grass at Alex's feet. "My number is first. Keep in touch."

Then he was gone, leaving clouds of dust hanging in the air.

Alex saw Baz haring up over the hill. He must be mad with adrenaline. Alex tried to think. Where would the others hide?

On the Run

It was an accident, I swear it. I didn't mean to shoot the soldier. But when that other one went for me I flipped. I didn't mean to activate the trigger. I was knocked. Now I'm running and running and my throat is burning and it feels like the gods have put a needle through me.

Nothing will ever fix this. I may as well be dead.

I remember how the gun felt when it belted back into my shoulder and the soft sound of the bullet hitting his face. Oh hell, his face. What have I done?

What if I've killed him? When I saw what had happened I freaked and ran. I'm still freaking. I've been running for maybe half an hour, harder and faster than I have ever done in my life. I have no plans but to get deeper, deeper into the moor.

I have to get away.

The ground is steep and uneven and the sun is ferocious on the back of my head. I look back and am almost floored by a lightning bolt of terror as I see the other soldier way back in the distance pounding the heather, swearing and screaming. I am outclassed. The soldier is inhumanly fast and is gaining all the time. Now I'm coming to a load of trees and a river. I should cross. There might be places to hide on the other side.

I'm panting like a dog as I splash into the cold water and my trousers get wet and cling to me, weighing me down as I wade. This is the mother of all living nightmares. And ouch! I stumble over a submerged branch but as soon as I pick myself up I slip on a slimy rock. My laces are undone but I don't dare stop and tie them. I claw up on the bank and run along by the water, wet trousers flapping, shoelaces trailing. The stream rounds into a valley and here's a hedge of bushy trees climbing steeply upwards. I duck behind the hedge and scramble up an uneven field, so steep my calf muscles feel like they are tearing and my heart is thumping in my throat. This is my only chance to get away. The stream forks here. There's a marshy valley beyond and this massive hill ahead of me. I have to keep going, I have to reach the top before the soldier sees me and comes blasting after me (does he have a gun? Isn't there supposed to be live firing this afternoon? I can see a red flag flapping in the next valley. The soldier might have real bullets). I whimper and pound on. The ground moves under my feet in slow waves. Everything hurts. Twice I fall, my head spinning, but I force myself on, digging my toes into the sun-baked ground, thrashing up through the yellow grass and breathing so loud I must be heard a mile off.

I am doomed. I can't stop swearing, over and over. And just when I think I've reached the top of the hill I turn out to be wrong; there is a new horizon, maybe fifty yards above.

I hear splashing in the stream below. Any minute the trained killer will turn the corner, look up, and pepper my arse with shot, or pound after me with his army-schooled body and catch me in a matter of minutes. I know what I'm up against. I've seen my brother transformed from a fit schoolboy athlete into a strong, muscled superman, with hours of stamina, like his bones have been coated in metal.

I never bothered with physical fitness and the only reason I'm ahead of this soldier is because I've had a massive head start and because I am running for my life and I have everything to lose if I don't push myself to the absolute limit.

At last I see a thin hedge running along the uppermost ridge with wind-blown trees bent over like the backs of crooked old women. I throw myself over a ruined stone wall, landing in tic tacs of sheep droppings, and my breathing is insane (do I need oxygen?). I raise myself slowly, slowly on my elbows and peep down the hill.

The soldier stands in the cross of water at the very bottom of the steep. He looks up and down the stream, then over the valley. I duck, count to ten slowly, then look again. Now the soldier has his back to me; his shoulders are heaving with effort. I crouch low, terrified. I cannot move, I just have to breathe for a few minutes. A long roll of moorland lies ahead. There is no cover, except the odd gorse bush and clumps of marsh grass.

Horror. The soldier is looking up the hill, seemingly right at me. Slowly, slowly I lower myself flat on the ground. Is he called Baz? Have I got that right? Baz? Baz? I'm running from Baz. I hear swearing and water splashing. I wriggle behind the wall for a small distance until I find a clump of bracken in a gap in the wall. I peer through. If the soldier chooses to come up here, I won't be able to move. I've done myself in. My legs have been damaged from the effort I just made. I don't know if I can walk, let alone run.

Now Baz has his back to me again I can see dark arms of sweat reaching over his T-shirt. Ahhhh. There's a trickle of relief as he starts wading up the second fork of the river, away from me. Away!

I lean against the wall, still trying to calm my crazy, desperate breathing. I look up at a buzzard, circling the sky. Does it look calm from up there?

What have I done? One minute everyone was shouting; the next, the thing had gone off. There was blood; the soldier was clutching his face. I might be a murderer! I bite my finger out of sheer nerves. I don't know why I'm doing but it hurts and I draw blood.

Poor sod! I didn't mean to shoot him. I'm in hell.

I wish I could go back in time. It wasn't my fault. The soldiers were being so aggro. They'd started the fight (had they?). They'd thrown me in the shit pit. No one with any self-respect would have stood for that. No one.

I crawl on a little way. Acres of brown heath and craggy outcrops lie before me. I could easily lose myself on the moor, but where the hell should I go?

I've shot a soldier! I'll get locked up and beaten up. Soldiers are seen as heroes. Every so often there is a homecoming march in town and the streets are lined with flag wavers and bunting and trumpets. Everyone will think I am worse than some far-off enemy.

The birds wheel the sky like vultures waiting for a kill. I'm shaking! I make myself look back through the bracken. Baz-soldier has vanished from view so he could be anywhere. He could be nearly *here*. I struggle to my feet. Everything hurts so much but I have to keep moving.

I run into the moor.

I think I've been moving for two hours now. My throat is so dry and thirsty it feels like it is cracking. My head is boiling with heat and every crack, every rustle, makes me freak.

I slump against a stunted tree with prickly leaves in a low valley. I have no idea where I am. An emerald green beetle crawls over my shoe. It must be about one in the afternoon? The sun blazes, beating through the spindly leaves on to me. I can't formulate a plan. What to do next? Where to go? The panic still hasn't left me. If that soldier finds me, I have little doubt I would be ripped limb from limb. I shot his brother for goodness' sake. I hate to think what I would do to someone who hurt Simon like that.

What's that? I look around sharply but nothing moves, save the tiny clouds floating overhead. There's nothing here, nothing to see, only a few big old stones poking out of the horizon. I flick away the beetle and take off my shoe. I've got a blister the size of a fried egg on my instep. I wedge a tissue inside my hot, damp, strong-smelling sock and replace the shoe. I kid myself that it hurts less now.

My instincts are to go south, as far away from the army barracks as possible. They'll have the whole blasted regiment after me by now, swarming over the moor like locusts. They'll be practising on me for their military training. Jesus, I'm screwed.

I hear water trickling somewhere not far off. If I don't drink something soon, I'll pass out. My lips are dry and my mouth tastes foul.

What am I going to do?

Oake Tor

The army truck spun dust into the air, coating Alex's trousers and filling his nose and throat. His first instinct was to run like hell, not after the boys and Baz, but to grab the dogs and get out of here, to go home and leave the lads to sort out their own mess. But he wouldn't just abandon them. He had to try and think straight. It was like a farce, with everyone chasing everyone else. And did Max know where he was going? Alex doubted it. He wouldn't be surprised if Baz had caught up with him already. That decided him. He had to go after them, and try and stop whatever Baz was going to do. Alex fetched his binoculars from the truck, then shut the dogs in the latrine, as the truck was far too hot.

"Sorry, boys," he said at their downcast faces.

He raced through the farmyard and down through the paddocks and over the marsh to the fence. He crawled through the hole and pushed past the trees to open moorland. The others must have also come this way, as all the undergrowth was trampled. Here was the stone track, heading south. Alex found a bloody tissue on the ground and pounded on.

As he reached the bend of the hill he slowed. To the right of him lay a great marshy valley and in its centre he saw a small figure moving along the riverbank. Alex picked up his binoculars. It was Baz. He was heading south-west, in the direction of Mill Tor. Alex looked and looked but could not see Max or Levi anywhere. But Baz must have had a reason for going in that direction. He must be tracking the others. Alex walked a little way round the bend. The moorland behind him climbed up and up, dotted with sheep and stones, but no Max, no Levi.

So this suggested that his friends were not in immediate danger. Somehow they had lost Baz. How had they done that? Alex watched the soldier progress with terrifying speed along the valley, but there was no one ahead of him, not unless Max and Levi had managed to conceal themselves.

Alex looked over to the fork in the river. He walked on a little further and gazed at the steep, brambled hill that rose up from the water. A drystone wall ran along the ridge near the top. Alex thought he detected a movement. Yes, there was something moving. It was too far away to see exactly what, but every so often Alex glimpsed a dark shadow, like the curve of a back, scooting along, and it wasn't a sheep. Yes, that must be Max; there was something about the way he moved, with sudden jerking movements, like some kind of scurrying rodent, that made Alex sure it was him.

This was good. Max, the target, and Baz, the hunter,

appeared to be heading in opposite directions. This bought Alex some time. God knew where Levi was. But he wasn't the one who shot Baz's brother.

He wasn't the target.

Alex didn't want to go up on to the baking hot moor like this: tired, thirsty and with nothing to eat or drink. That was madness.

Jesus. It was bad. Max was heading right into the artillery range. And there was live firing tonight. But presumably an order would have been given by now, and the exercise would have been cancelled. Saul was radioing the Quartermaster Sergeant as he was leaving Strangeways.

Alex ran down the track back to the farm. He freed the dogs from the latrine and ushered them into the back of his truck. He turned and roared out of the yard. He was home in ten minutes. There had been no patrolman at the entrance of Strangeways, no sign of any activity at the barracks. Saul must have taken Baz straight to hospital. As it was, surely the police would be out here soon; you couldn't shoot someone in the eye and get away with it. But what about the army itself? What orders would the soldiers be given? Would a patrol be sent out to hunt down the boys? If so, Alex wanted nothing to do with it. But he knew he was the only one who could possibly reach Max before Baz did. Even now the soldier might be circling back. Even now he might have hold of Levi.

Alex jumped out of the truck and the dogs followed,

their claws clattering on to the stone yard. Inside the cottage everything looked so ordinary and safe. But outside, the world was going mad. His friends were running for their lives from a maddened soldier. And Max had shot a man in the eye. It was as shocking as it was unlikely. Max should have stayed. Everyone there would have sworn it was an accident. But he went and ran (and if Alex had Baz coming at him, he would have run as well) so now Max looked guilty, guilty, guilty.

Alex took the two litre canteen from the kitchen cupboard and filled it with cold water. He checked his pocket for his penknife and took a box of matches from the hearth. He grabbed a loaf of bread and a couple of bars of chocolate. He checked that his phone and the one Saul had given him were charged and unhooked the slim torch from the wall. He took a compass, the small lightweight binoculars and a map from the kitchen drawer. Alex pulled his sweatshirt and a thin waterproof from the back of the door. He shoved all this stuff into his rucksack. Then he drank two pints of water.

His quad sat square in the log shed. Alex fastened his rucksack to the back and roared up the track to the moor. Coming out from the shade of the trees was like walking into an oven. The heat was intense and pressed against his skin. Alex weaved through boulders and outcrops of stone. He bounced over the hot yellow grass, scattering sheep and bumping over grooves and hollows in the ground. He passed the stone fields, the marshes, the stone row. He revved hard and belted up the tor. A stone cairn sat at the top of Cosdon Hill.

Alex climbed off the quad and put the key in his pocket. Then he scaled the cairn. The sun glazed the landscape, baking it hard, making the air shimmer with heat. Alex stood against the sky, his feet firmly planted on the hot rocks and the breeze nudging him. He put the binoculars to his eyes and scanned the vista, searching the moor for his friends. Alex shuffled round three hundred and sixty degrees. Below him, to the south, spread the moor, vast, yellow-brown, hot moorland, rising and falling, littered with boulders and granite. In the clefts of the valleys were lines of deciduous trees: holly, hazel, ash, alder, wind-stunted and bent. A line of pine scored the path of the river. The tors rose around him, their crazy craggy peaks dominating the landscape. Here and there were moor ponies, brown and white, grazing on the dry vegetation. To the north-east, the moor sloped down to the town and then blurred into green fields, narrow roads and hills stretching on and on into the haze.

Thirty minutes later and Alex had scaled Belstone. He stood, as before, sweeping the landscape, searching for anything that moved or looked unusual.

Down to his right, he saw the grey silver glitter of Strangeways, wedged in the cleft of the valley that fell away from this very tor. The farmyard was empty. Then he trained his binoculars on the distant army camp. A military flag fluttered in the breeze but the road leading up to the camp was deserted and apart from a lone figure strolling between buildings, the place was quiet.

Where was everyone?

Miles of empty moorland reached on and on in front of him and then he heard the faint crack and rumble of gunshot. They must be training on the southern ranges. Surely it should have been stopped?

Alex focused his binoculars on the farm and retraced the path Max had taken, out of the yard, down to the river, along the valley, then up the steep hedge to the drystone wall. Where had he gone?

Suddenly, there was a black speck running hard. Not up the slope of Mill Tor, but back along the valley. Alex caught his breath. There was Baz, eyes to the ground, making steady progress. Every so often he'd stop, check the ground, look around. He'd changed his mind. Now he was heading in the right direction.

Now he was tracking.

Alex unfolded his map and marked the spot with a B. He reluctantly dragged his gaze from Baz, whose bare arms seemed to burn red as he waded through long, dead grass.

Did the soldier have a radio? A phone? It was tempting to climb back on his quad and tear blindly over the moors looking for the lads, but he had to be patient. He had acres of moorland to search and this, Belstone Tor, was the very best spot. Or was it? Alex suddenly felt exposed, the wind nudging him and the sun blazing down.

Maybe Max could see him now. If so, what was he thinking? Alex wasn't even sure he wanted to find Max. He'd shot someone, for God's sake. From the minute Alex had met him he'd sensed there was something damaged and frightening about Max. So what would Alex do with him if he did find him? Harbour him or arrest him? He wasn't sure if his motivation was protecting Max from Baz or protecting Baz from Max. Sure, Max had no army training, but he was a dangerous bloke. He was completely unpredictable and had never shown any sign of giving a stuff about anyone other than himself.

And what about Levi?

Shoes

My foot is agony. It's like someone is holding a lighter to it. At first the blister was possible to ignore but now, three hours later, it's hideous. I'm not good with pain. I'm hiding in a thicket of reeds, like some kind of amphibious creature. The tall, spiky fronds hide me. It's a relief just to sit and stare at my foot and finger the raging wound. If I were at home, I'd have taken myself to A&E by now. I'm in the middle of a broad, dryish marsh in a deep valley. If the soldier came tunnelling down, he probably wouldn't see me, so I should just stay here. Now I need to piss, but I don't want to stand up, I'm TOO TIRED. I've been running for hours and I'm still hungry and thirsty. I don't know where I am and am slightly confused as to which direction I've actually come. About an hour ago I came across some striped military poles, the ones that sometimes fly the red flags, but they didn't help me locate anything.

Ah! How long have I been sitting here? What have I just been thinking?

I can't remember. I clasp my hands over my head;

anything to keep the sun off for a minute or two. I really do need to drink something. I've lost the soldier but I'm also sure he won't give up until he's found me. But won't he have to return to his barracks soon?

Maybe the best plan (the only plan) is to hole up somewhere; lie low out on the moor for a couple of days, then decide what to do. What's that? I spy something white sticking out of the bog. It's a sun-hot rock with sharp edges like glass. I think of Baz-soldier as I pick it up and put it in my jeans pocket. I'm not as scared any more. I think I've gone beyond fear. I just feel numb (apart from my foot). It's like I'm looking at it all from the outside. And looking at my surroundings, maybe I DO know roughly where I am. I trained for the Ten Tors walking challenge with The Risings when I was fifteen (though I never actually did it). And now I believe I'm somewhere in the middle north of the moor, maybe between Yes Tor and Kitty Tor. I have to find water. I put my damp, dirty sock back on over my swollen hot foot, wincing as the cloth touches my blister. Putting my shoe on is torture. It's so unbearable I have to take the horrible thing off again. I'll walk in my sock. I rise and try to ram my shoe in my pocket but it won't fit so I shove it down the back of my trousers, but it slips right down and digs into my bum and I STILL CAN'T WALK. I dangle my shoe by the laces and step out into the marsh, immediately treading in soft, deep mud that covers my foot. I swear and fling the shoe into the marsh as a red-hot rage comes over me.

Why is this happening? And now I've lost my shoe. Huffing and puffing, I stumble through the reeds, treading on prickles, my sock dragging itself off my foot.

When will this end?

The sun is getting lower in the sky. It has been the longest and hottest day of my life.

Now I'm lying prone under the belly of a cracked old tree that gives me much-needed shade. I'm sucking a stone like a leper. It tastes salty but it makes me draw up saliva, which I can then swallow. I'm so thirsty I would gladly drink my own piss.

My remaining shoe, now an orphan, stands beside me. It is so caked with dirt it looks like a clog. At home I have cupboards full of shoes: trainers, scuffed and comfortable; welly boots, round-toed and waterproofed. Even my old Risings school shoes are better than this leathery torture. The soles are as slippery as glass.

Has the sun really got lower, or have I just *moved*?

Bits of skin are flaking from my lips, like I've eaten too many sugary doughnuts. DOUGHNUTS! I've got a crazy headache bouncing around inside my skull. It's like another being is in there, a spiky little alien. I dream of fluids: a pint of cold white milk, a glass of iced water with the ice cubes clinking against the glass. I remember the snap and hiss as you pull the ring from a can of Coke. I imagine the hit of cold against the back of your throat when you drink it. Mother is always asking, "Do you want a cup of tea?" which was always oddly bothersome and I always answered NO. But imagine a mug of tea, served in the green earthenware mug Mother has owned for ever. I imagine a spoonful of sugar, chink chink, the spoon stirring, the steam curling up, droplets of silver in the air. Think of a black, thick coffee, so strong it makes your heart race, or the muck of a vending machine hot chocolate from the common room at The Risings, the burn on your finger and thumb as you grip the hot plastic. I think of the sugar sludge at the bottom of the cup.

Wow, my head is getting tighter and tighter and tighter and tighter, like it is bound in string and someone is hauling in the nets. I have to move. I have to find water. But as I groan to my feet and step out into the lengthening shadows, I see Baz quite distinctly on the far hill. He's coming for me. It's like being electrocuted. He's maybe two miles away? Things are bad again.

Baz runs with methodical, trained steps. He's fit, strong and wearing boots – not just socks like me. A bitter substance rises in my throat as I watch Baz tear down the moorland path, the sun glinting off his fair hair. The path will lead, in thirty minutes, maybe less, to just below my cave tree. Muscles all over my body tense in fear.

I hear a shout on the wind and feel hatred coursing towards me on the airwaves. I've been seen, I've been seen! But where to go? There's no cover along the valley floor, but the hill beyond the valley is littered with boulders and stones like they've been dropped out of the sky. I could hide there. Decision made, I belt through the grass in my socks. When I reach the marshes I look behind and see that Baz has increased his speed. I flounder through the marsh and spy a sweet wrapper, Jelly Tots, which must have fallen out of my own pocket hours before. Have I really only got as far as the tree? And now I'm back again. I plough on, realizing that in my panic I left my remaining shoe under the tree. I can't go back for it. My legs are rubbery and useless and my stomach is clawing inside. I'm so scared I just want to lie down and have it done to me, the beating, or whatever, because at least then it would be over, this fear.

Maybe Baz would give me a drink before he killed me if I begged very hard?

I keep going, the ground nipping my feet with every step. The grass is rough like wires and my socks are so wet they are slipping off and tripping me up. I'm like a clown running with pom-poms of mud bouncing on the end of my feet. I don't dare look behind me, but I know I'm finished. I can't outrun this man-machine. He is trained for this. Lots of little flowers grow up from the marsh, bright little sunny faces, as yellow as egg yolks.

Does Baz-soldier have a gun?

Onwards. There's a big gorse bush up ahead. If I can get behind that . . . if I could just move faster. . .

"OI!" The yell bounds down the valley and slams into my ears. "OI, YOU! YOU ARE DEAD."

I pull myself on, yellow flowers flying under my feet in a blur and my legs moving by themselves. I'm a man centipede scurrying from a killer boot. But now I have arrived at the gorse, I'm through the marsh and at last here is the bank and a river! Come from nowhere! A stream of bright white and clear and silver water, gurgling over dark stones. I splash over, allowing my hand to trail through the water and cup a precious handful into my mouth before I fall into the hill, my legs driving me up and up and up to the field of boulders that crowd the hill. Up and up and then I dare myself to look back and Baz is at my shoe-tree. I have ten minutes, no more. I push through the stones, some huge, some tiny, my raw feet stinging, needles of fire and ice inside my skin.

I need to hide. Now. There's no other choice.

"OI!" The voice flying at me from over the valley is stuffed with rage. It makes me shudder. This is so frightening I might cry. There's a sudden sharp pain in the sole of my foot and I see blood. I realize I don't want to see any more blood today; mine or anyone else's. The rocks are getting larger the further up I go. This is like a maze in the middle of the moor, a maze of boulders and rocks.

I look round and see Baz barrelling through the marsh. It's down to minutes now. No one is going to come and save me. I choose a fat rock shaped like an enormous armchair and wedge myself into the crevice between it and the next outcrop. I lie still, letting my breath run out. I am largely hidden but there is no escape route. If I have chosen badly, then God help me.

I quietly examine the specks and patterns in the stone all around me. I hear footsteps coming closer. Baz's heavy, army-trained breathing is clearly audible.

I am finished.

Then I hear him muttering and cursing. I lie as still as a bone. Should my life be flashing before me? Should I try to attack him back or will that just make everything last longer? I'm not going to win, after all.

I nearly squawk as a boot arrives on the very stone I am crouching beneath. The scored brown rubber of the sole is scuffed and dirty. I smell wet leather. In just a few seconds this boot could be kicking the life out of me. I shut my eyes, but when I open them again, Baz is still here. I can see all of him. Does he know where I am? Is this the beginning of a deliberate torture? The soldier's trousers are tucked into thick socks and are made of some heavy-duty material. Baz also wears a khaki T-shirt blotted with sweat patches. He's holding Alex's air rifle. I feel a fresh torrent of fear. I didn't know he had that. And here is his mottled-red pink face with a bitten lip, furious eyes scanning the valley.

Don't look down.

I put my hand over my mouth, worried I'm so tired, scared and mad I might blurt something out. It's not unknown for me.

"I know you're round here somewhere, you little creep," says Baz. "Come out before I have to drag you out."

Time has run out.

Survival

At first the voices sound like they are on the radio – faraway high-pitched voices – punctuated with giggles, like a tribe of fairies on the move.

There's a thump as the soldier lands. I try not to exist.

The voices come again in a wave, loud and high, like children. The soldier grunts.

"What the. . .?"

I agree. I need to see. The voices are crowding into my rock, chattering, laughing, whistling and shouting. Happy little voices, animating the speckles on the rocks, making them dance.

Is this madness? Have I finally got here?

I hear the soldier clatter away over the rocks. This is incredible. I don't want to believe it in case I am wrong.

I wait for as long as I can bear before I move. Then I shift my aching body upright and smack my head on the rock but hold my tongue. I ease back.

The squat, muscular shape of the soldier stands silhouetted against the deep blue sky. He's watching two women walking at the head of a ragged line of brightly clad girls. All carry heavy rucksacks and wear map pockets around their necks. The girls are maybe twelve or thirteen years old and I count twenty of them. I'm so surprised I can think of nothing to think.

Baz-soldier swears under his breath as the party catches sight of him. The leaders stop dead and stare. They look scared, and rightly so. They confer and consult a list. Finally one of them gives a hesitant wave, to which Baz doesn't respond. The women look at each other and walk on, incurring waves of giggles from the girls.

I hide again as Baz turns and gazes round before heading off between the field of rocks, up towards the summit. I watch with great satisfaction as the soldier climbs further and further away from me, finally vanishing over the horizon.

They camp on the flats beyond the marshes. There are nine tents grouped round in a circle. A campfire burns through the darkness and torchlight stars the valley. Giggles and shrieks punctuate the air. There has been group chanting, odd songs about the seasons and even a prayer.

"MONKEY!" shouts a voice in the darkness.

"OOH OOH OOH," reply all the girls manically.

Watching from under my stone, I decide they must either be Girl Guides or witches. The smell of their stew heating up over the fire is making me crazy. That and the midges, who have come out in force and are eating me alive. I feel like a freak, a monster in the dark, but I also feel safer than I have for ten hours. I watch the fire and follow the shadows running across it. The elders tell stories about Dartmoor ghosts and legends. Their voices ring clear in the stillness. I don't believe in headless hunters or malevolent hairy hands but a cold uncomfortable feeling steals over me as I listen. The girls, too, creep closer to the fire.

When I'm certain they are all welded into their circle with their steaming bowls of stew, I creep forward. Treading lightly over the ground in my socks, I slide over stones and wind round brambles until I reach the nearest tent. I unzip the flysheet. The noise is too loud, but no one at the fire seems to notice, so I stick my head in the tent and am assailed with strong-smelling deodorant and a waft of feet. I feel in the dark for a rucksack and when I find one, I burrow inside. Here is a toothbrush. No good. Here a pair of socks; way too small. Then, at last, a bar of chocolate and the dull glow of a mobile phone. It has no signal but plenty of battery. I turn it off and stuff it in my pocket.

Next I find a carton of juice and rip it open, spilling some on the groundsheet. I drink greedily but it doesn't quench me. I move on to the next bag, pocketing a torch, cereal bars and a pack of plasters. Here is a canteen of water, half full and tepid, but I swallow it down like it is ambrosial fluid.

Clutching a stolen box of sandwiches and a pilfered sleeping bag, I dare to go in the next tent. Here the booty includes a scarf, some blankets and more food. I empty clothes out of a bag and replace them with my new stuff. Here I am; a killer and a thief within twelve hours. I tiptoe to the next tent. This must be one of the leaders' tents, as everything is stowed neatly and there are no freakin' cuddly toys. I find a pair of very large socks, a large sleeping bag, a compass, a map, a full canteen of water and a whole packet of biscuits. It's a pity these are all small-footed females, otherwise I would have stolen some shoes. Aha! What's this? My fingers close over something plastic and soft and rubbery. Flip-flops! I'm about to throw them down when I realize they are quite big. They might fit. Anything would be better than walking in socks.

The singing has stopped. I slip out of the tent and retreat into the shadows. I'll stay close. Surely Baz wouldn't murder me next to a camp of Girl Guides? There would be too many witnesses.

Back under my now-favourite rock, I wrap soft, stolen blankets round my shoulders, pull on the new socks and assemble the food. First I attack the water, drinking so deeply that when I put the empty canteen down I feel light-headed. The sandwiches are dry and salty and the cheese has a metallic, artificial tang, but I demolish every crumb. When I've finished I realize I have never been so hungry. I watch the flames flickering over the plateau below and see torchlights bobbing as the girls cross the murky ground to their tents. There is lots of laughing and shrieking from the tents, and the talking goes on for hours. The high-pitched voices and complaints (the missing sleeping bag causes many arguments) and furious giggles carry up to my nest. I sit, dazed with food, letting the noise buzz over me.

Finally I snuggle down on the blanket between two rocks, the sleeping bag stretched tight over me. I use the other blanket as a pillow. I feel myself relax. Even now in the dark the stones feel warm, having been baked to boiling by the midday sun. The Guides' fire is dying down, now just a mass of red embers. My eyelids flutter. I'm exhausted. But now I have a moment, I must think what to do, where to go. Presumably Baz would have returned to base. I know enough about army discipline to realize that soldiers aren't allowed to disappear without explanation. Going AWOL, Absent Without Leave, is a military offence. No, Baz will have churned home, fuming. Now the police will be after me instead (and the army too?). But I think I am safe next to these chittering girls for now.

My eyes start open. The fire has gone black and grey moonlight lights the rocks. The wind has got up and whistles eerie notes. I shiver. I heard a noise; something has woken me. I hear a step and feel the back of my neck prickle. *I can hear someone.* Male breath comes pulsing out of the gloom, slow and steady.

A voice comes out of the darkness, hitting me like a bullet.

"Hello, stranger. I knew I'd find you in the end."

Under Long Meg

There ought to be a huge police operation. From Alex's vantage point he should be seeing blue lights flashing from every angle. The army, too, must have been deployed. There should be lines of fast-moving trucks bouncing along the rutted roads. Men in camouflage gear ought to be saturating the moor.

But there was no one out here except him, unless they were all being very, very stealthy and secretive, which would also be logical.

Alex had hidden his quad between a stone wall and a rack of gorse, and now night had fallen and the moors were in darkness, lit only by a half moon. There was no noise, no movement. It was eerily quiet. Alex believed Max had headed south-west, towards Lydford. If he was walking and running, he could have covered as much as twenty miles.

Baz still had not returned to the barracks. Alex knew exactly where the soldier was; there were two fires flickering between the rocks below Dinger Tor. It was a good choice as it was sheltered, and Alex knew there was a spring nearby. He'd have lit the two fires so he could lie between them and stay reasonably warm even though he had no blankets. Doubtless Baz knew the moors from all his training. He was a soldier. He was trained in survival. But Max and Levi must be desperately tired and hungry by now. He hoped they'd found water. He thought of the group of campers, young girls, deep in the valley. Had Max seen them too? Alex wondered if he ought to warn them about everything or just leave them alone.

Far on the other hill the fires died down to a red glow and Alex watched the darkness deepen over the moors. He checked his phone. It was half past ten at night and he had a signal at last. He phoned Sasha.

"Where the hell is everyone?" she said. Her voice was comforting in the darkness. "Neither you, Max or Levi were in class today. What are you up to? Is there some kind of conspiracy?"

"It's tricky," said Alex carefully.

"Is it about the guns?"

"What?" Alex was stunned. As far as he knew, Sasha had never been told about them.

"Levi told me. He's useless at keeping secrets, especially from me."

"What did he tell you?"

"Everything."

Alex blinked. He wondered if Levi had told anyone else.

"He swore me to secrecy, but I don't like the sound of it. This evening, when we were supposed to be walking together, I was going to try to persuade you to go to the police. Guns, Alex! You don't mess around with things like that."

"I know," said Alex. He bit his lip. He'd completely forgotten about a walk he'd planned with Sasha.

"Levi hasn't been answering his phone. AND I've had Levi's mother on the line, asking me if I know where he is. As if!"

"Sasha, have you seen the news?" interrupted Alex. He wondered if there had been something mentioned about Riley and Strangeways. If there was a major manhunt under way, surely it would be all over local radio and TV.

"I've just watched the news and the weather," said Sasha. "And it's going to be very hot again tomorrow. Alex, where is Levi? He usually always answers my calls. And what about you! You stood me up, you rat! You were supposed to take me walking this evening. I turned up like a tit at the car park, with my ordnance survey map and everything. I waited for TWO HOURS, Alex."

"Sorry," said Alex. "I've got a good excuse. We all have."

"Like hell you have," said Sasha. "Were you too busy catching rats?"

"Not quite," said Alex. "Listen, Sasha, there's been a problem."

Quickly he told Sasha about the accident, about Max running off into the moor, with Baz and Levi chasing after him.

"Sasha? Are you still there?"

"Wow," Sasha breathed. "That poor soldier, I hope he's OK. I knew Max was deranged. You know when you just know?"

"Look, Sasha, are you sure there's been nothing on the news?"

"Nothing. I just watched *Devon Today*. There was nothing about a manhunt."

This was all very strange, reflected Alex. This should be big news unless it had been hushed up. This made him feel uneasy.

"Shall I come out and help?" asked Sasha.

"No," said Alex quickly. "Definitely not. There are too many people tearing round the north moor as it is. You really wouldn't want to be out here with Baz on the warpath. He's got my air rifle."

"No," said Sasha thoughtfully. "But what about Levi? You've got to find him. He's out there, now, probably lost. He's not like you, moor-man, or Max, who has the survival instincts of a cockroach. Levi's just a big softy, despite all his fitness stuff. He has to EAT, Alex, or he gets low blood sugar and passes out."

"I know, I know." Sasha was speaking so loud Alex held the phone a little way from his ear. What was it about Levi that made women want to mother him?

"Where are you?" she asked. "I should definitely come out. I'll bring some food. Mum will look after Sammy." She was half talking to herself.

"No," said Alex. "It's not safe. There's a dangerous

armed man out here. Stay away." He wished he'd never rung her, but he had to find out what was going on.

"Look, keep me in the loop, OK?" said Sasha. "Or I swear I'll come and find you."

"Just let me know if Max or Levi call you," said Alex.

"Should I let their parents know?" asked Sasha.

"I don't know," said Alex. "Yes and no." He couldn't understand why they hadn't been told already, but there was a danger they would come out looking for him, and the less people on the moor tonight, the better.

"I'm going to phone the Quartermaster Sergeant at the barracks now," he said. "He'll know what's going on."

Sasha made him swear that he would phone her, and promising not to say anything until she heard from him, she rang off.

Alex sat against a tall standing stone and ran his fingers through his hair. The stone was called Long Meg. All the standing stones up here had names. Dad knew most of them, as he liked archaeology and stuff. He wished Tim was here now. He'd know what to do. The wind had got up and blew over his skin, making him shiver.

Alex held up his phone and examined the screen. He hated phoning people up, especially someone like Quartermaster Sergeant Furzey. But what could be more important than this? He should have phoned him hours ago, rather than chasing over the moor, but he'd been unable to get a signal.

Alex dialled the number he'd been given and it was answered immediately.

"The Jebb boy?"

"Yes. Is your man OK?"

"Thank God you've called. Private Hurley has damaged his eye, very badly. Where are you? Have you found the perpetrator yet? Can you confirm his name?"

Alex stumbled through his answers. "Has anyone come back yet?" he managed to ask.

"No, but I've sent two platoons and a small patrol out to look for you all." Quartermaster Sergeant Furzey paused. "When Lance Corporal Powers and I returned to Strangeways, we found something very strange. We found a sack, lying in the middle of the yard, containing weapons. Can you elaborate?"

"Oh," said Alex. He bit his lip. Levi and Max must have left it there.

"Do you know about these weapons?"

Alex took a deep breath and explained how he and Levi had found them in the ruined barn, how they had dug them up and had wondered what to do about them.

"There are more guns?" The Quartermaster Sergeant sounded incredulous. "Why didn't you report this to me at once?"

"I didn't want to get involved," said Alex, at which Furzey swore.

"I always thought you were a sensible lad," he said. "Tell me everything now."

"There's not much else to add."

"Then tell me everything again."

Alex felt the wind chill him as he talked. When Alex mentioned the laser equipment, Furzey swore over and over.

"Right," said Furzey when Alex had finished. "This is shocking. But right now, we need to get you bloody kids off the moors. Private Baz Hurley, unlike his brother, can be erratic. Do you know what I mean? He has a temper. He's a good soldier and the army is the right place for him. But you wouldn't want to be on his wrong side. I expect he'll be back in the morning, once he's cooled down, but I don't want my soldiers at risk of getting into trouble over you kids."

The phone went quiet for a few seconds.

"I need your help. You say you can see two campfires now? Can you tell me where they are on the map?"

Alex explained as best he could. They were somewhere between Dinger Tor and Kneeset.

"You'll be maybe a mile from the tin mines?"

"I guess. It's hard to tell in the dark."

"I'll instruct my rapid response unit to come directly to you. In the meantime, do not let the soldier out of your sight, but DO NOT approach him. OK?"

"OK." The situation was becoming increasingly surreal.

"I'll be in touch. If my soldier moves position, you must contact me immediately. Understand? Don't say anything about the guns to anyone, do you understand?

I don't want a media circus out here." The Quartermaster Sergeant rang off.

Alex leaned back against the standing stone. So an army patrol was on the way. That felt reassuring. All he had to do was wait for them to find him.

The stone was warm against his back. He leaned and looked up at the stone, shining pale in the darkness. The story went that this stone was the scene of a wedding between a fairy and the devil, who had disguised himself as a prince. When the fairy found out the truth, she cursed the place and threw herself in the marshes. Alex wasn't one for fairy stories. But out here, in the dark, with strange lights flickering over the moors and the wind playing a tune through the granite maze, anything seemed possible.

Toad Rising

I roar and hit out in the darkness, making contact with a clump of stinging nettles.

"Easy, boy. It's me. It's Levi."

Is it really him? It's his voice. But nothing feels real any more.

Gradually I make out the dark contours of Levi's face and the pale shape of his T-shirt as he stands before me.

"Am I ever glad to find you. I've been completely lost. I only found you because I heard you coughing, and I thought to myself, I know that cough, even though I was worried it would turn out to be a sheep or something. I've been following you. I keep getting glimpses, then losing you." Levi sounds as cheerful as ever.

"But how did you find me?" I'd almost forgotten about Levi.

"I saw the girls' fire and I was going to ask them for help, but was worried they'd be scared of me. As I was fiddling about, I saw you sneak into the tents. I couldn't believe it. I thought, 'What is that boy up to now?' Now here I am. Do you have anything to eat? I'm starving."

"I shot him." I don't know why I say this, it just comes out.

"It was an accident, wasn't it? Why did you run away? You've only made it worse."

"What the hell am I going to do?" I whisper.

"God knows," says Levi. "But you can't hide out here for ever." He steps closer. "You stink real bad."

I sink back against my stone. "Do you think the whole army is after me by now?"

"Probably," says Levi. "If I was you, I'd hand myself in. They'll find you in seconds. Do you have anything to eat, by the way, or were you raiding those little girls' tents just for kicks and teddy bears?"

Remembering my recent starvation, I draw out a squashed foil-wrapped packet of sandwiches and reluctantly hand them over. I'd allocated them for my breakfast.

"Thank you," says Levi, cramming them into his mouth. Despite everything, I get a surge of amusement. Here I am facing torture, death and exposure and Levi is still minding his manners. His mother would be proud. I watch him eat. It's good not to be alone.

"What's happening with your feet, man? Jeepers, what IS going on?" Levi holds up one of my old mud-balled socks against the gloomy sky.

One of my feet is wrapped in the thick socks of the guide leader. The other is bare. I'm hoping the fresh air will dry up my sores.

"You're in a right state. You're worse than me." Levi

explains how he has drunk lots of water from a stream and hopes he won't get the runs. He's had more luck than me; he found a hot, melted Mars Bar on a trig point.

"How lucky is that?" says Levi. "It was, like, liquid. I had to drink it. Ewwww! But it turned everything around. And now I've found you. And now. . ."

"Now what?" I ask. I'm so tired, my voice sounds deep and scratchy.

"Now we've got to go and face the music," says Levi, ever-so-gentle. "You're only making things worse, hiding out here like a highwayman."

A brief image of my mother's face flits across my mind. I see the tremble of the feather on her hat.

"Never," I say.

"Come on, Maximus. What's your plan? What will you eat? You'll get caught soon enough by that squaddie. And the bloke you shot is a soldier, tough as nuts. He'll be OK."

"Maybe." I hunch into my sleeping bag. "But I'm not going back."

"Come on, what are you going to do? Become a tramp?"

"I don't know," I snap. Levi is crowding my head. How can I go back? I'll be thrown into prison, or worse. I'll have the whole British army after me. And what would Simon say? I picture my brother's puzzled face. And Dad – well, Dad would have me killed. After what happened at The Risings, he'd physically thrown me out of the house. I slept in the garden shed for the night, before creeping in the next day. Dad didn't speak to me for nearly two weeks and he withdrew all my allowance money and all lifts. And then came the real punishment.

"So is it true, then?" Levi's voice comes at me out of the darkness."You were the Risings Bomber?"

"The bombs weren't real," I say. "They only looked like it. Everyone got it all way out of proportion. It got out of hand," I say.

"Totally," says Levi. "Why did you do it?"

Why did I do it? Why do I do anything? The Risings is a joke. The place is stuffed with smug sycophants. I had an idea and then I had to do it. There were many occasions when I dreamed of blowing the place sky-high for real. One such occasion springs to mind. I was showing my homies my trophy, the prize for coming second in the North Devon Hip Hop Competition, when Mr Able, the music master, informed me I was "as talented as a dungball" in front of the whole class. And that "listening to my raps" made him feel "medically depressed". It's no coincidence the biggest "device" was placed in the wind instrument cupboard. But I have a million other reasons to hate the place: the teachers, most of the students, the boring grind of it all. And I only meant to tickle, to get under the skin of the school with a wasp or two; i.e., a few small packages resembling explosive devices, strategically placed around the main school building to cause a little stir. I didn't think it would shake it to the rafters with mass evacuations, army deployments, SWAT teams and government ministers buzzing down in helicopters. They overreacted!

"I wish I hadn't," I say. I rest my head on my knees. This is the bit I've been trying to forget.

Two weeks after I'd been expelled, Dad took me to the barracks to talk to the Quartermaster Sergeant and some of the bomb disposal experts who had been called in to deal with the incident. I remember being nervous, but not overly so. I've been on the receiving end of many a telling-off, after all. But after Dad was waved through the checkpoint, he drove straight up, round the back of the camp, and parked outside a small, isolated brick building.

As we went in, I remember thinking it was odd that there were no windows. I quickly began to panic as Dad directed me to sit on the concrete floor in the centre of the darkened room. Then soldiers filed in. There were six of them, including Quartermaster Sergeant Furzey, all togged up like they'd been on parade, all carrying their personal weapons. I was so scared I didn't move. They looked at me like they wanted to kill me. Then it got worse. I was shown pictures of the damage bombs can do, the danger faced by bomb disposal experts. I was told of ruined lives and despairing families. I was shown pictures of children whose fathers had been killed, dismantling bombs. Then I was shown the dead fathers. A soldier switched on a projector and I saw huge colour slides of bomb injuries. I was sick on the floor and the Quartermaster Sergeant yelled at me and I had to mop it up myself, in front of all of them, before the ordeal continued. I watched films of real bombs exploding and real people being injured and killed. I saw photographs that now dance in my head and won't ever go away, horrible images more terrible than anything I could ever imagine.

And then the Quartermaster Sergeant got on his knees, put his face close to mine and screamed in my face, about how stupid and useless I was. About how I was a worthless piece of crap who deserved to be shot. I broke up and cried and bawled in front of them all like a kid, I was so scared and shocked. And my dad was sitting in the corner the whole time and didn't lift a finger to stop them.

This was something my dear father, with his military connections, had organized just for me. I think he got the idea from *A Clockwork Orange.* Dad has always liked the book. I'd only seen the film.

Now I'm having to fight to stop the tears swarming out of my eyes.

On the way out, Dad said he had to do it. He said I "had to be fixed".

That's when I ran away.

And now I've done this, God knows what my father will organize for me. Whatever it is, it will be terrible. Dad will not believe the shooting was an accident. I can never go home. This time, my father will kill me. But then something sparks in my brain.

Could I go home after all?

Levi makes me unzip the sleeping bag so it spreads over the sharp grass. He lies on one side and pulls one of my pilfered blankets over himself. In ten minutes, despite the discomfort, he's sound asleep and snoring so loud I worry the Guides will come up to investigate.

Levi's feet are a little bit bigger than mine. He's still wearing his big, soft, grey trainers. I look at them in the moonlight. I won't get anywhere without shoes. After a few more minutes of thinking about this, I make my move and lean over Levi. My friend's mouth is ajar and his eyes are shut tight. The first knot is tricky. It is sodden and dirty and my fingers are stiff, but I gradually work it loose. Then, holding my breath, I slip it from Levi's foot. I shuffle back and try it on. The difference between this big, soft shoe and my crippling patent ones is incredible, like walking on pillows. Even my blisters seem dulled. Without hesitating, I start work on the next shoe. This is more difficult, as Levi's foot is tilted slightly to one side. He stirs and moves and now the leg is on the wrong side. If he wakes, I'll say I thought I'd take his shoes off for him. Levi would never suspect what I'm about to do, would he? The shoe slithers off, damply hot, and I feel the warmth coming from Levi's foot. I look at Levi's sleeping face for a moment, deliberating. Then, gently, I unhook the watch from my friend's wrist and fasten it on my own. I leave the thick, woolly socks for Levi, but put all the food together in the stolen bag and hitch it on to my shoulder. Levi will understand. He can ask for food from the campers. He'll be OK, but everything is at stake for me.

I creep away round the hill, into the darkness.

At Four a.m.

The watch reads four a.m. I have been walking for five hours, stopping now and then to eat something from the bag or to shine the stolen torch on my stolen map. My legs ache like hell. The shoes are soft and comfortable. I have a momentary qualm about Levi. What will my friend do when he wakes up in the middle of Dartmoor with no shoes, food or watch? But Levi is a good bloke. He knows I'm in deep trouble. He'll probably find it funny. When all this is over and we're back in college, we'll all sit round our favourite table in the canteen and laugh about it.

". . . And then . . . you nicked my shoes!" Levi will say, his voice cracking as it does.

A few more steps and my legs really hurt, rather than just ache. Each step feels like I am stretching the muscles in my calves and thighs to snapping point. I'm in a flat area of moorland where the bracken grows in clumps and the grass is cropped close to the ground. To the west, the sky is beginning to turn pink and the birds are singing.

I have to stop. I'm fairly sure I'm not being followed.

I've come too far, and I've lost that funny prickling sensation on the back of his neck, the feeling that makes me stop and look, and imagine a face watching me. I unfold the map and spread it on a large flat boulder, flicking away the sheep droppings. That peak ahead, that could be Sharp Tor, and to the west, that must be Hare Tor. If I keep heading south-west, I will hit the A386, probably in another four or five hours between Tavistock and Lydford. Then I'll really know where I am.

But I have to rest. If I keep walking now I'll damage myself. There's a depression in the ground a few metres away, lined with heavy, flat, almost rectangular stones. I know enough from my enforced Risings school walks that these are called cists and are prehistoric. I refold my map and cross the heather. I sit by the cist and eat my remaining damp cheese and tomato sandwich. Then I curl myself into the cist like I'm planning to die. Now, at least from a distance, I am invisible. I pull the sleeping bag up around my ears. The wind is growing stronger. Bits of grass and heather keep blowing on to my sleeping bag. Above me, the morning clouds race against the lightening sky. I shut my eyes.

Alex hadn't really slept. The night had been too cold. He'd wrapped himself in every item of clothing he had, and it still wasn't enough. He figured Keeper's Cottage was only three hours away, but he couldn't lose Baz, and the Quartermaster Sergeant had told him to wait here at this rendezvous point. Every now and then Alex would sit up, check the soldier's fires, smell the air for smoke and scan the moorland for any movement, any sound. But he was fairly sure Baz had holed up for the night. Through his binoculars, by the light of the half moon, he thought he could make out the shape of Baz's boot and his dark outline slumped between two smouldering fires.

"Make contact with my patrol as soon as you see them," the Quartermaster Sergeant had ordered. "Talk to no one else."

After ordering Alex to telephone immediately if there were any changes, he'd rung off.

That was two hours ago and now, at four in the morning, Alex had had enough. He ate half of the block of cheese and drank most of his remaining water. There was a stream in the valley; he'd refill it from that. He took out his gun and thought of the rabbits, small nibbling shapes, only a few metres away. He could be eating roasted rabbit within an hour, but the gunshot would alert everyone to his presence. He bit another mouthful of cheese.

His phone beeped, making an odd digital sound amongst all the wildness. Alex read the message. It was from Sasha.

Can't slp. What's goin on? Any nws. PLZZ!

He texted back.

NOTHING HAPPENING. GO 2 SLEEP B4 SAM WAKES U UP.

He immediately got a reply.

Sam awke 2! We wurrid abt u. Come home.

Alex texted back.

AM GOING 2 SLP. ALL FINE. ARMY PATROL ON WAY. DON'T WORRY.

Then he put the phone away.

Alex put the binoculars to his eyes and swept the dark valley. It was nerve-racking stuff, waiting for a horde of trained soldiers to find him, even though he was on their side.

He waited, unable to sleep and watching the sky gathering light.

Something touched his shoulder.

"You must be Alex."

Alex leapt up in alarm to discover an armed soldier standing right behind him.

"How long have you been there?" he spluttered, completely taken aback.

"Long enough," replied the soldier. He was dressed in camouflage gear, complete with helmet covered in reeds and grass. His face was dark with smeared-on mud so the whites of his eyes gleamed. He was carrying an SA80 assault rifle and several rounds of ammunition. He looked savage and frightening.

"You are Alex?"

"Yes," said Alex, still in shock. He prided himself on his hearing and his ability to sense changes and movement out here in the wild. It was his job. But he'd had *no idea* someone was behind him. How terrifying.

Now he recognized the soldier, criss-crossed with webbing and hung with a radio, backpack and various unidentifiable bits of kit. It was Lance Corporal Powers. In other words, Saul. Why had Furzey sent him?

Saul took a metal canteen from his knapsack and drank deeply.

Then, to Alex's surprise, he offered him some.

"No, thanks." Alex indicated the quad, where his own supplies were. He looked around, expecting more soldiers to materialize. Hadn't Furzey said a whole platoon was on the way?

"How's the bloke who got shot?" asked Alex bluntly. He knew the Quartermaster Sergeant said Riley was OK, but he wanted to hear it from someone else.

"He'll live," said Saul, calm as you like. "But he's lost an eye. His army career is probably over, thanks to you lot."

Alex said nothing. He resented the implication that he was responsible for the accident.

Saul watched him. "Where's Baz? Or did you make that up?" he asked gruffly.

Alex bit his lip. Then he unhooked the binoculars from round his neck and handed them to the soldier.

"Under that tor – see the wooded area, holly trees? Hazel? Just below those three sheep. There's a depression in the ground, surrounded by rocks. See it?"

"No," said Saul. "What am I looking for?"

"Smoke," said Alex. "You can see where he's dug into the ground – see the blackened sticks? Last night it was glowing red. If you look to the left, you'll see another fire. It is still smouldering. Then you'll see his boots. He's sleeping under the bush, between the two fires."

"I can't see him," said Saul. "You're making this up, aren't you? You haven't got a monkey's where he is."

"We could reach him on foot in about an hour," continued Alex. "The quad won't make it up there. The ground is too boggy, too stony; besides, it will give us away when he hears it."

"I see him," said Saul in surprise. He took the binoculars from his face and glanced at Alex. "Fantastic. How did you do it?"

"Fluke," said Alex. "I heard him talking to himself. On a still day, sound carries for miles." He didn't mention the other things. The fact he'd been tracking him more or less since he left Strangeways. Just before he'd spotted Baz he'd smelled a whiff of cigarette smoke coming downwind. Also he'd found an empty carton of juice with flies swarming over it and he'd seen a flock of rooks rise suddenly from a copse of trees in the valley. The rest had been guesswork and a lot of standing still, sweeping the landscape with his binoculars, then belting off on his quad to the next peak.

"What about your mates? Have you seen them?"

"Levi, no." Alex swallowed. He was getting really worried about Levi. There had been no trace of him. "But I think Max is camped just on the slopes of the next tor. I've been tracking both of them. But it's hard because of the quad."

"All right," said Saul. He sat down. "All right, all right." He adjusted his radio mike and tapped at the box hanging from his waist. Alex moved away, but Saul didn't seem to care about his presence.

Whoever he was contacting answered straight away.

"Powers calling, Sergeant. Contact with Alex Jebb. I repeat. I've made contact with Target A. Fit and well. Position." He gave a grid reference. "Affirmative. We have a definite sighting of a person wearing army-issue footwear, probably Target B. He's asleep, Sergeant. No confirmed position for Target C, though Jebb has a predicted location." Saul glanced at Alex. "He's been pretty accurate so far, Sergeant."

He listened. "Copy that, Sergeant. Will you, er, send in the squad now?"

Whatever the Quartermaster Sergeant said next made Saul's face fall.

"Say again. . .? . . . Affirmative. Wilco." He rubbed his chin. "Over." He ended the transmission.

Alex waited.

"Well done," Saul told him.

"Did Furzey tell you to say that?" asked Alex incredulously.

"No, I said it," snapped Saul. He took another drink, wiped his face again. He sat squarely on the rock and looked through the binoculars again.

"Are the rest of your lot on their way?" asked Alex hopefully.

"Not any more," replied Saul, tersely. Alex waited.

"It's a sensitive situation," he said at last. "Q thinks too many men on the ground will upset Baz." From the way he spoke, he didn't seem to agree with his superior.

"But Max is running scared," said Alex. "We need to find him and Levi before they get dehydrated."

"I'll worry about those goons later," frowned Saul. "It's Baz I'm after. I don't want him getting into trouble."

That was exactly what the Quartermaster Sergeant had said, thought Alex. The army certainly looked after their own first. Saul sniffed and looked at him. "Q told me to explain the situation to you, so you understand.

"Baz is a man who, in the civilian world, would probably be described as having a personality disorder. Whatever. In the army we can utilize his skills. He is usually a good soldier, but we have to keep a watch on him. His brother, Riley, is good at calming him, making him see sense. That's why we keep them in the same squad. As a team they are formidable."

Saul cleared his throat and spat.

"But as Baz has effectively gone AWOL, my job is to either disarm him, or if he is unapproachable, to lead him to a designated point where a team should be waiting to arrest him."

"But what about Max and Levi?" asked Alex.

"We'll find them next," said Saul. "With your help."

He asked Alex if either of them had mobile phones. Alex replied that if they did, they hadn't answered any of his calls. He knew Levi owned one, but he didn't know if he had it with him.

Saul blew his cheeks out.

"We'd better get on with the job," he said. "Baz won't be any trouble. He'll have cooled down hours ago. We just have to follow a few procedures. You'll need to stay out of sight to begin with, while I do an assessment."

"Fine," said Alex. "I'll wait here."

"Oh no, I'm not losing you now," said Saul. "You're following me every step of the way. My orders are not to return unless I've got you three lads as well as Baz."

"Why are you on your own?" Alex couldn't help asking.

Saul shrugged. "Unfortunately, that's not for me to ask. Orders is . . . anyway, I told you. Baz might be freaked out by a whole platoon charging down on him."

"But you said he's got a personality disorder!" protested Alex. "I'm not going anywhere near him."

"Oh, chill out," said Saul. "There's nothing to worry about. Nobody's perfect."

"I think I'd be more useful looking for Levi," said Alex, unconvinced. "I'm worried about him."

"We'll do that next," said Saul. "Let's just look after Baz first. You've got to learn to take orders, mate."

"But I'm not in the army," said Alex.

"You are now," said Saul.

"What's happening about the weapons at Strangeways?" asked Alex.

Saul looked at him then. Something passed over his face, an expression that Alex couldn't read.

"Now that is something to talk about," he said. "When we've detained the target, I suggest you tell me everything you know."

Simon

I stand on the Corn Ridge, blazing with glory. I've been walking for an eternity. I don't know how I've made it this far, but I have. Only an hour ago I was ready to lie down in the heather and let the buzzard-vultures eat me, but now I'm on fire. The last few hours have been a daze of walking up endless hills, map-reading and worrying that I've been going in the wrong direction. But at last I know exactly where I am. It's eight in the morning and beneath me is a vast valley with the A386 winding through. The wind is blowing through my clothes. I watch the faraway cars trawl up and down. I hope the people down there are not looking out for me. I must be a wanted man by now. But I think I'm safe. The moors are always littered with walkers. I won't stand out, at least not from a distance.

I have a plan but have no idea if it will work. I pee on a rock. There's not much fluid and the smell makes me gag. I've got poison pee.

OK. It's now or never.

I jog steadily downwards, my bones creaking. As I get closer to the road, the moor gives way to a series of fields. I skirt along the side of these. I'm beginning to feel the heat again. I reach into my swag-bag and wrap a scarf round my head to keep the sun off. I watch a series of caravans crawl along the road below. My esteemed parents have gone on holiday this weekend. They've gone to the Black Mountains in Wales. It is one of their many eccentricities to holiday in a place that is nearly identical to their own home. Never mind, the important thing is that the house ought to be deserted, unless they've heard about me and have come gunning back. This is unlikely because when they go on holiday they make a point of not taking any mobile phones with them. I guess it's roughly two miles into Lydford, where, if I get hold of some money, I could catch a bus up the A386, around the edge of the moor to home. Alternatively I could pay a visit to an old friend. I decide the latter.

If my plan goes wrong, in a few days I'll be incarcerated in Dartmoor prison, amongst the most terrifying characters in the country. I'll be banged up for GBH. But at least the cell would have a bed, and blankets. There would be food and water. I shake myself out of my stupor. I've shot a soldier. I'm the lowest of the low in the prison. No one will have mercy.

I walk on.

After another half an hour I have had enough. Even Levi's pillow-soft trainers are beginning to rub. I'm hungry too, so hungry my stomach is cramping. The inside of my arms are chafing against my damp, dirty T-shirt. I have to walk swinging my arms out so they don't rub. But at least I've made it off the moor alive.

I'm walking through a field with nothing in it but long, long grass, which buzzes with hideous insects. Now I'm only a few steps away from the road and the hamlet of Beardon.

Gerry lives here.

Gerry – my so-called best friend from The Risings, the same friend who hasn't been answering my calls since I was expelled. As it is now Saturday morning, Gerry will be at school, playing tennis. He is a champion tennis player and has a bedroom full of shields. His younger sister, Rachel, will also be at school doing whatever her preferred sporting torture is today. Their mother will be at lunch with her cronies. Every Saturday they meet at the Two Bridges Pub for lunch. The place will be empty. I should be there in twenty minutes.

I'm here. I know this place very well. Up to a couple of months ago I used to come round nearly every weekend. Now I am an outcast. I get a glitter of anger.

Damn them. I step through the gap in the hedge that's been worn down by Gerry and his sister and look through a crack in the back gate. There's the old swing and the hosepipe (water fights). And here is the house: large, white, detatched, bay windows. I stare at it and my insides turn sour. Gerry should have called me. Someone is moving around in the upstairs bathroom;

there's a dark shape against the blurred glass. As I watch the shape vanishes, then reappears downstairs at the back door in the form of George, Gerry's father. He is a slightly fat, dark-headed man, with very brown eyes and hairy wrists. He laughs a lot, but is quick to switch to a shocking temper. He never had much time for me. Gerry's dad walks round to the side of the house and out the front. In minutes, I hear a car start and drive off.

He'll be going to The Risings to collect his beloved and adored children from their morning of wholesome sport. In another life, he'd be bringing me home too. We'd make huge bowls of vanilla and strawberry ice cream, layer it with chocolate sauce, and go and eat it, lazily, in the garden. Or we'd spend the entire afternoon killing each other online.

I climb stiffly over the low, sculpted wooden fence, drop into the garden and creak over the grass. I open the door of a small shed and reach inside for a key. I look at it and the anger surges up again. Riding it, I unlock the back door and let myself in.

Gerry's kitchen! It's so calm and cool in here, and so clean. The glass sparkles with spray-on hygiene and the noble stainless steel surfaces shine. I reacquaint myself with the sink, operate the cold tap and dunk my swollen head under. The hit of cold water is fantastic, like an ice-maiden is stroking my temples with her silky fingers. Until now, I've never thought about how amazing it is to be able to turn on a tap and have clean drinking water gush out.

"You look awful!"

I start up so fast I brain myself on the tap. I turn, dripping water on the floor. A dark-eyed girl of about fourteen stands in the doorway.

Rachel. She isn't part of the plan.

"Sorry," I say. "I didn't mean to scare you." Rachel is four years younger than Gerry and I have always found her annoying in many ways. Like how she stands, a kind of amused slouch.

"You've been banned from this house," she announces. "And I'm not scared," she adds.

"Banned?" I'm suddenly so tense I don't know what I'm going to do. But I don't want to scare her.

"Oh yes. Mum said Gerry wasn't allowed ever to contact you again."

"Oh." Isn't this a tad extreme? I'm *furious* Gerry hasn't bothered to tell me this.

"She said if she caught him communicating with you, then she'd stop his allowance for six months," goes on Rachel. "And you know what Gerry's like about money."

I nod, still trying to manage this information without making another mess.

"You still haven't told me why you look like you've just crawled out of a drain." Rachel moves towards me. "You smell disgusting."

She looks older. She's wearing silvery jeans and a black vest. Oh hell! Still, she's a lot less scary than Baz-soldier, who may still be out there hunting me down. He could be outside now.

"I'm in trouble," I admit.

"Surprise, surprise," says Rachel. "You'll be in even bigger trouble if you're still here in forty-five minutes when Dad gets back." She obviously hasn't heard about the shooting. I really thought my evil face would be all over the news by now.

"Don't tell him," I beg.

"Of course not." Rachel goes to the fridge, takes out a Coke and hands it to me.

All is forgiven. She is my number-one favourite girl. I snap open the can and drink the cold fizzing liquid. My throat soaks it up.

"I'm on the run," I say, feeling better already. "There was an accident." I eye her speculatively. I suspect Rachel has always had a bit of a crush on me. How can I use this to my advantage?

"Can I have a sandwich?" I begin.

"Sure," says Rachel. "Ham or cheese?"

Twenty minutes later, I'm belting off on Gerry's pro mountain bike. It has eighteen gears, 120 mm aluminium frame, a two-litre water bottle, twenty-six-inch wheels, souped-up suspension and hydraulic brakes. As far as I know, Gerry never rides it anywhere.

I turn off the main road up a small, steep lane. I'm energized by the food and the Coke. If I cycle hard, I could be home in forty-five minutes. I've done this journey thousands of times. But before I get too far, I take out the stolen phone and dial my home number.

On the last ring, just as I'm about to give up, the phone is picked up.

"Hello?"

I recognize my brother's voice. This is what I have been hoping for. Simon was coming home today for lunch with just me, before he spent the rest of his leave with Andrea.

"Hello?"

All at once I feel overwhelmed by everything and I can't speak.

"Max, this has to be you. Where are you? I thought you were supposed to be here! Some welcome home reception this is."

"Haven't you heard?" I croak. This has to be a wind-up.

"Heard what?"

"Nothing. Listen, are the folks there?"

"Of course not. They're in Wales. You know this."

"They're not on their way back?"

"No. Look, what's this all about? Are you coming home? Only I'm supposed to be spending the afternoon with Andrea. I'll go earlier if you're not coming home." He sounds irritated.

But why hasn't he heard about the shooting?

"Are there any police about?"

"What?"

"Police. Could you look out of the window and see if there are any police cars."

"Max. . ."

"Just do it."

A pause.

"No, Max, there are no police cars here. Why. . ."

"I'm on my way," I say. "Don't go to that bitch's house till I get there."

"Sorry?"

"Don't go until I get there. I need your help, Simon."

"What have you done now?"

I pause. "Later."

It takes me an hour to get home, pedalling through the narrow lanes outside Lydford and up to my house in Sourton, and by the time I get there my legs are numb with exhaustion.

My house stands by itself in a big garden, down a short gravelled track. I climb off the bike before I reach my turning and wheel it into the hedge. Then I creep forward. It is possible that the police have staked the place out and Simon hasn't noticed. If so, I'm stuffed.

Spying through the hedge, I see no police cars, no nothing, just as Simon said. And my parents' car is not present. The weekend away is still live.

"Jesus, man, look at you," Simon gapes as I hobble into the back garden. He's sitting under the sun umbrella, wearing flip-flops, red shorts and a yellow T-shirt and tapping something into his laptop.

"I could do with a shower," I say.

"You need disinfecting," says Simon. "What happened to you? You look like a crusty."

"It's a long, long story." I sit at the garden table.

"You reek," says Simon, shifting away.

"You're going bald," I counter. But then a groan escapes from me. I didn't commission it, it just erupts of its own accord. I'm home. For the moment I am safe. I am not lying dead out on the moors. Dad is tucked away in Wales and for some reason any official manhunt hasn't reached Sourton yet.

If I don't lose my head I may be able to steer through this thing after all.

"Has anyone called you recently?" I help myself to Simon's smoothie.

"No," says Simon. "Go take a shower. No. First tell me where you've been."

"In a spot of bother," I say. "I gotta pee."

In the hallway I kick off Levi's shoes and take the phone wires out of the socket. Next I rifle in Simon's jacket for his mobile, which I turn off and hide under a pile of dishcloths. I am completely calm doing this. Step one. Buy some time. I venture upstairs to my bedroom and look at all my stuff: the expensive trainers, the designer shirts, the games consoles and devices, it is all mine, and is now all useless to me. But I look lovingly at my very comfortable double bed. What wouldn't I give to get under the duvet and fall into a deep, deep sleep?

Instead I go into the bathroom, bolt the door and pull off my rancid clothes. I stand under the shower, feeling the hot water pummel my tired body.

As I'm drying myself, I check out of the window and watch Simon scratch his ear and gaze into his laptop. All clear. Pulling on a clean T-shirt and shorts, I cross the landing into my parents' bedroom. I crawl under the bed, lift a section of loose carpet, and find the safe hidden there. I tap in the code, open the door and remove four credit cards and one thousand pounds in cash. I stash these in a small black pouch I was given as a kid and have never got round to throwing away. Then I fill my rucksack with T-shirts, jeans, underwear and a light jacket. I add my passport, a pair of sunglasses and replace the Girl Guide's mobile phone with my own. Then I take everything downstairs.

"I need a lift to Plymouth."

My brother doesn't lift his eyes from the screen. "What for? When are you going to tell me what's going on?"

"On the way."

"What have you done?"

"PLEASE, Simon." My voice trembles. I'm not being as cool as I thought. The panic is just below the surface. "Just give me the bloody lift. I've screwed up, OK. And when Dad gets home he's going to kill me. I don't want to be here."

Simon finally tears himself away from the virtual world and looks at me suffering inside the real one. "It must have been something pretty bad. I'm not taking you anywhere until you tell me everything."

"Then I'll get the bloody bus." I start to walk out but Simon grabs my arm.

"Get in the car," he says. As we drive, I put on the sunglasses. I knew I could count on Simon. I always could. Even as a child Simon always covered for me. I get a wave of feeling for my brother. He's a star. We skirt round Tavistock and join the main road to Plymouth.

"What is it, then?" asks Simon.

"You'll find out soon enough," I reply, fingering my passport inside my jacket.

Sausages

The fires either side of Baz had burned out. He lay, snoring heavily, his face mottled and stubbly in the morning light. He had Alex's gun tucked under his arm.

Saul and Alex were crouching behind a rock twenty yards away, directly in front of the rising sun. Alex's palms were sweating with nerves. He was aware that this could go very wrong.

"We have to wake him up on tour," whispered Saul, retying his bootlace. "Otherwise the noise might give our position away to the enemy." He glanced at Alex. "Have you ever considered a career in the army?"

"Yes," replied Alex under his breath. "But I prefer to shoot things that can't shoot back at me. Rabbits, for example."

Saul shook his head. "You're wasted doing that."

Alex was surprised and secretly gratified.

"Honestly," said Saul. "The army needs people like you. People with a cool head. Brains."

"I haven't got what it takes," admitted Alex. "I like being on my own. All that team spirit stuff is not me."

"I wouldn't say that," whispered Saul, switching off

his radio. "What have you been doing for the last twenty-four hours if it hasn't been looking out for your mates? You're not even getting paid for it!"

Alex grunted. He was surprised at how differently Saul had started to treat him – all this banter, almost like he was one of them!

"I'm going in," said Saul, handing Alex his radio set and his pack. "Remember what I said: any difficulties and you are on to Furzey instantly. As soon as I make the signal, you come over and retrieve your weapon. Understood?"

Alex nodded. This was completely terrifying.

"Watch closely, because this is what we will be doing when we catch up with Cosgrove."

Saul took a rope from his pack and hung it over his shoulder. Then he enabled his weapon. Alex put his hand to his mouth and watched as Saul ran a short distance, then dropped to his stomach and crawled with impossible speed. He stopped short of Baz, behind a gorse bush. It was like watching a machine. A moment later and he had extracted the air rifle from Baz's armpit, grabbed his knees and flipped him on to his front. Baz groaned and lashed out as Saul sat on him, ramming his head into the ground.

"HANDS ABOVE YOUR HEAD," Saul roared, grabbing them, twisting them back and roping the wrists together.

Alex watched, mesmerized, grateful that Saul hadn't done this to him earlier.

"Get OFF," yelled Baz, coming to his senses. He kicked out, but was unable to shift the soldier sitting on his back.

"LIE STILL," Saul bellowed. Alex cringed. The Lance Corporal was unstoppable. Baz kicked again, lamely, then went still. He groaned.

"It's me, you daft bugger," said Saul in a completely different voice. "Calm now?"

"Riley?" gasped Baz.

"He's OK. He's sitting up in hospital showing his bruises to the nurses. Are you going to behave yourself?"

"Yes," spluttered Baz.

Saul jumped off Baz and went round to his head.

"Any crap and you'll be court-martialled, soldier."

Baz groaned again and spat out a mouthful of dirt. He rolled over and sat up, his hands still firmly tied behind his back.

"Did you have to make me eat dirt?" he complained. Saul gestured for Alex to approach. Nervously Alex stepped out from his hiding place.

"JEBB, HURRY UP AND RETRIEVE YOUR WEAPON," Saul bellowed and Alex broke into a run.

When Baz caught sight of him his face tightened.

"What's he doing here?" he roared.

Alex took a step back.

"Calm down," said Saul, passing Alex his air gun and gesturing for him to step back. "He's with us now."

He looked at Baz for a moment or two. "In control?"

"Yes," moaned Baz. "Undo the ropes." He blinked. "I'm thirsty."

Saul gave him a drink from his canteen. The water dribbled down the sides of his face.

"What the hell were you thinking of?" said Saul. "Charging after that kid, disobeying orders. Not coming back. You were AWOL, mate."

"I lost the gunman," said Baz. "There were all these little girls. It was surreal, and then he just vanished." He coughed. "So are you going to arrest me or not? Only I'm dying for a piss and I need my hands for the job."

"I'm not going to arrest you now," said Saul. "That will probably come later. Though everyone understands the provocation, you can't charge off like that." To Alex's concern, he untied Baz's hands.

Baz stood, rolled his shoulders and winced at the sun. Then he took a few wobbly paces away and peed. Saul took the radio set and earpiece from Alex and put them on. He switched the set on.

"This is Lance Corporal Powers to Quartermaster Sergeant Furzey.

"Good morning, Sergeant. Target B detained. I repeat Target B for bravo is secured. Over."

The Lance Corporal took a few steps away, never letting Baz out of his sight.

"Say again. . . Say again. . . Affirmative. Reading you loud and clear. . . Sergeant, the platoon. . . Negative. . . Negative. No sighting of Target C for Charlie or Target D. He can't have got much further. Affirmative. It's blowing north-westerly. OK." He walked further away and Alex couldn't hear any more.

Baz sat down, staring at Alex, who couldn't help staring back.

"Do you know where he is?" Baz asked gruffly.

They both knew he meant Max.

"No," said Alex.

"He's a headcase," said Baz. "He's dangerous."

"I know," said Alex.

They both looked round as they heard Saul give a shout.

"Up there, look." He pointed at the vast hill beyond them. About three quarters up there was a figure picking its way up the hill.

"It's Levi!" said Alex in delight as he looked through his binoculars. "He's OK. Shall we go after him?" He was too far away to shout at, and the wind was blowing in the wrong direction. Alex focused on his friend. This was fantastic! He grinned as he watched him pick his way up the hill. But why was he limping? When he trained his sight on his feet he saw why. Levi was wearing no shoes.

"Yes, Sergeant, definite sighting of Target D. Heading away from us."

Alex couldn't stop grinning. This was fantastic. Suddenly everything was looking up.

But after Saul had ended his transmission he was shaking his head. He stepped over to Baz and the pair had a hushed, private conversation.

Almost immediately Alex's phone rang.

"Is that you, son?" It was Quartermaster Sergeant Furzey.

"Yes," said Alex warily.

"Well done," said the Quartermaster Sergeant. He cleared his throat. "I can't talk about this on the radio. About the other thing, the weapons you found. I hope you haven't mentioned this to the military personnel you are with now?"

"Only Saul," said Alex, feeling confused. "But he was with you when you found the gun anyway, wasn't he? Only I think he's telling Baz about it now."

"Of course," said the Quartermaster Sergeant briskly. "Who else has been involved in this?"

"No one except Max," said Alex.

"But no one else knows? This is important, Alex. They may need protection."

Alex felt a sudden chill. He thought of Sasha.

"Why?"

"This is a delicate situation that I don't expect you to understand. But until we know who is behind the cache, everyone is a suspect. Even military personnel. Do you get my drift? Do not tell anyone else about this. Not a soul."

"OK."

"Those guns are registered as being despatched to the bottom of the Argentine Sea after the Falklands War. They are the confiscated weapons of the enemy. How the hell they got into a ruined barn in the middle of Dartmoor is anybody's guess. And by the look of it, they've only been there for a few months at the most."

Yet again Alex wished he'd never laid his eyes on them. He simply did not want to be involved with this.

Furzey continued. "Are you sure you haven't mentioned the guns and equipment to anyone else? Your dad? Come on, Alex, this is important. You've messed up by not saying anything. Don't mess up again. People's lives may be in danger. We are dealing with some nasty people here."

"Nobody else knows," said Alex.

"What about that girl?"

"Sasha knows," said Alex. "But she won't say anything."

"Sasha?"

"Sasha Tavey. Look, I could phone her and. . ."

"Address?"

"Somewhere in Bloomfield Close." Alex couldn't remember the number.

"Not to worry. I'll find out and send one of my chaps round to have a word. Until we catch the culprits, we all need to be very, very careful what we say and who we talk to. This is a major security issue. Those guns were hidden on our property. It beggars belief, it really does."

"What will happen to Max?" asked Alex bravely. "Will he be arrested?"

"Of course he will," said the Quartermaster Sergeant shortly. "The sooner he is apprehended, the better. Now stick with Lance Corporal Powers and do whatever he tells you." He went silent, which Alex took to mean his interview was over.

Alex put away his phone. It felt like the Quartermaster Sergeant was far more interested in the guns than what was going on out here. Whoever hid them there might be dead by now. They could have been forgotten.

"Was that Quartermaster Sergeant Furzey?" asked Saul in a casual voice.

Alex nodded.

Saul muttered something under his breath as he took Alex's binoculars from him, focusing on Levi's retreating figure for a minute or so. Then he handed them back and picked up his rucksack.

"This is one of our most essential bits of kit," he said, drawing out a mess tin and a small gas stove. "Time we had some breakfast." He reached in his bag again and drew out a brown paper parcel. "I'm pals with the chef," he said, unwrapping fat coils of sausages. He lit the stove and dropped some oil from a tiny bottle into the mess tin. "I'll pass out if I don't eat something. I've been up all bloody night. And after a good breakfast, Baz will be as happy as a little rainbow."

Baz looked up from a rock, where he was attempting to clean his boots. "Where's the eggs?"

"Still up the chicken." Saul poked the sausages with his penknife. They were already beginning to sizzle and the smell was making Alex's mouth water. He was unsettled by the change in the soldiers' attitude. One minute they were these shouting, aggressive soldiers; now they were bantering with him and cooking sausages. But as he bit into a hot sausage wrapped in white bread, he was happy to go along with it, although he couldn't bring himself to sit too close to Baz. Alex still felt very nervous of him and couldn't help wondering how the squaddie would react when they finally found Max. Alex knew he wouldn't be able to relax until everything was sorted out, though Saul and Baz were munching away like they were having some kind of holiday picnic. It occurred to him that the men sharing their breakfast with him were used to much more dangerous and frightening missions than this one. This must feel like nothing to them.

Saul took up his radio and had a brief conversation. From the sound of it, it was the Quartermaster Sergeant again.

"Your crazy buddy has been spotted making for Lydford," Saul said, grabbing the last sausage from the tin. "Orders are to try and catch him up. Q says there's another patrol coming in from the east and another squad coming up from Princetown, just in case the target is completely lost."

Baz nodded. "Good," he said, stamping out the last smouldering embers of his fires. His face fell. "I'll get hauled in when we meet the patrol, yes?"

Alex waited anxiously for Saul's response. He really didn't want to see Baz riled up again.

"I don't know," said Saul. "Let's get on with it."

Lydford was at least another ten miles over steep moorland. Alex would have to leave the quad behind, as the terrain was way too rough. Besides, he wanted to go after Levi, not Max.

"We'll pick your mate up first," said Saul, looking through the binoculars again. "He looks like he could use some help." He started packing the breakfast things away.

Alex cleared his throat. "Look, I know nothing about army procedures and stuff. But now you've found your man." He nodded at Riley. "Isn't this a job for the police?"

Saul shrugged. "Orders is," he said. "We're the men on the ground. I can't see a copper in a Land Rover being very useful out here right now. Can you?"

"They'd have to do a risk assessment first," grunted Baz.

"I wonder if Max's dad is involved," Alex said, scurrying behind the others as they set off over the valley. "He works for the army. uite high up. He's an ex-soldier. I wonder if he's involved. I mean, might it get hushed up?"

"It won't get bloody hushed up," said Baz angrily.

Alex looked at him in alarm. Was he going to go mad again?

Saul didn't seem to be worried about Baz. "If Cosgrove were my dad I'd never stop running." He told Alex about the fake bombs and the punishment that Max had had to undergo. "I wasn't there but everyone was talking about it. I mean, he was just a kid, but his dad wanted the lads to let him have it with both barrels. The stuff they showed him wasn't suitable for kids."

Alex felt an unexpected stir of pity for Max. Tim wouldn't treat him like that in a million years. Shortly after, they passed the quad, parked up behind a boulder. Alex reluctantly removed the keys. He hated leaving it behind but it seemed he'd been given no choice.

"Come on, we need to move quicker," barked Saul.

They walked fast. Alex thought he was pretty fit, but he was finding it hard to keep up. Especially now it was getting hotter. The sky was all blue, not a cloud in sight. It was going to be boiling again, though it was windy. He thought of the pheasant chicks. Damn! He needed to be at home to water them. If they ran out of water, the whole lot might die.

Alex swore.

"All right?" called Saul, looking behind him.

Alex said nothing, but fished out his phone as he walked. He rang Jason's number. As he expected, it was just a voicemail, but Alex left a message, as brief as possible, asking him to water the chicks. Then he phoned his dad. The numbers dialled and Alex waited. He felt a wave of worry as it too clicked into the answerphone.

"Dad, it's me. I've had to help out a mate who's stuck on the moor. I'm still here and the pheasants haven't been watered and I can't get hold of Jason. Dad, I'm worried about them. It's so hot. Could you keep trying Jason for me? The signal is patchy." He hung up and sighed. He desperately hoped he wasn't responsible for the deaths of thousands of chicks.

Alex was out of breath already. The air was so hot, everything smelled of charcoal. The ground was brittle and sharp. All the water in the earth had evaporated.

Far ahead, he could see Levi, struggling on, now nearing the top of the rise. If he turned round, he'd see them following him. The sky above Levi was getting hazy. Maybe it was going to rain!

"Can you smell smoke?" Saul asked Baz, who shrugged.

"I was born with no sense of smell."

"Burned sausage on the pan?" suggested Alex.

They walked on. Alex didn't think he'd be able to keep up the pace for very long but was nervous about saying so. Nor could he stop worrying about the pheasants. They needed fresh water twice a day in this heat. Then Alex had an idea. He still had some juice in his phone. He dialled Sasha's number.

"Alex, at last! Any news?"

"Yes." Alex told her he could see Levi, right now, just below the dull, grey horizon.

"That's wonderful. And Max?" It was hard to hear her over the wind.

"He's been spotted heading for Lydford."

"Oh, thank goodness. How are you?"

"Fine. Look, Sasha, I need a favour. . ."

Alex put away his phone, relieved. Sasha said she would drive up to the game farm straight away and sort out the water for the birds. She said she'd work out what to do. Energized, Alex quickened his step to catch up with the others. He would never have guessed that Saul had been walking all night – he was storming ahead.

"That looks weird," said Saul. The grey cloud over the ridge was deepening and seemed to roll towards them. Alex stopped and stared. There was an odd noise too, a breaking, crackling sound that he couldn't place. Suddenly Levi turned round and started running back towards them. He was flying down over the hill. The men stopped and watched, baffled.

"Has he seen us?" asked Alex.

"He was crippled a minute ago," said Baz. "Now he's going for Olympic gold."

"Shit," said Saul.

A line of orange tinged the horizon. Alex stood still as the crackling noise grew louder and louder, and watched in horror as flames rose over the crest of the hill. The fire, fanned by the gusting winds, raced down the hill. Wildfire! Alex watched with mounting fear as Levi pelted away from the flames.

"Levi!" he screamed. "Levi!" Dropping everything, he ran towards him.

Ponies

I'm in the passenger waiting room at the docks. Most of my fellow Francophile travellers are belted into their cars, waiting to board the ferry, but I'm seated on an orange padded chair, flicking back and forth through my passport. The pages are almost full. Here is the oval stamp I got when we went on a two-month holiday to America last summer. Here is the triangular stamp added three months ago when I travelled to Austria on a school ski trip. I look at the next blank page. This would have had a South African stamp by now if only I hadn't pretended to blow up my school.

"So I'm assuming you've pulled another spectacular Max Cosgrove stunt." Simon commendably drains his vending machine tea. "And now you're bricking it. Correct?" I don't answer, though I know I must. How can I tell my brother that I've shot a soldier and I'm on the run?

I can't expect him to cover for me this time. Simon is an army officer, for goodness' sake. He's one of *them*! The marrow in his bones has been honed with discipline, routine and honour.

"Don't tell me the Risings Bomber has struck again?"

He is sitting on the chair opposite mine and is trying to make eye contact.

I stuff my passport in my pocket, unable to answer or look at him. Crunch time.

"Max," says Simon. "Am I doing anything illegal, bringing you here?"

Maybe he is. Will Simon get done for this? For aiding and abetting a criminal? I look at the cars lined up outside with huge baggage holders on top. Simon might lose everything because of me.

The sea churns in the harbour. The wind is very strong. It will be a messy crossing over the Channel.

"Max," says Simon. "Come home, yeah? It can't be that bad, whatever you've done."

Oh yes it is.

I been bad, bro / Deep down bad
Done a bad deed / Sowed evil seeds
Got the need to flee / and ahm running on empty
Cross the soup and sail to an eternity

I tap the beat on my thigh and try to concentrate on the TV screen, up high in the corner of the waiting room. In my other hand I clutch my ticket. Escape is the only way I will get through this.

How was I to know / a piece to kill crow / could make a man fall / make him call out / call out / call out. . .

I and I stole an eye from this guy
He was dissing me / shaking my reality / breaking
my vitality / shaming my identity
The latrine was extreme / I still feel unclean
This bad dream is ending on the sea. . .

I'm so caught up in the rhyme I don't take in the news item for a few moments. The screen shows an enormous hellfire raging somewhere. There are huge leaping flames, maybe forty feet high. It must be in Australia.

But the landscape looks familiar.

"No." I cross the room to the TV. Ignoring the few other passengers, I stand on a chair and turn the volume up loud.

"Simon, look."

The fire is happening now, on North Dartmoor. People and livestock are being evacuated. Here's an interview with a Guide leader who is surrounded by a pack of chattering girls.

"It's lucky in a way that we were robbed, otherwise we would have still been on the moor."

That was me! I saved her life!

We watch, mesmerized, as an aerial view shows the extent of the flames.

I'm so shocked I can hardly breathe. The fire is raging where I was walking just a few hours ago. Now the moor is engulfed in smoke and flames. I take a shaky breath and allow my thoughts to flicker to Levi and Alex, not to mention the soldier, Baz. Surely they aren't still out there.

"No," I whisper again.

Levi has no shoes.

The commentator speaks. "The fire brigade have not ruled out that these fires were started deliberately."

Simon gives me his most searching look.

"NO," I say. "It was NOT ME."

There's a murmur from the other passengers.

My feet are still encased in Levi's trainers. They're so much comfier than any of my shoes that I hadn't wanted to take them off, even though they are grubby. And now my friend is out there with no shoes. I, Max Cosgrove, stole them from his feet.

"We've got to go back," I say.

"But you've just bought a ticket to Roscoff," says Simon, clearly confused.

"We've got to go back," I repeat. "I've got friends out there."

The air was full of dark, choking smoke. It rolled over them, down their throats, up their noses and into their eyes.

"Back," shouted Saul, grabbing Alex's sleeve. Alex stopped dead.

"Levi," he bellowed, hurting his throat.

He heard a tiny thread of a voice in the distance.

"Help."

Just then, incongruously, his phone rang, the ringtone playing a bright melody.

Alex answered. "Dad?"

"Get the hell off the moor," bellowed Tim. "There's wildfire spreading from Cocks Hill. It's been burning for three hours and is raging out of control. GET OFF NOW."

"I know," said Alex. "I can see it."

There was a pause. "Where are you?" asked Tim, calmer now, though there was tension in his voice.

"Below Rough Tor. Dad, Levi is up there."

"Is he?" Dad's voice wobbled. "Don't do anything stupid, please, Alex. Make for the marsh."

The phone was snatched from him by Saul.

"Lance Corporal Powers speaking. Have you seen an aerial view of the fire? Which is the best way for us to proceed? We're unable to get a radio signal. We're south-facing, downwind." He gave a grid reference.

Alex watched dumbly as the smoke swirled round.

He couldn't hear what Saul was saying to his father. His ears were full of the sound of burning. He watched as a small hawthorn tree, not four hundred yards away, started to smoulder and then a yellow-blue flame licked up the trunk.

Saul rang off.

"Come on," he said. "We need to head north, out of the wind." He stared at Alex, who was unable to move. "If you go up there, you'll be a dead hero. Levi can run down. He'll be OK. We'll never find him in this smoke.

If you go up there, we'll all have to follow and that will be three dead heroes."

Alex bit his mouth.

"Come on," shouted Baz, shoving him in the back. "RUN."

They could see the flames clearly now, and feel the heat; intense, merciless heat. It was like the whole world was on fire. Alex's throat burned and his eyes watered. He wiped black tears from his cheeks.

He felt Saul and Baz each take hold of his arm and run with him so he had no choice.

"To Boulder's Marsh," shouted Saul. "The fire will encircle us if we go back the way we came."

"Why the bloody hell did Q send us up that way?" shouted Baz as they stumbled on.

"No idea," shouted Saul. Now the smoke was clearing, Alex could see they were headed for an outcropping of rocks. Beyond that, he knew, was Boulder's Marsh.

How were they going to survive this? "I can't just leave him to burn," shouted Alex.

"And we can't let you burn," shouted Saul. "It's out of your hands, mate."

Alex was dragged along, and soon he felt his body begin to work and he ran hard, along with the two soldiers, away from the waves of fire that flooded after them.

Was it screaming he heard? Or just the sizzling sap of a million plants, the whining and singeing noises all around?

Saul stopped.

"Wait," he said. "What about the other platoons? They'll be caught up in this too." A dense, choking fog of smoke billowed around them. Saul tried again to work his radio but got nothing. He took Alex's phone, dialled a number and had a garbled conversation. Alex tried to think.

Dad said they should run for the marsh. Why? The damp wouldn't stop the flames; the reeds and tussocks would go up just like the scrub and bracken.

Then he remembered there was a small stream that crossed the marsh. It wouldn't stop the flames, but it might slow them down. This stream never seemed to dry up, despite the heat. It eventually fed into the West Dart River, a few miles to the south.

But which direction to go?

"I don't understand," yelled Saul. "I called my mate, Corporal Higgins. He said his patrol is approaching Grimspound. He says there is no other patrol out."

"But that's in the south," said Alex. "And Furzey said there were two squads."

A flurry of flame rolled towards them.

"Come ON," yelled Baz, dragging Alex's arm so hard it felt like it was coming out of the socket. They ran blindly away from the flames to the place, always just ahead of them, where the smoke seemed to be thinner. They ran bent double with hands clamped over their mouths. Alex felt his lungs grow hot and his throat tighten. And now none of them knew where they were.

Alex tried to identify large rocks and boulders as he passed, but could not. He felt his legs grow heavier and heavier. He knew if the others hadn't been pulling him along, he would have stopped by now. Running seemed to be pointless. He felt a great fear creep up his back, into his head, numbing him at the shoulder.

Was this the end?

Alex coughed and spat. The ground seemed brittle under his feet, like there wasn't a drop of moisture in it. There was a new noise: squealing and thudding. Just ahead, through billows of smoke, he saw the backs of stampeding moor ponies.

"Look," he called.

There was a small path at his feet, a pony path, worn to mud. It was going in the right direction. Saul nodded; he'd tied a handkerchief round his mouth. The men ran together in the direction the ponies had taken. Alex knew that these ponies were intelligent. Maybe they could sense a way out of this. He felt a sharp pain on his shoulder and cried out. A burning ember had fallen on him. He patted his shoulder vigorously. Now the sky was full of embers, mostly grey but some blazing orange. There were sparks filling the sky behind them.

Alex heard his phone ringing again, and, as he ran, he grabbed it out of his pocket to answer it.

"Alex?"

"Dad," grunted Alex.

"It's really taken hold." Dad's voice was high and panicky. "Are you at the marsh yet?"

"No," gasped Alex. "We can't see much." It was like night around them.

"Alex, I'm watching the footage on TV. The fire is heading south, but there are other fires coming up from the west and the north."

"So where should we go?" Alex shouted into the phone. He was biting back the panic.

Dad shouted, "Head for the marsh, right? Downwind. There's a river there."

This must be where the ponies were heading.

"We need to get to the marsh." Alex felt his lungs fill with smoke. "From there, it's not far to the army road."

But Saul was shouting into his own phone.

Baz grabbed him; his face was streaked with dirt and ash. "Which way, mate? You're supposed to be the moor boy."

Alex gazed around. There were no landmarks, nothing. They stumbled on after the ponies and then Alex saw them, humping out of the smoke, a line of standing stones.

"These will lead us to the marsh," he said.

Saul took his phone from his ear, looked at Alex. "Sure?"

"Yes," said Alex. Here was Gladboy: a tall standing stone with a distinctive curve. Now he knew exactly where they were. Quickly he relayed the information to Saul as they stumbled along by the stones, who in turn shouted it into his phone. The men put the old stones between their bodies and the flames. At last, coughing and choking, they were treading on reeds, uneven soft ground.

"I don't understand," gasped Saul. "No one at the base knew we were out as far as this. The CO didn't know I'd found you guys. Q has gone missing and the checkpoint radio is dead."

There was no time to process this information; they had to keep moving away from the raging fire. The ponies were grouped a little way off; beaten back by the heat and the smoke and unsure which direction to run, they huddled together, whinnying and snorting. The smoke seemed to be blowing right over them as the marsh dipped in a bowl. The fire was curling round the outskirts of the marsh. Instinctively, Alex knelt and began tearing at the ground, ripping up tussocks of grass to get at bare earth. The others watched, then joined in. Saul had a knife; Baz had keys. They scrabbled at the earth, rolling back the turf to expose the damp peat below.

"Don't they burn peat on the fire in Ireland?" asked Baz. "Are we just setting up an oven here?" Nobody answered. They moved back, away from the heat, towards the ponies, pulling and scrabbling at the soil. Now there was a metre or so of bare soil, now twice as much. The dry grass came off easily, peeled off like a layer of dead skin. Alex kicked and booted at the ground. Now more damp earth was exposed, maybe three metres. The men worked frantically, silently, until they had an area of approximately four metres in a rough circle, surrounding them. Then they shunted back and began to clear the ground behind them, widening the circle.

Alex looked up from his work and gasped. Through the black smoke a wall of flame appeared, sizzling the bushes that ran close to the standing stones. The flames grew taller and taller and the blackened air was thick with sparks.

The men moved back, but on the other side of the stones, a wall of flame was approaching. The heat was more intense than anything Alex had ever known.

"Keep digging and keep low," ordered Saul. Alex kept going, but he felt like something inside him had just broken. This was it. The ponies stamped and neighed, doing their own job of flattening the undergrowth.

Then the flames were on the stones. They curled over them with a horrifying intensity. The men dug on, deep into the soil, peeling back layers of dry gorse. Saul came up to Alex with a handful of wet mud and smeared his cheeks and hair with it. Alex felt the wetness drip down his clothes. He watched as Saul and Baz covered themselves with wet mud and then carried on scoring the earth. The heat from the flames was incredible, like standing in front of an oven. His face, despite the protective mud, felt like it was already singeing.

A spark landed by his boot and began to burn. He stamped it out. But then another appeared, and another.

He stamped hard, and watching the others, saw they were having similar battles. Behind him, the ponies were whinnying, and snorting, unable to escape. It seemed like the flames were hotter than ever.

Alex stamped for his life.

Water

It wasn't working. Scratching the scrub down to bare earth slowed the fire, but the flames swarmed closer every second. Alex had never been this hot and now even the inside of his head seemed to be filling with smoke. He ignored the ringing of his phone. Dad wouldn't want to hear this.

But then the sky seemed to explode and he was knocked over by a force so strong he was flattened. Alex lay coughing on the steaming ground, unsure what sensation he was feeling but finding it impossible to breathe. Stuff had got into his throat, choking him. He clawed at himself and his hands felt wet. His face was dripping with water and his hair was soaked. Confused, Alex sat up, and water trickled down his spine. He was wet through, like he'd been hit by a swimming pool. Around him was a sizzling noise and the smoke had cleared. He heard a thundering and drumming and watched as the ponies charged out of the steaming circle. Why was he so wet? He had heard of cloudbursts but didn't know they were really real. But how could there have been a cloudburst when there hadn't been a cloud in the sky?

"Get up," yelled a voice in his ear. He was dragged skywards by the shoulder by Saul.

"Come on. We're not waiting for a bus." Saul shoved him through sizzling steam.

At once, like it had only just appeared, Alex heard something like thunder and roaring and the ground seemed to tremble and the noise was deafening.

"It was a water bomb," shouted Saul. He must have realized that Alex was utterly disoriented. "Helicopter," he pointed at a swirling mass in the smoky sky. "Come on, this way."

Alex fought to regain his senses as they tracked through the drifts of grey smoke and steam after the ponies. The fire was still raging on the hill, but now the smoke had cleared a little and Alex could see another helicopter dangling a container, he guessed full of water. As he watched, the water was unleashed, and it fell through the air like a rain of bricks, bombing into the fire.

"Come on, dozy," snapped Saul. They scrabbled further into the marsh, stepping on hot, wet rocks, and as he watched, a vast search and rescue helicopter appeared on the horizon.

"I hope you've got a head for heights," called Saul. "They're going to have to lift us out."

What happened next was a confusion of noise, smoke and yelled instructions. One minute Alex was waiting on a hot, flat rock, looking up into the underbelly of the massive, beating helicopter. The next, a man in orange overalls was being lowered towards him. Alex stood, utterly bemused, as the man came level with him. He had red hair and green eyes. Alex could only stare at him. The man buckled him in and gave him a pat on the back.

"I'm Ben. Don't panic and you'll be fine," he said. "Just hang on to me." Alex felt the tug of his harness and the utter madness of his feet leaving the ground. Now he was dangling in the air, hoisted higher and higher over the burning plains. The worst thing was how they swung in the hot air, the wind buffeting them as they climbed higher. He felt tiny and weightless as he was winched through the sky, thinking, Is this me? Is this really happening? It was all very well for Ben to say "Don't panic." How do you stop yourself from panicking? How do you stop yourself shaking? How do you slow your breathing? The smoke bowled up after him and he saw a line of ponies galloping beyond it. The rough stuff of his rescuer's jacket bit into his cheek and he smelled the sweat of his body. His chest felt so tight with fear he could barely breathe.

He was going to survive.

Now he was strapped in the helicopter, listening to the men shout to each other over the roar of the engine. (It was so loud!) Alex felt he had never been so tired in his life. Everything ached and his hands wouldn't stop trembling. Saul and Baz sat close by, smeared with mud and ash.

"But what about Levi?" he shouted above the noise.

Ben, the man who had rescued him, put a hand on

his shoulder. "We've got two teams out looking for him. We're doing our best."

But it was hard not to scream at them to fly faster, try harder. Anything. He gazed out of the smeary window at the moor below, saw the line of flames and the blackened devastation. It was impossible to imagine how anything could survive that.

The hardest thing to understand was that the Quartermaster Sergeant hadn't passed on any of their radio messages. The manhunt for Max Cosgrove was taking place in the south moors, miles and miles from the position Furzey had told Saul. The water-bombing teams had flown in from the coast and discovered Alex and the two soldiers after being alerted by Corporal Higgins, Saul's colleague.

"Maybe Furzey was too busy with the guns," shouted Saul.

Ben looked at him blankly.

"Guns? Nobody's talking about guns. Everyone is talking about arson. We believe no less than three fires were started in different locations within half an hour of each other."

Then the noise got even louder as the door was opened and air rushed in. Another crew member perched by the open door of the helicopter, scouring the landscape. Alex, unable to take it all in, leaned heavily against the window. The noise felt like it was blasting his ears away. Then the world went muffled as Ben positioned ear protectors over his head.

Then they were flying back over the flames. The burned moor looked like another world; through a layer of smoke, twisted black trees clawed out of the ground. He was plagued by the awful fear that Levi hadn't made it. He willed himself to calm down, but another voice in his head was nagging at him. What if the fire had been orchestrated *because of them*?

What if this was connected to their discovery of the bog rifles? An image of Quartermaster Sergeant Furzey flashed before him.

Do not tell anyone else about this. Not a soul.

Now the helicopter had pulled back, flying low over the north moor, where the ground was yellow-green and unburned. Alex recognized landmarks: there was Rough Tor, and Cosdon Hill. He looked down to see Gold Combe and there, to the left, lay Strangeways. As they flew over the farm, Alex did a double take. There was a car parked in the yard; a scruffy white hatchback. He pressed his face against the window. Then he saw a tiny blonde figure in a green T-shirt, walking round to the back of the house. It was definitely Sasha. He recognized her top. Why was she here, of all places? As the chopper flew over she looked up to watch. Alex fumbled in his pocket for his phone, but doing so, he saw a military vehicle belt down the track. It had a distinctive dash of orange paint on the bonnet. Alex put his hand to his mouth. This was Quartermaster Sergeant Furzey's vehicle, being driven as fast as it could possibly go over the uneven road.

Are you sure you haven't mentioned the guns to anyone else? Your dad? Come on, Alex, this is important.

"Oh God," said Alex. This was hideous. Was Furzey behind the bog guns? Why else would he have directed them into the flames? Why hadn't he told anyone else about the hidden weapons? It all added up. Alex had no concrete evidence, only a strong feeling of dread.

"Sasha." Alex craned his neck to see as the chopper circled back towards the fire. "Sasha," he shouted as Furzey climbed out of his truck. Alex tried to stand up in his seat and was held down by his seat belt. He found his binoculars, miraculously intact and hanging round his neck. Putting them to his eyes, he had a clear view of Furzey, bare-headed and armed, running to hide behind the lambing shed. Why would he do that? He rammed his head against the glass as he tapped in Sasha's number. He pulled off his ear protectors and the noise was incredible. He couldn't hear if she was answering, and now they were leaving Strangeways behind.

"GET OUT OF THERE. QUARTERMASTER SERGEANT FURZEY COULD BE DANGEROUS. PLEASE."

The screen showed him he'd been cut off. Whether she'd get the message, he had no idea. Saul touched his arm and made the signal for OK with his finger and thumb.

"NO." Alex wildly shook his head. "We've GOT to go back," he yelled. "Sasha's in danger. FURZEY is after her, at STRANGEWAYS."

Saul and Baz looked at him, puzzled. Ben drew back from the door and held up his palms. "What?" he mouthed.

"GO BACK," yelled Alex, pointing furiously. "SASHA IS BACK THERE. HE'S AFTER HER. FURZEY. HE'S BEHIND THE GUNS."

Saul shook his head. "I don't understand."

"FURZEY'S DOWN THERE," Alex howled. "HE'S BEHIND IT."

Saul spoke in Ben's ear, who said something in his mouthpiece to the pilot.

After a few agonizing moments, Ben placed his headset over Alex and the pilot spoke to him.

"We understand you've seen your girlfriend. But we can't go back now. We're looking for the lost boy. His life is in danger. We must try and save him first."

"BUT SASHA'S LIFE IS IN DANGER," shouted Alex. "PLEASE, YOU DON'T UNDERSTAND. FURZEY MIGHT HURT HER." He watched as the soldiers exchanged looks and he groaned. They were miles away from the farm now. He could see nothing.

"I repeat, we must continue to look for the lost boy. These conditions are treacherous."

Alex covered his eyes with his hands.

White Noise

This call is a wind-up. All I hear is white noise and someone shouting from a long way off. Then I recognize a word.

"SASHA."

"Alex," I say. "Is that you?" Talk about mixed emotions.

Simon pulls up at a red light and bends in to listen.

"Alex, I can't hear you." Then I hear FURZEY and DANGER.

"Alex, where are you?" The noise in the background becomes thunderous. What is going on? All at once I can hear Alex speaking clearly. He sounds hoarse and frantic, but it's definitely him.

"Oh, he's-shut-the-door. Max. Can you hear me now?"

"Yes, Alex, are you all right – have you seen Levi?"

"I'm all right; Levi's still out there. But Sasha. . .'" SHHHHH SHHHHHH SSHHH. More interference breaks over his voice.

"—at Strangeways Farm. I'm sure the buried weapons are something to do with Quartermaster Sergeant Furzey.

D'you hear? He's there now, I've seen his truck, it's got orange paint. . ."

SSSSHHHHH SSHHHHHHHHH.

"—NOW, MAX."

SSSSHHHHHHH.

"—fire to cover his tracks. . ."

SHHHHHHHHHHH shhhhh.

"—I think he's g. . ."

SHHHH.

"—really hurt her. . ."

The phone goes dead and when I try to call back it won't connect. My skin starts buzzing. So Alex has got it into his brain that Quartermaster Sergeant Furzey himself is the weapons mastermind. That's so sly! Burying the stuff under the very nose of the army. Furzey IS the army. And now Sasha (Sasha! The girl who looks at me like she might look at a turd) might be in trouble at Strangeways. I don't like her but I can't abandon her like I abandoned Levi.

"Turn left here," I order my brother. Look at that, my hands have started to shake.

"Where are we going?" Simon asks as he flicks the indicator.

"There's no time to explain it all. You won't believe me anyway." I tap the window and jiggle my feet. All the time I'm looking out of the window expecting a SWAT team to pounce on me. I don't want to go back to that place. Strangeways Farm has ruined my life. But I must.

A short distance out of town Simon slows and pulls over.

"What are you doing?" I'm beside myself. "We've got to get to Strangeways Farm. Now!" I've just tried phoning Sasha but she didn't answer.

Simon switches off the engine and folds his arms. "Not until you tell me everything. Why won't you trust me?"

Because you'll think I'm a psychopath. You'll turn me in to the law and never speak to me again. I feel myself getting desperate. "You won't believe me," I say. "Please, Simon. I think my friend is in real danger at Strangeways Farm."

Simon pockets the keys. "And why is that?" he asks.

I groan. I have to tell him. I look at my brother, look at his decent, clever face, the very opposite of me. He'll have nothing to do with me after this.

"There was this accident." I hesitate. "I sort of shot someone. . ."

I have lost all sense of time and am light-headed as we approach Strangeways. Simon listened to my babbled story and halfway through, he'd started up the car. I was convinced he would ignore the stuff about Sasha and Quartermaster Sergeant Furzey and drive me straight to the police station, but to my amazement and relief, my brother continued along the moor lanes towards Strangeways.

"Let's go and sort this out first," says Simon, in his

infuriatingly calm manner. "There's bound to be a rational explanation. Then we'll see about the accident. I'll just phone my superior officer first. . ."

"NO," I say. "There's no time. You don't have to ask your superior officer everything."

Simon makes an annoyed noise but accelerates, sending a rabbit racing for cover. "You just can't stay out of trouble, can you," he mutters.

We arrive at the farm turning shortly afterwards. No one is here to stop us and the gate over a cattle grid is standing wide open.

"I am seriously sticking my neck out for you," says Simon, steering in. "I very much doubt a Quartermaster Sergeant has secretly hidden stolen weapons in a Dartmoor bog." He slows to negotiate the cattle grid. "And you think he's committed arson in an attempt to murder everyone who knows about them."

I frown. This is exactly what Alex suggested. "The guns are there," I say. "I've held them."

"That's why I'm coming now," said Simon. "But you wouldn't commit murder over a few guns."

"What about the laser equipment?" I say.

Simon nearly steers into the hedge. "What?"

"I forgot to tell you about it. Levi found boxes and boxes of electrical equipment in the barn too."

"I have to phone my CO," says Simon.

"Too late," I say. "We're here." I see the hedge, where, a lifetime ago, Levi and I left our bikes before skirting through the fields and moorland to the back of the farm and the derelict barn. "We have to help Sasha. If you phone him, it might be too late."

Simon doesn't like it. He's become such a dogsbody, but credit to him, he takes us down the rutted driveway of Strangeways Farm. A few minutes later and we've arrived in the farmyard. I'm relieved to report there's no sign of any army truck.

"There's Sasha's car." I recognize her scruffy white Fiat with the baby seat in the back. The baby seat. Surely she wouldn't have brought the baby out here?

Simon switches off the engine and looks out of all the windows. "You're right so far. But isn't there supposed to be a marauding Quartermaster Sergeant too? I can't see the mythical truck-with-the-orange-blaze."

"You have to take this seriously," I say.

"Why d'you think I'm here?" replies Simon. He looks back at me. "If anything happens, you've got to do exactly what I say. Understand? Exactly."

It is just as if we are six and ten again, with Simon giving commands.

I swallow. "Of course."

"Good, then stay in the car until I get back," orders Simon, climbing out.

"No way," I say, following him.

I'm so mixed up. I've got all these emotions crashing into each other; I've got guilt about shooting Riley, fear about what might happen to me here, and after we leave, and of course I'm worried about Sasha. I can't stop thinking about Levi. If he doesn't make it through the fire then it will be all my fault. I took his shoes! I shouldn't have done that. I should never have left him. Strangeways stands oblivious to me. I look at the old house, surrounded by its overgrown garden and crumbling outbuildings. It looks reproachful, or maybe I am just mad.

I point to the trees by the perimeter fence beyond the paddocks.

"That's where you'll find the weapons," I say softly.

"I'll check them out later," says Simon in a low voice. "First, let's locate your friend. Look." He picks something up from a clump of weeds. I look at my brother, aghast. It's a child's dummy. So Sasha must have brought the baby with her. I really don't like this. Why would anyone bring their baby here? I try to think what this means. Surely they can't be far? But wouldn't we hear them?

We walk carefully along the wall of a stone outbuilding and when I see the old army latrine in the back paddock I get an automatic urge of nausea. When Baz tipped me in there, it ranked along with the worst moments in my life. I'm gaining quite a collection of worst moments.

"So how far is the fire from here?" asks Simon, peering through a shed window. "I'm sure I can smell smoke."

"Oh, miles and miles away," I say. "On the telly they said it was raging over Cocks Hill." I'm wondering if I should call out for Sasha when I notice something odd about the old latrine. It looks different. I look more closely again and draw a sharp breath as I realize I'm seeing the very back of a truck, parked neatly behind it.

I feel myself grow cold with fear. "Look," I whisper to Simon. "Over there."

Simon frowns. "It looks like it's been deliberately hidden." He rubs his chin. "I don't like this." Nor do I.

"What do we do?" I whisper, suddenly certain we are being watched.

"We go and look," says Simon softly. "Don't make a sound." We cross the paddock to the latrine. I grimace at a pile of dead rats outside, covered in flies. Simon bids me to stay behind him as we creep to the back of the building.

The truck is empty. It also matches Alex's description, with the orange blob of paint on the bonnet. Simon takes out his phone and taps in a number and I'm so scared I don't try and stop him this time. I don't want to be here any more. This all feels too real. As Simon waits for an answer, he signals for me to stay put.

I check out the hill behind the farm buildings, but there's nothing but sheep, grazing peacefully. I carefully step out from behind the latrine and look beyond the buildings and the paddocks but see no one. The place looks deserted. Sasha may have walked off, looking for Levi. Furzey might have followed her. Or maybe Sasha left a clue in her car. I'm rubbish at standing still, so I head back to the farmyard.

A man is speaking behind me, and it's not Simon.

"Max Cosgrove. The boy who shoots war heroes in the face. I think you'd better come with me."

Spinning round, I'm looking right into the face of Furzey himself. His grey hair is matted and he has a smudge on his livid pink cheek. Sweat runs down his temples and in rivulets through his wrinkles. His face has so many lines he looks like an old man, though he must only be in his fifties. I remember him, oh man, I remember him. I've had his face yelling into mine. He wears a revolver in a holster around his waist and is in uniform but with no hat.

"You don't seem to learn, do you, Cosgrove. Is that your vehicle in the yard?"

I nod dumbly. Should I, could I run?

"What are you doing here? Are you alone."

"Looking for Sasha," I stutter. "I'm alone." I don't know what else to say.

"I'm looking for her too," says Furzey reasonably. He gives me a sideways look, so quick I nearly miss it, but I swear it was pure evil. I'm completely freaked out by it. His face sort of twisted then relaxed. It was horrible.

"Her mother sent me up here to make sure she's safe."

I say nothing. I know he is lying but I'm frozen here, my brain shooting with dark memories.

"I think you and I should have a chat," says the Quartermaster Sergeant companionably. He reaches over and grabs my arm. It is like being gripped by a robot. "Come with me." I don't want to go with him! I'm scared he's going to hurt me. I look wildly round for Simon but there is no sign. He must still be on the phone. Should I call out? Would that be putting Simon at risk?

"I expect you'll get off with a caution," says Furzey, propelling me over the dusty concrete. "Private Hurley's condition is stable, though he is blind in one eye." I'm half walking, half floating. I'm in a slow-motion nightmare and I'm unable to resist or change anything. I feel like I am being pulled towards something terrible.

Furzey forces me past a huge stone trough full of dead grass and a rotted old tarpaulin. I step over a little enclosure with the remains of a wooden kennel and into the paddock that runs alongside the drive.

"You've led us a fine old dance, Max. You've used up resources that would have been much better spent elsewhere. What came over you?"

I'm so scared my body is hardly working. I need to fire up and fight back, but I can't. I feel hypnotized by dread. We approach a large concreted circle in the ground covered with gravel. In the centre is a circular grill with a padlock hanging open.

"We go underground here," says the Quartermaster Sergeant, lifting the grill. He chuckles. "It's just like James Bond, really." He guides me forward but all I can see is darkness. A prickle runs up my legs, my back and up and over my head. I start to push back against the Quartermaster Sergeant's hands.

"See for yourself," says the Quartermaster Sergeant and as he gives me a great shove, knocking me off my feet. I finally regain my senses and lash out. I catch him on the shin as I fall and he stumbles backwards. But I am falling, falling towards the hole and my head enters the blackness but then I feel an intense pressure on my throat as I am grabbed by the collar and hauled upwards.

"Is there a problem, Sergeant?"

I lie on the concrete, coughing and gasping, and hear gravel splash in deep water.

"Second Lieutenant Cosgrove, Sergeant, Second Star Regiment. On weekend leave. Is my brother being a nuisance, Sergeant?" Simon stands beside me, his face expressionless. He kicks the grill shut. "I'll close this, seeing as my brother nearly fell in."

The Quartermaster Sergeant steps back from the hole, blinking and surprised.

"He's a hell of a nuisance," he says when he's gathered himself. "He nearly dragged me down too. I was trying to catch him when he lost his balance."

"No," I shout. "He tried to kill me! Simon! He tried to push me in." I back away from him on my bum. Oh God, Alex was right. Furzey is behind everything. He's trying to kill all of us that know about it.

"Son, you lost your balance," says Furzey. He wipes the sweat from his face. "I was trying to save you."

"You opened the well and tried to throw me in!" I shout, on the verge of hysteria.

"There's a raging fire on the moor," says Furzey after a breath. "I'm under orders to expose all water sources for the firefighters. There will be a helicopter along in a minute wanting to fill a water cannon." He sighs. "I could do without this."

"Sergeant," says Simon. "My brother's been spinning me a crazy story about arms caches and laser equipment and barns and shootings and God knows what."

I WANT TO KILL HIM! I can only stare at my treacherous brother. How can he not see?

"I wondered if you could help straighten him out," blunders on Simon, the innocent. "He's got some crazy notion that you know something about it and. . ."

Furzey holds up his hands. "Of course I know about it. I've just heard about it from the Jebb boy. I'm under strict orders to keep it a secret until we've had a thorough investigation."

"He's lying," I yell. I get to my feet and the ground heaves. "He just tried to kill me."

Furzey snorts. "This is the boy who planted fake bombs in a school full of children, the boy who shot a soldier in the face." He pauses. "The same boy who left his friends to perish in the fire. Now I would ask you two to kindly bugger off. I really haven't got time for this. Enjoy your leave, Second Lieutenant, and let me get on with my job."

Simon hesitates. "Could I . . . could I just. . ."

I groan in frustration. Despite everything, Simon is having trouble questioning his superior. It's ingrained in him to obey, not to question.

"Could I just see the guns? Only I'll need to make a report about this and. . ."

YES!

"It's not standard practice in these situations," says Furzey. "And to be honest, they are the least of my worries. There is an inferno on the moor. Lives and businesses are at risk." He claps his hands. "Go have a sightsee, but be quick. I want this place evacuated as soon as." He looks at me and I see the devil dancing in his eyes. "You can show him, but you'd better not abscond a second time."

"Where's Sasha?" I blurt out. "What have you done to her and her baby?"

Furzey rolls his eyes. "I think she must have wandered off on to the moor, which is bloody stupid, considering."

I look at the well in horror. As Simon and Furzey walk off, I bend low to the grill. "Sasha!" I shout. "Are you down there?"

Furzey simply throws his arms in the air in exasperation and keeps walking. In a few minutes he is out of sight.

Simon turns, embarrassed. "Max, for goodness' sake. I'm beginning to think you've told me nothing but lies all day. I'm beginning to think you know more about the fire than you admit. After all, you're the Risings Bomber, aren't you?"

"Simon, you really can't trust that man . . . he tried to kill me!" I scrambled to my feet and follow Simon through the paddock and into the farmyard. "I'm so worried about Sasha. I think he's hurt her. I think she might be down that well." We cross the lower paddocks. Furzey has vanished, for now.

"You know what your problem is?" Simon battles through the long grass. "You've got an overactive imagination."

"And you're a bloody yes sir, no sir, three bags full, sir. Just because you're in the army doesn't mean you haven't got a brain." I chase after my brother into a copse of trees.

"If Furzey wanted to get rid of you, he'd have shot you. Then me. He hasn't." Simon steps through the weeds towards the barn.

"That would leave evidence," I protest. "He'd have to account for the missing bullets. He's clever, Si; all that crap about water bombs."

Simon ducks under the collapsing roof and I'm too scared not to follow him.

"Holy cow!" He gasps when, through the gloom, he sees the rifles lying in the mud at the back of the barn. He bends and picks one up.

"This is incredible," says Simon and he swears.

A scraping noise above our heads makes us jump, but then a couple of rooks fly cawing past the entrance. Simon takes several photos of the guns on his phone. Then he presses a few buttons. I assume this is to email the photos to his superiors.

"OK," says Simon. He lowers his voice. "Now we're

alone we can talk properly. I couldn't say this before in case he was listening, but when you were having your rendezvous with Furzey, I spoke to my Commanding Officer, OK? I've said there's something going on here. He's heard nothing about these weapons. He says the military police are on their way. Now I don't know what Furzey is up to. He may be innocent. I do know that as he is a Quartermaster Sergeant, he will have more opportunities to steal equipment than most military personnel, but we just don't know. I need you to play along with me, OK?"

Why, the sly hound. Simon IS on track after all. He's been ACTING. So why isn't he more worried about Sasha?

"Simon, what about Sasha? Her baby?" I can't stop thinking about the well.

Simon shakes his head. "Listen, I need to get back out there and talk to Furzey. He's acting strangely and I want to keep an eye on him. He's probably innocent. But if he's not. . ."

A chill runs over my body. "He's not," I say, remembering the darkness of the well. "Of course he's not."

"If we're too late for Sasha, then we need to get the hell out of here. . ."

"But. . ."

"Be very careful, Max. OK? Help is on its way."

I follow my brother over the dead grass and bare earth to the entrance. A vision comes into my mind of me and him, aged eight and twelve, walking out of our grandparents' chicken coop. Simon in front, in green shorts, carrying all the eggs as usual.

Simon bends to get out.

"LOOK OUT!" screams a voice and I know it is Sasha. There she is, behind a tree, maybe twenty yards away. "ON THE ROOF." She points.

There's a man wearing a balaclava on the roof above us. He has a revolver aimed at Simon. I don't stop to think. I just dive for Simon, knocking him to the ground as an outrageous, agonizing pain rips through my leg.

"Back!" Simon shouts, dragging me inside the barn. "Where are you hit?"

"Leg," I gasp. The pain swirls around me. It's incredible. Hot, nasty and hellish.

We hear thumping on the roof as bits of moss and dust and wood fall on us.

The pain is like nothing I have ever experienced. Simon lifts my leg and rests it on a broken plastic container. He rolls back my trouser leg. We listen to the noises overhead as Simon clamps his hand over the wound.

"Just a scratch," he whispers, putting his finger to his lips. I want to yell out but through the blanket of pain a voice in my head is saying SASHA'S ALIVE. Simon removes his hand and wipes it on his shorts. He takes my palm and presses it to my injured leg.

"Keep it there," he says, so quietly I can hardly hear him. "Don't bloody pass out on me."

I watch helplessly as Simon uproots a rusting sheet of tin lying in the ground. He drags it over and gently stands it over me, leaning it against the wall so I have a makeshift shield. Simon crosses to the back of the barn and presses himself against the wall.

"THE POLICE ARE ON THEIR WAY," he shouts. "FOR GOD'S SAKE, STOP THIS NOW." The roof creaks and bends as the gunman moves in Simon's direction. I can only stare, totally terrified. The whole barn could easily come down on us.

Simon creeps back along the wall to me and gets under the shelter as another shot rings out through a hole in the roof.

"All right?" Simon mouths at me, but I can only grimace. Simon touches my shoulder. His eyes are darting round everywhere. He reminds me of a cat, twitching at every movement, every sound. He's clever; he's found an old car seat and is balancing it on his head and shoulders for protection. I wince as Simon removes my laces – I mean, Levi's laces. What is he doing?

"We're gonna shake him down," whispers Simon. "You've got to move your bum outside. Take your shield with you. OK?" I shake my head. I'm not OK and I can't move. I can only just bear the pain if I don't move.

"We're sitting ducks in here," mouths Simon. "Move it."

This is a side of Simon I rarely see. Gingerly I lower my leg, panting with the pain of it. I roll out of my shelter towards the light and hold out my hands to steady the tin sheeting Simon is lowering on me. Then I roll on to my stomach, just under the eaves of the building, as Simon grabs one of the central support pillars. It already leans inwards at a stupid angle. Simon begins to shake it hard, and the whole place begins to move and groan. Simon pushes, rhythmically hammering the pole with his body as the building seems to bend inwards even more. The movement on the roof grows more frenetic and detritus rains from the creaking beams.

Simon roars, lion-man, and shoulders the beam, and all at once the roof begins to cave in. There are splintering, scraping noises as the whole back end of the barn falls in on itself. I throw myself out as the building collapses and Simon lands beside me. I look at the sky between the treetops before Simon covers me once more with the protective tin. Then there is a hammering noise and shouting. I force myself to sit up and look back at the heap of tin and rubble that was the barn. The roof is now on the ground and the air is full of dust.

"Simon?" I whisper. "Simon?" There is no reply, only the sound of a man groaning. I can't see what is happening and I drag myself further back, away from the ruins. Then a figure appears amongst the beams and broken panels.

"Look after this." Simon opens the gun and empties out the bullets. He lobs it at me. "Furzey's trapped under a beam," he says. "I've tied his hands." Next he throws his phone at me. "Call the police again, will you? Tell them to get a move on."

He climbs back over the wreckage and out of sight.

"Pssssst." The noise comes from beyond the trees. I stare as Sasha pokes her head up, her hair all fluffy.

"You're all right," I say. "But your hair's a mess."

"I hid in the drinking trough in the yard," whispers Sasha. "Is it safe yet?"

"I think so," I reply. "Can you call the police now, please?"

"I called them twenty minutes ago," says Sasha. "They'll be here soon."

"Where's the baby?"

"I didn't bring the baby." She frowns. "What do you think I am, crazy?"

"I found a dummy," I whisper.

"Must have fallen out my pocket," says Sasha.

We both jump as the wail of sirens fills the valley.

Television

The hospital was as stifling hot as the thick of the fire. Alex felt the sweat pour off him as he sat up in bed, his throat burning, and grabbed for a plastic glass of tepid water. He felt stupid and his head hurt. He wanted to go home this morning, but apparently he'd inhaled way too much smoke and needed to be observed for another twenty-four hours. Saul was in the next bed, though he was off in another room being debriefed by his Commanding Officer and expected to be discharged from hospital shortly. Baz had a nasty burn on his leg and was being observed in a private room with a military guard at the door.

Levi's mother was in hospital too. When she'd heard Levi was missing on the moor in the fire, she needed to be sedated. Alex felt pretty hysterical himself. How would he ever climb out of this moment? He had survived, yes. But how could he even function, knowing that Levi, in all probability, had perished in the fire? No one had seen him since yesterday afternoon when he was running away from the fire. It was unthinkable. If Alex allowed himself, he might start yelling, and then he might not be able to stop.

Dad, Sasha, Sasha's mother, Jill, and Sammy-Joe, breaking the hospital visiting rules, sat on chairs at the end of his bed, eyes glued to the TV. They had wanted to switch it off, but Alex had insisted they kept it on. The local news was showing a live feed of the helicopters still combing the blackened moor.

"If I'd known it was that bad, I'd have never gone up there," Sasha was saying quietly. "It's an inferno. Oh, Levi." She buried her face in Sammy-Joe's neck, her shoulders shaking with grief.

Yesterday she'd given water to two thousand pheasants before she made the journey to Strangeways.

"I couldn't do nothing," she said. "I couldn't just sit at home. I knew Strangeways was a long way from the fire and I knew it was the place where everything kicked off. I thought one of you might make it back there. I phoned my mum to tell her where I was going." She was wrapped in a blanket, and shivering despite the heat.

The cunning of the Quartermaster Sergeant was frightening. Sasha's mum said Furzey had turned up at the door, asking for Sasha, and Jill had said yes, having no idea that she was putting her daughter in danger. The Quartermaster Sergeant then said he was in charge of evacuating the moors and he'd personally make sure that Sasha was safe.

Sasha picked up the story. As she spoke she held Sammy-Joe close.

"I was at Strangeways poking around the back when I saw the Sergeant arrive. I was going to speak to him, but then he saw my car and he looked really confused. He wound down the window of his truck and called out 'WHERE ARE YOU?' and he sounded really scary. I didn't know what to do. I stepped out and he saw me and he said, 'WHERE'S SASHA? SHE'S SUPPOSED TO BE HERE.' He looked strange, hot and angry, and his eyes looked dead. He started to get out of his truck. I wasn't going to tell him that I was really called Sasha, not Kate. I was too scared. I was so freaked out I just mumbled, 'I'll just go and get her, she's just round here somewhere,' and then I ran and hid. Then I got your message, Alex. I didn't really understand, so I hid in the trough in the yard under a stinking old tarpaulin."

Alex swallowed. He couldn't bear to think of what might have happened. That Furzey might have hurt Sasha. He felt restless. It was so hot! He wanted to walk down the corridor and see Max, who was in the next ward, but wasn't allowed as Max had just had an operation to remove the bullet from his leg.

"Thank God you're all right," repeated Tim from the window. That was all he'd said for the last twenty-four hours.

"We're not all right," said Alex. "We haven't found Levi."

Then he noticed Saul had come back. He was talking

to an army officer at the end of the ward. Then he made his way to Alex.

He had a dressing on his wrist where he'd been burned and his neck was dotted with small blisters where embers had fallen on him.

His normally clean-shaven face was dotted with stubble and he wore a T-shirt and tracksuit bottoms. One of his dark eyebrows had nearly been singed off.

"Unbelievable," he said. He came and sat on his bed, next to Alex. Ignoring the others, he began to talk.

He couldn't say much, he said, as there would have to be a major criminal investigation, but off the record, it appeared that Quartermaster Sergeant Furzey had been siphoning off weapons and equipment from the military for over twenty years. In his role of Quartermaster Sergeant, he had unchallenged access to the stores, and this he had exploited to the full, forging documents and making false inventories, and although the details were not yet clear, he had been distributing the stolen equipment to various groups and factions. Here Saul looked very grim.

"I can't believe any soldier would do that," he said.

"What factions?" asked Alex.

"There are always people who want to purchase weapons," said Saul, pale-faced. And on this he would be pressed no further.

The bulk of the bog weapons had indeed come from the Falklands conflict. Saul speculated that Furzey, who had been on duty there at the time, might have used his Quartermaster Sergeant status to gain access to the weapons, and then to arrange their illegal transportation over the seas, probably smuggled in ammunition crates in a Hercules aircraft.

"This is all speculation," said Saul. "But this is the general thinking."

He said that, having smuggled the guns back, Furzey might have distributed some of them, but had dumped the rest. He said all evidence suggested they had recently been moved to Strangeways, probably because a previous hiding place had become insecure.

"But what about the laser systems?"

Saul breathed in, obviously distressed. He glanced around at the assembled group. Alex got the hint and got out of bed and followed Saul a little way down the ward.

"We'd better not say too much about it at this stage," he said quietly. "But yes, in addition to the SA80 assault rifles, there is a substantial amount of sophisticated support equipment." He paused. "Worth millions of pounds. You lads uncovered something that goes much deeper than a few knocked-off souvenir rifles."

He touched the burn on his neck and lowered his head, upset.

"Doing that to your own men," he whispered. "It breaks all the rules."

Alex didn't know what to say. He noticed everyone had gone quiet, watching the TV above his bed, and, touching the Lance Corporal on the arm, he went to join them.

The TV presenter was blonde and beaky in a blue dress. "The fire is now under control but the moor is closed until the final blaze has been extinguished. Forensic experts are already combing the area after twelve empty fuel containers were discovered in a skip just outside Hammerton."

She turned to her co-presenter, a plumpish, dark-haired man.

"So, Bill, what are people saying about these cans? Are they suggesting that an arsonist is behind this terrible fire?"

"That's exactly what people are saying, Michelle. Sources suggest the police have taken a senior member of the armed forces into custody for questioning."

Alex watched as the helicopter filmed the blackened moor and wiped his eyes.

"Oh, Levi," said Sasha, and burst into tears again. Sammy-Joe looked at her curiously and wriggled off her lap. Before anyone could stop him, he grabbed a handful of flowers from a vase and offered them to her, making a smile flicker on her tear-stained face.

Now the helicopter was circling Cock's Hill. It circled low, then swept back, as the camera focused on an object on a flat rock.

"What's that?" gasped Alex and the TV presenter at the same time. The helicopter turned and flew back.

A solitary figure sat on a large rock, surrounded by

soot and ash. The camera panned in on his face. A boy looked up and grinned and gave a small, self-conscious wave. He was barefoot.

"Who's that?" gasped Blue Dress.

The boy stood and waved with both hands.

Beginnings

I repack my suitcase, trying to make everything as small and as neat as possible. It's ten o'clock in the morning. In one hour I'll be on the train. When I announced my plans six months ago, Mother burst into tears and said, "Thank God." Father gritted his teeth so tightly that a bloom of pink appeared over his face; this is his way of showing pleasure.

"The first sensible idea you've had for years," he'd said. He thought a minute. "Bar one."

This wasn't entirely flattering, but I gave up trying to please these people years ago. No, I'm doing this for myself. There's something in me, some kind of devil, that I can't switch off, but there will be no room for devils where I'm headed – at least, not my particular kind.

Eighteen months have passed since the fire and everything has changed. I took part in the inquiries, which are still ongoing. They are still investigating Furzey, his scams, and the fire. The others – Alex, Sasha and Levi – have sat and passed their exams, but I didn't go back to college. They didn't want me, even after the judge decided that shooting Riley had been an accident. I clawed back some points for my alleged bravery going to help Sasha. But Riley lost his eye. He's been discharged from the army. I don't know what he's doing now but I hope I never run into him. I think I may have ruined his life. I'll feel bad about it for ever.

After the tech gave me my last orders, Levi badgered his mum to put in a good word for me (she took some persuading) and I've worked at the supermarket, full time, for over a year. I've more or less managed to keep my head down, stacking vegetables and amassing cash. (I've also written some wicked tunes.) But it's definitely time to leave. I can feel Bad-Max stirring again and he needs to be suppressed.

I check my watch. At 10.05 Levi might be sitting in his university lecture, or cooking up a Levi-breakfast storm in his hall of residence kitchen. I picture him surrounded by newly minted friends. He's gone to Lincoln University so he can be near his dad.

Levi said that when the flames came over he was so terrified, he dug himself into the ground. He'd rolled into a kind of shallow well on the hillside. As the flames approached, he'd attempted to build himself a kind of shelter out of the stones.

"You do realize you were building yourself an oven," interrupted Sasha.

Levi shrugged. "I was desperate."

When he said that, I felt like a worm. I couldn't meet his eye.

Levi had scrabbled and pulled at rocks and then, to his amazement, he had found a hole in the side of the hill. He'd reached in and felt a bigger, deeper space behind. A scrabble of earth and suddenly the side of the hill seemed to give way and it collapsed with a gush of ice-cold water, soaking Levi to the waist. As the water flowed away, Levi found himself looking into the buttressed entrance of an old mine shaft. He'd crawled inside and after a few minutes he saw he was not alone.

"It was me and this hare, for maybe six hours," said Levi. "We were in it together. We sat and stared at each other. He had these beady eyes and huge ears and big legs. I had never seen a rabbit that big. And it was noisy in there, man. We crawled into the deepest part of the mine, deep, deep. I could hear the burning overhead. I was worried for you guys. I mean, what was the likelihood of me finding the mine? What about the rest of you?"

That made the others smile, that Levi, lost, dehydrated, hungry, in the face of a wildfire and with no shoes, had been worried about everyone else.

"When I came up the ground was still so hot I couldn't walk," said Levi. "I was more scared after the fire, to be honest. I thought no one would come. Why would they? I was bloody pleased to see the helicopter."

Everyone said it was a miracle.

*

Four p.m. I look out of the window of the train. There's a line of purple moorland rising from the distant horizon, but this isn't Dartmoor; these are the Yorkshire moors, my new home.

Alex, as predicted, is helping run the game farm with his dad. Tim tried to persuade him to apply for university but Alex just said no. I see him now, lying in a hollow on that bloody moor, gunsight to his eyeball, not aiming to kill, but watching the little birds scamper round the eaves of Strangeways. Funny how, after the fire, Sasha and Alex seemed to fold into each other. Nothing was formalized, nothing was said. But after everything, they just spent more and more time together. Now Sasha works with Alex, helping with the cooking in the shooting season, cooking stews for the guns and the beaters. She says when Sammy is a bit older she might do something different, but for now, she's happy driving up to be with Alex every day, her and the baby. I wouldn't be surprised if, one day, those two manage to buy back Strangeways. I can easily imagine them running a farm. Someday there'll be bacon cooking where soldiers now fire their rounds and practise their warfare.

The weapons arsenal in the bog was worth millions of pounds. There were hand-held explosives, mortar rockets, all kinds of weapons from every kind of conflict, all wrapped in oilskins and plastics. It turns out Furzey had to move them there in a hurry after a remote army outpost on Bodmin, the centre of his operations, had been sold off. Everything was illegal, stolen and smuggled. It was an old, dirty, secret business, done under the very eye of the military establishment. Quartermaster Sergeant Furzey, believed to be at the centre of a vast criminal network, was being held in maximum security in a military prison.

He had betrayed his fellow soldiers for years. The weapons he helped to sell to illegal groups and terror organizations may have harmed his own men. I imagine he's having a very rough time in prison.

I tug at the strap on my suitcase. Will I survive this? When the others find out who I am, what I am, will I make it through the sixteen weeks? Will they believe the judge?

Dad's reaction completely floored me. He said that he was glad I was alive, and when he heard that I'd taken the bullet meant for Simon, he wept (!). If that wasn't shocking enough, Mother actually hugged me. Imagine! For a moment it was like someone else's family and was all rather embarrassing.

One hour later, I walk through the car park, clutching my suitcase. I follow the other lads, some with parents (naturally I haven't brought mine). I step into a low grey building and wait my turn. This is like a dream – whether it will be a good one remains to be seen.

The man at the desk looks up at me. "Name?"

"Max Cosgrove."

I wait, but nothing bad happens.

The man hands me a document. "I need your autograph just here, please."

I sign my name on the dotted line before I can change my mind.

"Welcome to the army," says the man.

ACKNOWLEDGEMENTS

Thanks to

ACIO Taunton, for answering my very odd
questions about army life
David Welch
Sheila Braine
Anna Solemani and all the rest of the talented and
beautiful team at Marion Lloyd Books.

All military mistakes are very much my own.
(I fear the term 'military precision' may not apply
within these pages . . .)

Help for Heroes is a charity formed to help those
who have been wounded in Britain's current
conflicts www.helpforheroes.org.uk